I0452172

FLOWERS ARE RED

HART of ROCK and ROLL
BOOK ONE

MARY J. WILLIAMS

Copyright © 2016 Mary J.Williams

All rights reserved

ISBN: 099761613X

ISBN-13: 978-0997616132

<u>ABOUT THE AUTHOR</u>

Writing isn't easy. But I love every second. A blank screen isn't the enemy. It is the opportunity to create new friends and take them on amazing adventures and life-changing journeys. I feel blessed to spend my days weaving tales that are unique—because I made them.

Billionaires. Songwriters. Artists. Actors. Directors. Stuntmen. Football players. They fill the pages and become dear friends I hope you will want to revisit again and again.

Thank you for jumping into my books and coming along for the journey.

HOW TO GET IN TOUCH

Please visit me at these sites, sign up for my newsletter or leave a message.

http://www.maryjwilliams.net/

https://www.facebook.com/maryjwilliamsauthor/?ref=hl

https://twitter.com/maryjwilliams05

https://www.pinterest.com/maryj0675/

https://www.instagram.com/2015romance/

https://www.goodreads.com/author/show/5648619.Mary_J_Williams

MORE BOOKS BY MARY J. WILLIAMS

Harper Falls Series

If I Loved You

If Tomorrow Never Comes

If You Only Knew

If I Had You (Christmas in Harper Falls)

Hollywood Legends Series

Dreaming with a Broken Heart

Dreaming with My Eyes Wide Open

Dreaming of Your Love

Dreaming Again

Dreaming of a White Christmas (Coming in December)

(Caleb and Callie's story)

One Pass Away Series

After the Rain

After All These Years

After the Fire

Hart of Rock and Roll

Flowers on the Wall

Flowers and Cages

Flowers for Zoe (Coming in November)

Table of Contents

PROLOGUE

EVERY TEENAGER POSSESSED a certain arrogance. Youth will be served—and all that crap. Ashe Mathison was no different. He believed the world was his to conquer. At eighteen, there were no boundaries. No limits. He had talent, ambition, and endless drive. Dreams would be fulfilled. One day he would stand on a stage while thousands cheered his name. Ashe had no doubts. *If* never entered his mind. Success was just a matter of time.

Money was tight. Ashe shared a studio apartment with five other struggling musicians. The walls were paper thin. They froze in the winter and sweltered in the summer heat. Rats didn't scamper through the building's halls. They arrogantly loitered, waiting to snatch the first unattended scrap of food.

Ashe was accustomed to better. He grew up the pampered son of a wealthy man. Heir apparent. To say he tried fitting into that life would have been stretching the truth. Ashe knew what he wanted for as long as he could remember. Working in an office. Chained to a desk. The thought of daily donning a suit and tie gave Ashe hives. A noose— whether fashioned from silk or hemp—was still a noose.

In a perfect world, Randall Mathison would have accepted that his son wanted something different. Ashe had edges that couldn't be smoothed down to fit in a round hole. Two strong personalities. Father and son butted heads. Argued. Threats were made. Conform. Ashe wasn't given an alternative.

On the eve of his eighteenth birthday, a freshly minted high school graduate, Ashe walked away from his home. His family. The only life he had ever known. And for the first time in that life, he felt free. The air smelled sweeter. His steps lighter.

Pride made Ashe leave his childhood home with nothing but a suitcase and the saxophone he paid for with the money earned breaking his back at the local quarry—the family quarry—three summers straight.

He had some cash, but it didn't last long. Chicago was an expensive town. Ashe learned quickly to hold onto what he owned with an eagle eye. Thieves that included a few of his early roommates were every place he turned. It helped he looked older—tougher—than most of his contemporaries. The summers hauling rocks at his family's quarry matured him, filled out his body. The lessons his fellow workers taught him paid dividends on the streets of Chicago. Ashe had learned how to keep his eyes open. Most of all, he learned how to fight. Dirty, if necessary. No Marquis of Queensbury rules in the limestone pits. Or in a dark alley.

The average street thug thought twice before confronting Ashe because of his height and burly arms. Those that worked up the nerve never tried it again.

Ashe earned enough to get by working minimum-wage jobs. Anything and everything. He wasn't picky about hours which made him appealing to employers. Flipping burgers. Washing cars. Sweeping floors. Ashe did it all. Gladly. He was a young man who liked to eat. Money was necessary if he wanted to keep a full stomach.

The plethora of mindless jobs meant something else. Something more important. Ashe used the hours in between to work on his first and only love. His music. There were advantages to growing up rich. Little boys with mothers who supported the arts were given piano lessons. And violin lessons. Ashe learned from the best teachers in Boston.

The lessons were fine. Ashe wanted more. Classical training was a great jumping-off point. However, when he began to chafe at the rigid structure, his family-sanctioned lessons ended. Ashe taught himself the saxophone. And the guitar. And any instrument that caught his interest. Gifted. That was what his instructors called him. All he knew was that playing. Writing. Singing. Music. They were as vital as breathing.

Today found Ashe on a street corner playing for tips. On a good day, he made a tidy sum. Most of the time, not so much. Ashe enjoyed the interaction with people. When somebody stopped and listened—truly heard what Ashe was playing—he didn't care if he made a dime.

Ashe took his saxophone from the case, wetting the reed, adjusting the mouthpiece. Early June. The weather was mild. He played when it wasn't as pleasant. Seventy-two degrees and sunny was perfect. People were happy on days like today. Happy translated to a few more listeners—and a few more bucks dropped into his open case. Ready to begin, Ashe raised his horn to his mouth. That was when he heard it. Faint but distinct. Music played with skill on an acoustic guitar.

Drawn to the melody, Ashe abandoned the street corner. Keeping his horn around his neck, case in hand, he crossed the street and entered the small park to his right. Finding his fellow musician was easy. The notes became louder as Ashe drew closer. On a bench, head bent, a dark-haired man attacked the strings with complete abandon. He didn't play for tips. He simply played.

A kindred spirit, Ashe thought, lips quirked. Damn, this guy could make those strings sing. Then he stopped mid-chord. Ashe watched as the man retreated several bars, played the notes, stopping in the same place.

"*Son of a bitch*," the guitar player muttered. He tried again, but couldn't seem to make it past the series of notes.

Sometimes it took a fresh ear. Ashe played the same sequence, note for note. When he came to the sticking point, he continued, bridging the gap, adding his personal flourish.

"That's what it was missing." Nodding, the man's fingers flew, echoing what Ashe had played. "I've been stuck on that for days. Thanks." Setting aside the guitar, he held out his hand. "Ryder Hart."

"Ashe Mathison."

Getting a better look at his face, Ashe realized he recognized Ryder Hart. Chicago was a big city, but the music scene was amazingly insular. Ryder was making a name for himself playing small clubs and bars in the area.

"I saw you play at the *WFTW* a few weeks ago. You were good." *Working for the Weekend* was *the* place to be seen if you were a young musician trying to get noticed. Ashe thought it overrated, but Ryder made an impression.

"Thanks. Again." Ryder grinned. He was about Ashe's age. Kind of pretty but not effeminate. As he recalled, Ryder drew a lot of women fans. "*WFTW* is all reputation and no heft."

"That was my impression, too."

"Smart man." Ryder paused, obviously sizing Ashe up. "I want to put together a band. Equal partners. Equal say. Are you free Friday night?"

"Are you asking me to join your band?"

"I'm asking you to sit in for a set or two. It's me and Dalton Shaw. He plays drums. Hell, he owns the drums. What do you say? Want to see if we click?"

"Why not?"

Ashe had a feeling about Ryder Hart. A good feeling. Maybe this was the break he had been looking for.

CHAPTER ONE

"ONE-NIGHT STANDS are the best. No commitment. No chance of getting bored. In and out. What could be better?"

With a wink, Ashe Mathison ran his finger over the electronic keyboard, testing the sound.

"Is that comment supposed to be provocative?" Zoe Hart shook her head. "Get a new line. The bread in my refrigerator is less stale."

"That speaks more of your culinary skills than my wit."

"That's hilarious." Zoe flung a guitar pick at Ashe. When it landed three feet from its target, he didn't gloat. Not with words. The smirk on his mouth said it all.

"Asshole," Zoe muttered.

"Bitch," he shot back.

Simultaneously, they burst out laughing. Heated banter was their favorite way of working off pre-show nerves. They were veterans. They had faced an audience—some friendly, some hostile—more times than either could count. However, the jumpy feeling never subsided. Ashe understood that it was a good thing. The day they could walk onto a stage with a blasé sense of calm was the day to think about hanging it up. Nerves equaled passion. It meant they cared. They wanted to give their best—every time.

The Ryder Hart Band was playing a One Night Only concert at the Hollywood Bowl. The day the tickets went on sale, they sold out in minutes. More dates could have easily been added. As many as the venue allowed. However, volume was not the point.

The band was between touring. A new album was ready to drop the next day. The tie-in made perfect sense. Word was this would be their biggest release. Record breaking. Chart topping. The first single, *On Your Mind*, had been number one four weeks straight.

Ashe was damn proud of that song. He wrote it. The saxophone solo was one of his best. The first time he heard the final mix he knew it would be a hit.

"Tossing out insults already?" Ryder Hart joined them, his guitar in one hand. "Now I know it's going to be a great show."

"Damn straight. If Ashe and Zoe have sunk their claws in, we can't go wrong."

On his way by, Dalton Shaw tapped Zoe on the butt with his drumsticks. She slapped them away, shaking her head.

"Men have died for less," she warned Dalton.

"Died?" He raised an eyebrow.

"Fine. Walked funny for a week."

"When Zoe's knee hits a man's balls, he only wishes he were dead." Quinn Abernathy winked at Zoe, walking into Ryder's outstretched arms.

"When did you get in?" Ryder asked after a long hello kiss.

"About an hour ago."

Quinn spent most of her time in Los Angeles. As an in-demand celebrity photographer, there was more work than hours in the day. When she traveled, it had to be something special. A personal invitation from Bob Dylan qualified.

"The new album cover is going to be amazing."

"If you do say so yourself."

"Colleen." Quinn rushed to greet the newest member of the growing group.

"How come Quinn gets a hug before your fiancé?" Dalton demanded, pulling Colleen close.

"She moved faster." Colleen touched the side of Dalton's face, her green eyes filled with love. "You get a hug and a kiss." She

6

demonstrated to Dalton's satisfaction. He wandered to his drum set, keeping Colleen's hand in his.

Ashe watched all this play out with an indulgent smile. They had been a close group for a long time. First, it was Ryder, Dalton, and him. Then, Ryder's younger sister joined the mix. Zoe made an easy transition from the kid who watched from the wings to badass lead guitar and smooth backup vocals. But one never knew how the dynamic would change when a member—or two—fell in love.

First Ryder. Then Dalton. It could have been a disaster. Instead, Quinn and Colleen fit in so seamlessly, it was almost as though they had always been around. Funny, smart, sarcastic in the best possible way, and easy on the eyes. Ashe couldn't have been happier for his buddies.

There had been an unexpected side effect to all of this personal happiness floating around. Dissatisfaction with his own life. Not his love life. Ashe was fine with temporary. Women floated in and out. Quickly. With no remorse. Not his or theirs.

The small niggling feeling had to do with his family. The one he was born into. Perhaps it had to do with thirty looming in the not-too-distant future. Ashe wasn't concerned about getting older. However, as he aged, so did his parents. His father would turn sixty next month. Hopefully, Randall Mathison had many years left. That wasn't guaranteed.

Walking away from his family hadn't been an easy decision. But it had been the right one. Ashe vowed he would never return unless his father made the first move. Hateful words were said—on both sides. His father told him there would be no going back. Was that true? Ashe didn't feel the same burning resentment. His anger had mellowed.

Was it time to go home?

"Hey." Zoe snapped her fingers in his face. "Earth to saxophone boy. Are you with us?"

Shaking off the past, Ashe laughed. Looking around. Ryder. Dalton. Zoe. And now Quinn and Colleen. No matter what he decided, they would always be the family of his heart.

Slinging an arm around Zoe's shoulders, Ashe nodded. "Hell yes, I'm with you. What are we waiting for? Let's rock this place."

BELLE RICHARDS COULDN'T remember the last time she had such a good time. The music was fantastic. The band exciting. The crowd loud and just rowdy enough. Belle jumped right in, singing along. Yelling at the top of her lungs. What did it say about the state of her life that she had to cross the country to let loose? There were three thousand miles between herself and a job that left her cold and a fiancé who wasn't much better. Tomorrow she was headed back. She wanted to stay. Never leave. She should feel guilty. Instead, all Belle felt was regret that if she let things sail in the direction they were headed, this could be the last great night of her life for a very long time.

Somebody jostled Belle, reminding her there was a party going on. Forget next year. Or next month. Or next week. Tomorrow could go to hell. Tonight, Belle Richards was checking off an item on her bucket list. Number three. See *The Ryder Hart Band* live. Not only were they everything she dreamed they would be. They were more.

As the notes to the next song started, Belle let out a wild whoop. *On Your Mind*! It just kept getting better and better.

QUINN RAISED HER camera, randomly snapping shots. She loved standing backstage while the band played. But she always took the time to wander through the crowd. The photographs contained an energy she couldn't duplicate from a distance.

Aiming, she caught the excitement in each set of eyes. The joy. They knew every song. Had listened to each hundreds of times. This was different. *The Ryder Hart Band* put on a show few artists could equal. Topping it was impossible. If one loved the band's music—and who in their right mind didn't—one had to see them live at least once. There were fans who traveled from city to city. Continent to continent. Quinn had met them. Marveled at their devotion. Thought they were a little crazy. Of course, that was before she fell in love with Ryder Hart. Now, she understood completely.

Laughing at her thoughts, Quinn was about to head backstage when someone caught her attention. What it was about the woman that set her apart, Quinn couldn't have said. Not classically beautiful. Pretty. No. More than that. Arresting. That was the word. It was impossible to see the color of her eyes, but they were crinkled at the corners. Smiling eyes that matched the curve of her full lips. Quinn found herself drawn to the woman's utter enthusiasm for the moment. Taking her picture was a given. Ten photos later, Quinn couldn't resist. She struck up a conversation.

"Is this your first time?" Quinn yelled the words. She had no choice if she wanted to be heard.

"Yes." Beaming, she bounced in a circle, her arms in the air. "Amazing."

"I agree." It was like being drawn into sunshine. Happy and warm. "I'm Quinn."

"Belle."

Even her name made Quinn smile. "I take it you're a fan."

Belle nodded. "I used to know one of them."

Fascinated, Quinn leaned closer. "Used to?"

"My bedroom window looked into Ashe's." Belle laughed. "It's not as provocative as it sounds. Unfortunately."

If it had been Ryder or Dalton, Quinn would have moved along. Ashe might hate her for what she was about to do. But he wouldn't hold a grudge. Who knew? He might end up thanking Quinn.

"Would you like to come backstage and say hello?"

The color seemed to drain from Belle's flushed face. No longer bouncing, she turned her wide eyes toward Quinn.

"Are you kidding?"

"Nope." Quinn flashed the pass she wore around her neck.

"I shouldn't."

"You should." Quinn took Belle's arm, leading her through the crowd.

"He won't remember me."

"We'll remind him."

"I had a major crush." Hand flying to her mouth, Belle stopped in her tracks.

"We won't tell him *that*."

BELLE KNEW IT was a bad idea. Fantasy—even one as tempting as Ashe Mathison—was best when it stayed unattainable. She was setting herself up for disappointment. Why would Ashe remember the awkward girl next door? Two years older, he ran in different circles. They went to different private schools. Though their parents were friendly, they weren't the kind of people who had backyard barbecues or holiday open houses.

Nodding acquaintances. That was the best she could claim.

Coming to the concert was one thing. A fluky, unplanned opportunity. Only a fool would turn down a ticket to see the hottest band in the world—especially when it fell into her lap. *Stop this foolishness*, her brain commanded. After years of conditioning, Belle was good at listening to her brain. Logically, she should thank Quinn for the kind gesture, disappear into the crowd, and leave the lure of Ashe Mathison where it belonged. In her dreams.

For the first time in years, Belle's feet ignored her brain. Perhaps her heart had a bit to do with it. Before she could mount a protest, Quinn had them past security. The glances she received from some of the female concert goers helped to spur Belle on. It wasn't often women looked at her with envy. Why shouldn't she enjoy the moment?

"There you are." A gorgeous redhead greeted Quinn with a warm smile. "You were gone for most of the concert. How many pictures do you need?"

"Snapping photos is automatic. Vital. Like breathing in and out."

"If you say so. Who's your friend?"

"Colleen McNamara, meet Belle. I'm sorry. I didn't catch your last name."

Because I didn't throw it. It was an old joke. And might come off as snarky. Belle was a fan of some good snark, but under the circumstances, she simply held out her hand.

"Richards. It's nice to meet you."

"Belle is an old friend of Ashe's," Quinn explained. "Keep her company while I stow my camera bag in Ryder's dressing room."

"A friend of Ashe's?" Colleen's green eyes sparkled with interest. "Where from?"

"Boston."

Belle felt a wave of unease. Like Quinn, Colleen seemed genuinely interested. Nice. Open. But there was a layer of wariness in the emerald gaze. Was she Ashe's girlfriend? It was a possibility. One that made her stomach sink.

Belle didn't keep up with gossip. She loved *The Ryder Hart Band's* music. But she had no idea about their private lives. Not keeping track of Ashe had been a deliberate decision. The less she thought about him, the better. Which made her current situation all the more untenable. Turn and walk away. Forget Ashe. Go home to Boston. Your job. Your fiancé. Poor Theodore. Boring, nice, predictable Theodore. Though he never would say, Belle was certain he felt the same about her. She supposed on some weird level that made them perfect for each other.

"Boston? How long has it been since you spoke?"

"We didn't. Speak that is." When Colleen's eyes narrowed, Belle sighed. "I told your friend that I didn't think Ashe would remember me."

"Looks like we're about to find out."

The huge roar of the crowd drew Belle's attention.

"Thank you, Los Angeles. We've had a great time. Be safe. We'll see you soon."

Oh, boy. Surreptitiously, Belle wiped her palms on the slope of her denim-covered butt. This was a new feeling for her. Excited nerves with a tinge of the unknown making her stomach knot. Damn it. She was vice president of a billion-dollar company. She dealt with problems that

11

would have lesser women sweating through their designer suits. Meeting Ashe Mathison for the first time in over ten years shouldn't be such a stressful moment.

Pulling back her shoulders, Belle put on her best *I'm in control expression*. It wasn't true, but nobody else had to know. She did a quick rundown on what she was wearing. Fashionable faded jeans. A silk camisole. The heat meant her jacket was of the lightweight variety. Dove gray linen outlined in slightly darker piping. Wishing she had taken the time to check hair and makeup, Belle rolled her eyes, cursing herself for turning—even briefly—into one of *those* women. If her smoothly styled shoulder-length hair had turned into a rat's nest and her *Luscious Peach* lipstick was a distant memory, so what? Ashe could take her as she was or stick it where the sun don't shine.

Feeling better, Belle's shoulders relaxed. Her smile melted from forced to natural. Bright eyed with anticipation, she had no idea what her mental shakedown had done for her looks. This was the woman Quinn noticed in the crowd. Bright. Warm. She exuded a relaxed confidence turning her from pretty to breathtaking. Belle never thought of herself that way. When she perused herself in the mirror, she saw what most of her family, friends, and colleagues saw. Competent intelligence. Attractive in a slightly above-average way.

What Ashe saw as he exited the stage—the breathtaking Belle—stopped him in his tracks.

"TWO MINUTES. BE ready to go back for your encore."

The concert had flown by without a hitch. Critics liked to say that *The Ryder Hart Band* was at the top of their game. Ashe, Ryder, Zoe, and Dalton preferred the term 'better than ever.' That left room for growth. They refused to rest on their laurels. *Top of their game* sounded like there was nothing left to strive for. There would always be more. The day there wasn't would be the day they walked away.

Towel wrapped around his neck, Ashe grinned at something Zoe said. She had a wicked sense of humor. Dry. Sometimes a bit dark. It didn't always translate if one wasn't around her very much. Those who knew her understood that under her cool, polished exterior was a woman who loved to laugh—at herself as much as at others.

"I'm telling you," Zoe grinned. "There was a woman in the front row playing an imaginary saxophone. She kept mouthing, 'I love you, Ashe. I want to have your babies.'"

"You're making that last part up." Set up in the corner was a food service table. Ashe passed Zoe a bottle of water, grabbing another for himself. "There is no way you could read her lips."

"It's a gift," Zoe said, her expression neutral. "You wouldn't believe some of the things fans say from down there."

"Blush worthy?"

"I don't blush. But you?" Shrugging, Zoe masked her smile behind the bottle of water.

"Why haven't I heard about this before?"

"I didn't want to shock your delicate sensibilities."

"My ass," Ashe muttered good-naturedly.

Chuckling, Ashe turned to ask Ryder if he could confirm Zoe's bullshit. The question dissolved from his brain the second he saw her. *I know you.* There was something about the way she stood. The curve of her lips. But mostly, it was her eyes. Big, brown, and expressive. If he didn't know her, he wanted to.

"Ashe!" Zoe tugged at his arm. "Encore time. Maybe your prospective baby-mama will mouth her phone number. I'll make a note."

Ashe didn't give a damn about the woman in the audience. It was *this* woman that had his attention. Afraid she would disappear before they finished their encore, he took a step in her direction. Something flashed in her eyes. Ashe wasn't certain what it was, but it triggered his memory.

"Belle?"

"Hello, Ashe."

"Get your ass in gear, Mathison." Dalton shoved Ashe in the direction of the stage. "Hear those cheers? That's our cue."

Keeping his eyes on Belle as Dalton dragged him along, just before he lost sight of her, Ashe called out, "Don't you dare move. Understand?"

Belle didn't say anything, but her smile widened. Because he wanted it to be, Ashe took it as a yes.

Two songs—and what seemed like endless bows—later, Ashe rushed backstage. His gaze went to the same spot. When he didn't see Belle, he felt a wave of disappointment. And a flash of anger. Goddamn it. Hadn't he told her not to move? Hadn't she smiled? If not legally binding, it was an agreement reached by two consenting adults. That should have counted for something. What was wrong with people these days?

"If you're looking for Belle, she was waylaid by Alden." Colleen pointed to her right. "He recognized her from some charity he co-chairs. Or something like that."

Relief washed over Ashe. For two reasons. First, Belle. That was it. Belle. Second, he was grateful Colleen wasn't a mind reader. His thoughts were a little intense. And a lot embarrassing. Ashe had a reputation for keeping his emotions on an even keel. Never one to overreact. His response to Belle would have surprised his friends. Almost as much as it surprised him.

"She didn't think you would recognize her."

"I didn't at first." Ashe addressed Colleen while keeping an eye on Belle. "It's been a long time."

Shaking her head, Colleen let out a slow whistle. "I'll give it to her. Quinn has the knack."

"What are talking about?"

"Quinn decided there was something special between Dalton and me before we met. She's the one who plucked Belle out of the audience. For you."

14

"Jesus, Colleen." Ashe dismissed her words as crazy. "Never say those words to another living soul."

"Not a problem." Laughing, Colleen sauntered away.

"My advice is to grab a shower before you speak with Belle. You're starting to smell a little ripe." Quinn waved a hand under her nose. "A woman can overlook a lot. Body odor is a tough sell. Even for a man with your legendary charm."

"Did you and Colleen decide it was tag team Ashe night? I'm going to exchange a few words with an old friend. I don't need a shower for that."

"Belle told me you weren't friends," Quinn said before Ashe could move.

"What else did Belle say?"

"Not much. You were neighbors with bedroom windows that faced each other. And you never spoke." Quinn paused for effect. "Ever."

Was that right? It didn't sound right. Or possible. In all those years, he and Belle must have exchanged a few words. The fact that Ashe couldn't remember any particular instance didn't bode well for his theory.

Scratching his neck, Ashe frowned. The sweat that poured off him during the concert was drying fast, leaving a layer of sticky salt. Maybe Quinn was right. A shower would make him feel better and give him time to think. Why would he recognize Belle if they hadn't interacted? It made no sense.

"I should get cleaned up."

"I'll make sure Belle is here when you get back."

Nodding his thanks, Ashe headed to his dressing room.

The usual crowd milled about in the halls. Mostly crew members tackling after-concert duties. Breaking down equipment, packing it up, making certain everything made it onto the trucks. Ashe nodded at the familiar faces. These were the people he saw every day when the band

15

was on tour. He knew their names. If they were married. When new babies were born. In their own way, they were family.

Security was tight. Crazies came in every form. A few years ago, they had problems with a stalker. From the outside, she looked like somebody's grandmother straight out of a Norman Rockwell painting. However, her obsession turned bizarre. She swore she was pregnant with Ashe's love child, going so far as to show up at a concert with a fake baby bump. She charged the stage, screaming for him to do the right thing by her and their child. The media picked up the story, treating it as a big joke. The woman ended up in a local psych ward. Ashe didn't find *that* terribly funny.

"Great show, Ashe." Billy Boyd, head of their security staff, opened the door to Ashe's dressing room. "All clear."

Billy and his crew checked the band's dressing rooms before and after every performance. It wasn't overkill. More than once an industrious fan was found hiding in a closet or in a shower stall—clothing optional. Ashe liked a naked woman as much as the next guy. *Random* naked women were a completely different matter.

"Thanks, Billy. How is that new grandbaby of yours?"

Billy beamed, his burly chest swelling with pride. "Little Billie is an angel. Thankfully she looks more like Grandma than Grandpa."

"I can't wait to meet her."

The second he was alone, Ashe unbuttoned his shirt, tossing the blue silk on the nearest chair. He didn't worry about making a mess nor who would clean it up. It was one of the perks of success and money. It was the same at his house. Three times a week a cleaning service swept up his clutter. Ashe was good about getting his dirty socks into the hamper and filling the dishwasher. That was it.

Reaching into the shower stall, Ashe turned the faucets on full. Hot. Close to scalding. With a sigh, he turned his face toward the water and let the sweat slide from his body, swirling down the drain. One hand braced against the wall, he closed his eyes. Then smiled when Belle's face popped into his head.

16

Damn. Talk about a blast from the past. Ashe tried to remember the last time he had seen her. A specific moment. Try as he might, none came to mind. They hadn't been friends. She was younger. Not a lot. Maybe a year or two. They had attended different schools. Wealthy Boston families had many choices for the education of their children. Some might say endless choices if their only criteria were a strong curriculum and excellent teachers. Bragging rights counted for the nouveau riche. Getting one's kid into an exclusive private institution was a sign of acceptance—as long as the tuition was paid on time and in full.

For old money, it was all about tradition. Ashe was sent to the prep school attended by his father, his father's father, and so on. *Winsted Academy* turned out future titans of business. Congressmen and women. Senators. They hadn't managed to infiltrate the Oval Office. However, one graduate *had* received his party's nomination. All this was carefully chronicled. The picture-lined corridors were daily reminders of how much could be achieved with a *Winsted* education. Ashe doubted he would find his face on those hallowed walls. Rock stars—no matter how successful—were not brag-worthy material.

It didn't matter which school Belle attended. The names changed, the snobbery was interchangeable. That thought gave Ashe pause. Grabbing a towel, he stepped out of the shower. Belle was from the world he walked away from. Had she stayed or broken away? Would he find a stuffed shirt housed beneath that unique beauty and warm smile?

Running the towel over his head, Ashe grabbed a clean pair of jeans followed by a blue cotton button-down shirt. Lovely Belle Richards. Perhaps they had never exchanged more than a few words. Subconsciously, she made an impression. One that stuck with him all these years.

Wiping the steam from the bathroom mirror, Ashe gave himself a quick once over. He wore his dark hair short, the ends curling slightly where they touched his neck. Gray eyes that were more often filled with good humor than anger or doom and gloom. Sometimes he shaved. Sometimes he didn't. The stubble on his cheeks had more to do with his mood that morning than a desire to look fashionably unkempt.

"When was the last time a woman made you think this hard?" Ashe asked his reflection with an ironic twist to his mouth.

All ego aside, not surprisingly, the answer was never. Women liked him. They always had. And Ashe liked them. He liked the way they sounded. The way they smelled. Most of all, he liked the way they felt in his arms. Soft and smooth. Curvy was his preference. Uncomplicated was his style.

No random hook-ups. Ashe was a fan of the wine and dine. Sex was better with mental as well as physical foreplay. A few nights. A fond farewell. That was his style. While the encounters were nice—very nice—they weren't particularly memorable. Ashe knew how that sounded. What could he say? He wasn't against forming a long-term relationship. Nor was he looking. Someday. Maybe. For now, he was happy with the status quo.

Which brought him back to Belle Richards. She interested him. The reasons were easy to figure out. A reminder of the past—a subject that had been on Ashe's mind with growing frequency—Belle represented a part of his life he thought he had left behind without regret. Now, he wasn't sure.

Was there more? The attraction? The pull? Ashe was interested to find out if it would last beyond a proper hello. With one more glance in the mirror, he shrugged. Maybe. Maybe not. Grinning, he ran his fingers through his hair. Either way, it would be fun finding out.

CHAPTER TWO

"BOSTON? GREAT CITY." Dalton Shaw's blue eyes held an expression that could only be termed *faintly bored*. Any second, Belle expected him to yawn.

"Very historical," Belle said it with a straight face, but her lips twitched. "Should I launch into a lengthy discourse on Paul Revere? My father owns an authentic silver paper weight forged by the man himself."

"Really. That's fascinating." Surreptitiously, Dalton scanned the area as though hoping the cavalry was on the way. He must be cursing Colleen for leaving him with the task of entertaining Belle.

"It is fascinating." Belle paused for a beat. Her next words were accompanied by a laugh. "If you are a collector. Or a historian. For the rest of us, it is boring as hell."

"God, yes." Air rushed from Dalton's lungs. Relief seemed to waft from him in waves. With a laugh, he pulled Belle in for a quick, friendly hug. "Thank you. I can't do small talk."

"I can." Belle's words were self-deprecating. She was a master at making a discussion of the weather last longer than what should be humanly possible. Walking in a no-bullshit zone was a nice change of pace. "May I ask you a personal question?"

A shutter came down over Dalton's blue eyes. "You can *always* ask."

Belle leaned closer, her whisper conspiratorial. "Would it be possible for me to trade this bottle of water for a beer?"

There was a beat of silence before Dalton burst out laughing. "Hey, Ashe. While you're at it, grab a long neck for Belle."

Swallowing, Belle followed Dalton's line of sight. Ashe. Freshly showered, looking relaxed and refreshed, he nodded, sending her a friendly smile before taking two beers from the small refrigerator. Though enjoying herself immensely, Belle couldn't help feeling the moment was slightly surreal. Here she was, standing in a room with *The*

19

Ryder Hart Band. She had met them. Exchanged words. They looked like, like… well, like normal people. If normal people were insanely attractive and charismatic. Okay, Belle admitted, Ryder Hart, Dalton Shaw, and Zoe Hart weren't close to resembling normal people. But they were a surprise. She had expected an air of entitlement. Standoffishness. Instead, they were open and friendly. Welcoming her. Not with open arms. That would have seemed strange—to say the least. But Belle felt that she *could* become close to them. Given time and opportunity. That couldn't be said for the majority of people she met.

"Here you go."

Taking the bottle, Belle smiled, trying hard to think of something to say. It had been a breeze with Dalton. Nerves didn't stop her. Those had dissipated long ago. It was the realization that she didn't know this man. She never had. Ashe had always been a concept more than a reality. Quinn invited her backstage because Belle claimed a connection. But what they had was superficial at best.

"I'm sorry about this." For something to do, Belle took a sip of the beer. "I should have stopped Quinn. I've been foisted off on you with no warning."

"Hardly foisted."

Ashe's warm gray gaze hadn't wavered. It made Belle intensely aware of everything. The way her heartbeat spiked and her breaths became shallow. Heat rushed over her skin. Belle knew what attraction felt like. At least she thought she did. This was different. It was… more. Wonderfully potent. She wished it were possible to pack the feelings in her suitcase and take them with her back to Boston.

"I'm barely an acquaintance. Not even that. It's kind of you to pretend otherwise."

"What makes you think I'm pretending?" When Ashe smiled, Belle felt a lovely warmth in the pit of her stomach. "I recognized you almost instantly."

"That was a surprise." *To say the least.* "I didn't think you knew I was alive back then."

"Back then, I was wrapped up in a lot of family drama. *And* I was a self-centered teenage boy. However, only a blind man could fail to notice you."

Ashe brushed her hand with his. One little touch. Less than strangers passing on a crowded street. Belle knew it was silly. Juvenile. But it left her slightly breathless.

"Come on." The reaction of her body was one thing. Her brain worked fine. Fully grown with a woman's maturity and intelligence. She knew a load of bullshit when she heard it. "In all the years we lived next door to each other, we barely spoke. Now you expect me to believe I made a lasting impression?"

"Ah ha!"

Belle jumped. Literally. "Excuse me?"

"You told Quinn that we had never spoken. *Never.* I wondered how that was possible. Now you admit we did speak. Hence, ah ha."

Hence? Belle laughed. It wasn't a word she heard every day. However, she wasn't going to let that sidetrack her. Ashe looked mighty smug. Time to knock him down a peg. Or two.

"Until just now, you weren't certain, were you?"

"No. But—"

"You can't recall a single conversation. Not a single moment when we interacted."

"That may be true. Still, I—"

"Is it any wonder I was surprised that you recognized me? And knew my name?"

Belle enjoyed the disconcerted expression on Ashe's face. At this moment, he wasn't a world-famous rock star. He was the boy next door. Only, Belle had no reason to blush or duck out of sight every time he passed by. They were on equal footing as adults. No. Not equal. For once, Belle had the upper hand. It brought a smile to her lips.

"Whatever you have on your mind, think again. The point—the only thing that matters—is that I knew you."

Yes, he had. The knowledge didn't diminish Belle's enjoyment of their light banter. Just the opposite. All that time when she was dreaming in her bedroom—wishing he knew she was alive—the truth was, Ashe Mathison *had* noticed her. Belle wondered what her fifteen-year-old self would have done with that exciting bit of information. She didn't have to search very hard for the answer. What would she have done? Absolutely nothing. She had been too shy to make the first move on any boy. Experience wise, Ashe had been so far out of her league it was mind boggling to even contemplate. Belle wouldn't have known what to do with him. If she had worked up the nerve to try, the only outcome would have been complete and abject humiliation.

However, Belle was curious. If Ashe liked what he saw, why hadn't *he* done something about it?

"You could have asked me out."

Slowly, Ashe shook his head. Again, he touched her hand, lingering. "There were so many reasons why that would never have happened."

"Give me three." Belle couldn't help herself. She wanted to know.

"Ashe!" From across the room, Dalton called out. "It's closing time, brother. The folks at the Hollywood Bowl want to put the old girl to sleep."

"Right behind you." Ashe met Belle's gaze. "Your question will have to wait."

Until when? The last thing Belle had was time. At nine tomorrow morning, her plane would leave for Boston. This strange interlude would be over, and she would never know. If one of them had stepped left instead of right, was there a possibility—even a minuscule one—that her life would be different today? More important, did she want to know? *What if.* It was a dangerous game to play. Especially for a woman who was already trending toward dissatisfied with her life.

Who was she trying to fool? Belle had passed dissatisfied long ago. A few hours and a few questions answered. It wouldn't make things worse. It couldn't. Maybe, if she were lucky, Belle would return home with an imperceptible spring in her step. It didn't matter if nobody noticed. She would know.

"Do you have someplace to be?"

"No." Ashe tipped his head to the side, his lips slowly curving up. "What did you have in mind?"

"Nothing *that* provocative." At least that was what Belle told herself.

"Too bad." Laughing, Ashe took her hand, tucking it into the curve of his elbow. "The rest of my night is yours."

"Two old acquaintances catching up?"

"If that's what you'd like. Sure. Why not?"

Belle knew she was playing with fire. Everything that came out of Ashe's mouth sounded like a come on. *The rest of my night is yours. If that's what you'd like.* Deep in her secret desires, Belle knew what she would like. Was she capable of taking it? She was about to find out.

"Ashe?"

"Hmm?"

"Let's go to your place."

THE LUXURIOUS DOWNTOWN condominium was so perfect, Belle was speechless. She imagined Beverly Hills. A huge mansion behind a security-tight gated community. A man of Ashe's high profile needed to keep out the crazies. He deserved the sense of well-being a place like that would provide. That was what she had expected.

Not that the condominium was scaled down. The wide-open living room was huge. Hardwood floors gleamed from corner to corner, flowing into a kitchen that made her drool with envy. Belle loved to cook. It was something she discovered when she moved into her own place. Without her parents' full-time cook to provide meals, it was either learn to make her own or rely on going out and order in. Surprising

23

herself—and her friends and family—Belle became a talented amateur chef. As with most things, she learned cooking was as much about confidence as skill. As soon as she lost her hesitancy, she flourished. Baking was her latest favorite activity.

"I covet your double oven." Belle ran her hand over the professional-grade appliance.

"I've never heard that one before." With a chuckle, Ashe handed her a glass of brandy. "Most people go straight for the view. You're the first visitor to fondle my stainless steel."

Not the least bit embarrassed, Belle moved from the oven to the counters. "Poured concrete?"

"So I understand."

"Sub-Zero." Belle sighed when she caught sight of the refrigerator. Inspired, she took out her phone. "I need a picture. This is practically my dream kitchen."

"Practically?" Ashe stood behind her, taking it in from her angle. "What would you change?"

"I want a huge island. One with a cook top and sink for prepping vegetables and so forth. The rest would be tweaking. Color schemes. A different backsplash. But the layout is fantastic. Very cook friendly."

"Good to know."

"Are you laughing at me?" Belle put her phone away. When she looked at Ashe, his smile was warm, not derisive. "I tend to get carried away when something interests me."

"Come with me."

Naturally, as though he did it every day, Ashe took Belle's free hand. Large and strong, it felt good in hers. He led her down a well-lit hallway. The walls were covered with pictures that another time Belle would have loved to spend time perusing. Ashe's life. Friends. Fellow musicians. Unlike the photographs in her parents' home, they didn't appear to be professionally posed portraits where the subjects stared glassy-eyed at the camera, their smiles wooden. What drew Belle the most was the candid nature of the shots. They made her wish she had been there to hear the music. To share the good times.

At the end of the hall, Ashe opened a door, flipping on the light switch.

"Passion, Belle. You find it in the kitchen. This is where I find mine."

Carefully, Belle entered. The room was wall-to-wall instruments. Some were tucked in corners, others hung on the walls. There was order to the chaos. Though crowded, everything appeared to have its place. In the center of the room, in a place of honor, sat a grand piano.

Unlike the appliances, Belle was reluctant to touch. As though sensing her dilemma, Ashe took her hand, placing it on the smooth surface.

"It's beautiful, Ashe." For some reason, Belle felt the need to speak in hushed tones. She circled the piano, sitting on the bench. Her gaze took in the filled room. Most of the instruments were familiar to her, others, not so much. On the far wall was an intriguingly curved horn, the wood from which it was crafted meticulously polished to a dazzling finish. Belle had never seen anything like it.

"I began collecting before I could afford to. Some are priceless. Some I bought for a song—literally." The memory brought a smile to Ashe's face that took Belle's breath away.

"Can you play them all?"

"Yes." There was no bragging in Ashe's tone. Plain and simple. Fact was fact. "Do you play?"

Belle plucked out an awkward tune. She had taken piano lessons for about a month. Though she sometimes wished she had stuck with it, she hadn't the patience. Lips curving into a self-deprecating smile, Belle did their ears a favor, pulling her hand away.

"Does that answer your question?"

Setting his glass to the side, Ashe lightly laid his long fingers on the keys. There was nothing awkward in the way he played. Just a few notes and she was drawn in—wanting more. The tune was unfamiliar, but it enveloped her in its beauty. Belle closed her eyes. She cupped her brandy in both hands, sipping the warm liquid. Simultaneously, the alcohol and music entered her blood. Heady, they mixed, swirled, making her giddy.

"This song is a little rough. I can't quite get a handle on it."

"It's beautiful."

"It will be. Eventually. You, lovely Belle, already are. You always have been."

Belle didn't know if it was the music, the brandy, Ashe's words. Or the way his breath caressed her cheek. She didn't want to think too hard. She didn't want to stop or worry about the consequences. All she wanted to do was feel. For once, Belle wanted to jump. Safety net be damned, she closed the small distance that separated them and kissed Ashe.

It was a bold move—at least for Belle. She wasn't a virgin, but her experience was limited. Because it wasn't her nature to let a man know when she was interested, she waited for them to make the first move. While there had been a fair share of propositions, most she turned down because there was no overriding need to say yes. There was no question of that with Ashe. She wanted him. From the way he kissed her back, it seemed he felt the same.

"This isn't what I expected." Ashe touched the corner of her mouth with his tongue.

"No?" Belle had hoped. She had tried to talk herself out of it. But the effort had been half-hearted at best.

"I wanted to get to know you. Conversation before carnality." Ashe slipped his hand under the hem of Belle's shirt, his calloused fingertips playing with the soft skin at the base of her back.

"Carnality? Good word."

Descriptive. Appropriate. For the first time in her life, Belle felt her body taking over from her brain. She always thought too much before sex. And during sex. After, she thought that sex was much ado about nothing. Telling herself to let go was one thing, doing it was another. With Ashe, she didn't think about anything beyond his taste and touch. Belle smiled when she heard Ashe groan. It was a good sound. Better, knowing her hand cupping him through his jeans was the cause.

"You're killing me *and* my good intentions, Belle."

"Do you want me to stop?" *Please say no*, Belle begged silently.

"What the hell." Ashe scooped her into his arms, heading across the room and out the door. "Conversation is overrated."

"You can talk to me during." Belle like that idea. It wasn't a novel idea, simply one she had never implemented.

"Dirty talk?" Ashe kissed her, his lips perfectly firm. "Is that what you like?"

Belle had no idea. But it sounded good. One night. That was all she had. That meant no holding back. On anything.

"How dirty can you get?"

Ashe's gray eyes twinkled mischievously. He tossed her onto the bed, following close behind. "Foul. Think you can take it?"

"Try me."

"Remember. You asked for it."

The words weren't unknown. At one time or another, Belle had heard—or read—them all. What made her blood heat and her bones melt was the way Ashe strung them together. Talk about imaginative. Belle's skin flushed, then burned—in the best possible way. Words were great. However, when Ashe added action, she wondered if the world would fly off its axis. Or perhaps it was only her. Gravity was no longer an issue. She defied the laws of nature. Belle wasn't floating. Ashe was teaching her how to fly.

Magically, Belle's clothing disappeared. One second she wished she could feel Ashe's skin against hers, the next, her desire became reality.

"You're a magician," Belle declared with a sigh.

When had her breasts become so sensitive? The second Ashe kissed the tips, moving from one to the other, drawing the straining peak into his mouth.

"Now you see me." Ashe slid down Belle's body. "Now you don't."

It wasn't that Ashe dematerialized. Belle knew exactly where he was. And what he was doing with his mouth—between her legs. Seeing him did become a problem. With her head tipped back in abandon, her eyes closed and her senses concentrated on the center of her pleasure. One little spot. Expertly manipulated. If that wasn't magic, Belle didn't know what was.

"Talk to me, Belle."

Clutching at Ashe's hair, holding him close, Belle struggled to form a coherent thought. Words? How did they work? She opened her mouth, but all that came out was one long, heartfelt moan. It must have been what he was looking for.

"There you go." Ashe kissed the ultra-soft skin on the inside of her thigh. "Music to my ears."

Belle wanted to laugh, but Ashe chose that moment to renew his ministration. A lick followed by his teeth, and an amazingly erotic bite to just the right spot, sent her bursting over the edge from amusement to orgasm in the blink of an eye. Or in this case, the lap of a tongue.

Like a feather. That was how Belle felt as she came back to Earth. Light. Breezy. Free.

"I think the top of my head blew off. And you know what? I couldn't care less."

"Nope." Ashe slid his fingers through her hair, massaging Belle's scalp. "Completely intact. Good thing, too. I am not nearly finished with you."

"Is that so?"

"Ready for round two?"

In spite of feeling like a very satisfied limp rag, a surge of adrenaline shot through her. Belle watched through barely raised eyelids as Ashe rolled on a condom. Thoughtful. They hadn't discussed protection—much to her chagrin. Thank goodness one of them had maintained the sense to play it safe.

"I was taught to always be polite." Belle brought Ashe in for a long, lusty kiss. "Thank you. For before. As for another round? Yes, please."

"So sweet." Moving to his knees, Ashe entered her slowly, keeping his eyes pinned on hers. "This is my way of saying you're very, very welcome."

It didn't take long for polite chit chat to fly out the window. Down and dirty. Hard. Fast. There wasn't time to breathe, let alone talk. Ashe took Belle up, up, up. Higher than the first time until she was certain she saw stars. And a burst of sunlight. Was that possible? Scientists might scoff, but Belle would have sworn to it. Not that she planned on telling anybody. This was between her and Ashe. Wonderfully, completely private.

No more imagining how it might be. Ashe had given Belle a perfect memory to treasure. And she knew she would. Forever.

CHAPTER THREE

ASHE HAD ALWAYS been a morning person. As a child, he was always the first one up—except for the cook. She rose before dawn to start the dough for the bread his father insisted she bake fresh every day. Ashe would sit, eating his cereal, not terribly interested in what she was doing. His mind was already racing ahead toward the day's activities. The whys and wherefores changed as he grew older. But the process never had.

The desire to rise with the sun wasn't the best fit with Ashe's adult lifestyle. He was a musician. That meant late nights. Concerts. Recording sessions. After parties for both. His job screamed night owl. His internal clock had never gotten the message. No matter how late his head hit the pillow, Ashe woke early. However, there were exceptions. Between the concert and Belle, last night turned out to be one of them.

Opening his eyes, Ashe frowned when the burst of sunlight blinded him. What the hell? He never closed the bedroom curtains because he was always awake to greet the dawn. Unless he was just getting in. Either way, it was disconcerting to find the sun so far up in the morning sky. Ashe was about to roll out of bed when he remembered why he was still there.

Grinning with anticipation, Ashe reached out, expecting to find Belle. Instead, he found cold sheets and a piece of paper. *Well, shit.* Neither discovery boded well for a pleasant start to his day. Pulling himself to a sitting position, Ashe rubbed the rest of the sleep from his eyes. With a resigned sigh, he picked up the note.

Ashe,

I know how this looks. Sneaking away in the middle of the night is rude and juvenile. One-night stands aren't my forte, and I didn't have time to look up the proper etiquette.

Thank you. It's all I have, but believe me, the words are sincere. We were never friends. Old acquaintances is pushing it. But I will never forget last night.

One more thing. I'm completely healthy. I should have mentioned that before you performed oral sex on me. I was a bit distracted.

Belle

Short, to the point, and so utterly ridiculous, Ashe almost expected Belle to pop out of the bathroom, calling out *just kidding*. Reading it again, he crumpled it into a ball, hurling it across the room. To be honest, Ashe didn't know what to think.

Belle was gone. On her way back to Boston, he supposed. Had he gotten around to asking if that was where she still lived? Ashe didn't think so. They hadn't gotten around to much. Except for one hotter than hell night of sex. With the lady long gone, that made it a one-night stand. His first in how long? He couldn't remember.

Ashe rolled from bed. *You performed oral sex on me*. No argument there. And he enjoyed every second. Licking his lips, he picked up the note, smoothing out the edges. He could still taste Belle's sweetness.

One night. Ashe had to admit it was disconcerting. He fell asleep thinking of more. Woke with sex on his mind. Sex with Belle. But she made it clear in a few succinct lines that she hadn't felt the same.

Thank you. Ashe chuckled. Polite to the end. Belle was... unique. Heading toward the bathroom, he laid the note on the dresser. This was one he would have to chalk up to experience. Move on. No mistake. No regrets. Well, maybe one. Ashe glanced at her words with a sigh. He would regret never again having Belle Richards in bed.

THE RECORDING STUDIO was silent. Normally when the band was gathered in the acoustically friendly area, there was music. Or singing. Or both. Either live or on playback. It was an expensive space. When *The Ryder Hart Band* stepped through its doors, they were there to work. Not goof off. Not socialize.

And definitely not argue. Yet here they were, doing exactly that. At least, Ryder and Zoe were arguing. Ashe and Dalton were checking their emails. Surfing the internet. Playing video games on their phones. In other words, waiting for the tempest to play to its conclusion.

31

"We don't need another headliner," Zoe insisted for the third, or maybe it was the fourth, time. The heated discussion had been raging for over half an hour. When the brother and sister started repeating themselves, Ashe tuned them out. "We sell out every venue we play. Taking on someone of equal stature—and I use the term loosely—would be nothing but an unnecessary headache."

"This isn't about filling seats, Zoe. It's about reaching a different audience. And," Ryder interjected before she could interrupt, "It wouldn't be a full tour. Just a few dates scattered throughout next summer. Half a dozen."

"I don't see the problem," Dalton threw in his two cents for the first time. "Smith Carson is a good dude."

"How do you know?" Zoe stopped pacing, crossing her arms over her chest, her voice cool.

Add an intimidating icy blue stare and most people backed down rather than take her on. Her bandmates weren't most people. They were her friends. Her family. And they knew her better than anybody. That stare only worked when she was in the right. Today, Dalton didn't think that was the case.

"I will admit, I don't know Smith well. But his reputation is solid. In this business, assholes are identified quickly. We would have heard if he was a prima donna."

"Dalton is right, Zoe." Ryder picked a few chords on his guitar. It was how he gathered his thoughts. "Smith Carson is known as a nose-to-the-grindstone artist. He works hard and expects the people around him to do the same."

"Fine." Zoe resumed pacing. "He's a stand-up guy. That doesn't mean we want to litter our shows with his—"

"Trash?" Ryder chuckled. "You couldn't say it, could you?"

Zoe's gaze emblazoned. Never a good sign. "I will admit he knows his craft."

"Smith has a different sound than ours, but it is still first rate. He will be a good complement to us. Dalton? Are you on board?"

"I vote yes."

"Ashe?"

Ashe stared at his phone, unaware that he had become the center of attention. A text had just arrived. To call it unexpected was putting it mildly.

"Hey." Dalton knocked Ashe's leg with the tip of his custom-made boot. "Put down the phone for five seconds. We're taking a vote."

Frowning, Ashe raised his head. "I've been invited to my father's sixtieth birthday party."

That quieted the room. Fast. Ashe rarely spoke of his family because there was nothing to say. He and his oldest sister remained close, but only communicated by phone or email. She would update him on births or illnesses. It wasn't an ideal situation. He loved his sister. But their father's dictates ruled her world.

"Do you think your father is behind the invite?" Ryder asked, setting aside his guitar.

Family was a touchy subject for all of them. They knew each other's stories. If somebody needed to talk, there was always a sympathetic ear available. However, it didn't happen often. Ryder had come to grips with his childhood. As had Dalton. Zoe? Sometimes Ashe wondered if anybody—even Ryder—knew what went on behind her intense blue eyes.

As for him, Ashe thought he had made peace with what happened. His father had given him a choice. Stay with his family or leave and face almost total estrangement. At the time, it had been easy. Now, he wasn't as certain. Not that Ashe believed it had been a mistake. This was the life he was meant to live. But he would have handled it differently. He would have tried harder to make his father understand. Over the years, he would have kept trying.

Sometimes, it felt like it was too late. Years passed, making the divide seem wider. Impossible to bridge. This might be his last chance to try.

"I can't see my old man bending. But I would have said the same about myself."

"You want to go." Dalton nodded, understanding. "If nothing else, a trip back to Boston will give you some closure."

Dalton had gotten his own closure not long ago. It hadn't been easy. There had been people in his past who tried their best to trip him up. But he did it. In fact, things had worked out better than Dalton could have anticipated.

"Hell, it should be a piece of cake. Unlike you, I won't have half of a town against me," Ashe kidded.

Dalton chuckled. Not that long ago, he wouldn't have found any humor in such a joke. "They were the stupid half. You won't be that lucky."

It was true. Nobody would call his family stupid. Ashe came from a long line of successful entrepreneurs. The Mathisons didn't make their many, many millions by engaging in foolish behavior—in or out of the boardroom. They were bone-deep conservatives and proud of it.

"I need to go." There was no waver in Ashe's voice. He had made up his mind—as usual—with the support and input from his friends. Grinning, he added, "However, I won't mention that I vote Democrat."

"Great. Lovely. We are all on board politically. Call us if you need us."

Ashe turned to Ryder. "Why do I get the feeling Zoe wants to rush me out the door?"

"She'll miss you. We all will." Ryder's lips twitched when Zoe let out a frustrated growl. "How are you voting?"

Confused, Ashe looked around. "I told you how I'm voting. Liberal."

"Jeez." Zoe threw her hands up. "Not in November. Do we or do we not ax the idea of touring with Smith Carson?"

"Oh." Ashe had forgotten all about their potential touring partner. "Sorry, kid. I'm with Ryder and Dalton on this one."

"Fine." In a huff, Zoe picked up her guitar case. "Mark my words, you'll regret this decision."

"She'll cool down," Ryder assured him as the echo of Zoe's exit rang in their ears. She might not yell, but she was a master door slammer. "About your trip. Do you want to take the plane?"

"Damn straight," Ashe declared. "If I'm going to see my father, I'm going in style."

DAY AFTER DAY, all over the world, before they leave the house, there were people who donned a uniform. Mail carriers. Fast food servers. Men and women who serve in the Armed Forces. It became so much a part of their routine, after a while, it was done without special thought. Nobody stopped to contemplate what they did. They simply did it.

Before her trip to Los Angeles, Belle had reached that point. It was true that she had more options than most. The color, cut, and style of her suits were up to her. That didn't make them any less a uniform. If she had shown up at the office in t-shirt and jeans or thigh-high leather boots. Or, on a swelteringly hot day like today, a flirty sundress in the color of bright yellow daisies, more than a few eyebrows would be raised. Within minutes of her arrival, the big boss would have called her into his office for a firm talking to. If she weren't the boss' daughter, it might result in her termination. *That* was how strict they were at *Richards Inc.*

A month ago, Belle would have taken her shower. Dried her hair. Applied the usual light coat of makeup—another thing the company had strict ideas about—and pulled Thursday's outfit from her rigidly organized closet. Medium-heeled pumps in a complementary neutral shade. Stockings weren't mandatory, though a woman just starting with *Richards* was smart to wear them. Archaic and arbitrary it might be; these things were noticed.

Belle felt the flush of indecision. Blue? Beige? Summer green? Why couldn't she grab and go the way she always had? As long as the jacket was tailored and the skirt pressed, nobody cared. *She* hadn't. And that was the problem. Long before California or a certain rock star, Belle had stopped caring. No. That wasn't fair. She cared about doing her job to the best of her ability. She cared about the people she worked with. Most of all, she cared about her family—as frustrating as they could be.

To rephrase, Belle cared. Too much sometimes. Right now, she cared that she was an automaton when it came to her clothing. Be bold, a little voice urged. Forget the conservative suit—just for one day. The company balked at the idea of casual Friday. Be a trendsetter. Call it Breakout Thursday.

Who was she kidding? Certainly not herself. With a sigh, Belle blindly grabbed a seasonally appropriate uniform, a plain, no-nonsense blouse, and boring shoes. At least they didn't pinch her feet.

Setting the ensemble on her bed, Belle padded to the kitchen for a quick breakfast. On the weekends she liked to splurge with an omelet or blueberry pancakes. In Belle's book, living alone was no excuse for not getting creative with her meals. However, during the week, she seldom had time for more than a bowl of cold cereal.

Grabbing a spoon, Belle settled at her sweet antique table with the wonderfully mismatched chairs. Her place. Her taste. It was such a joy to pick and choose as she liked. Two years ago when her mother remodeled, Penelope Richards hired the most exclusive decorator in New England. Out with the old, in with the overpriced and pretentious. Belle shuddered when she thought about the paisley and dark chocolate color scheme. It wasn't her mother's taste. As far as she knew, it wasn't anybody's taste. However, it gave her mother bragging rights—and a photo shoot in some magazine Belle had never heard of. It was read by the right women who lived in the right neighborhoods who frequented the right parties. The gossip at these parties could be brutal. The preferred sport was ass kissing one second, backstabbing the next. Penelope—and her décor—received plenty of both.

For her last birthday, Belle was offered the services of that same exclusive designer. Not for Belle's apartment. According to her mother, what would be the point? This gift was for the future. For Belle's home *after* the wedding. The wedding to the perfect man. The wedding that had been postponed. Twice. Each time, Theo had an excuse. Business.

The flu on top of more business. Not terribly viable excuses in the scheme of things. Since their families wanted this match, they were giving him a lot of leeway. Since Belle would have been happy to delay until the next millennium, she didn't push. She had her suspicions as to why Theo's feet were turning from cold to blocks of ice. If he didn't fess up, she would have to call him on it.

When it happened, the fallout was going to be huge—mostly on Theo's side of the family fence. Though Belle imagined more than one finger would get pointed her way. It was inevitable. But it wasn't going to happen today. She had too much on her plate. Belle had plans to shake things up—just a little to start—at *Richards Inc*. To do that, she had to keep on her father's good side.

As Belle raised and lowered her spoon, not really tasting what she was putting in her mouth, she tapped the screen on her iPad, scrolling through her personal email. It was the usual. A sale at *Williams-Sonoma* caught her eye. Saving it as a treat for later, she moved on. Nothing caught her eye until she came across her mother's usual subject line. *I need to see you A.S.A.P.*

And good morning to you too, Mom. Smiling, Belle put the tablet aside. She rinsed out her bowl, put it in the dishwasher, and headed toward the bathroom to brush her teeth. The email would only be the beginning. Before lunch, her mother would add a text—sent by her personal assistant. That afternoon would see another email and finally a phone call. It didn't matter that Belle shot back a response to the original message promising to stop by after work. This was her mother's method. Always had been, always would be.

Belle took one last look at herself before leaving her bedroom. It was a nice suit. And it flattered her figure as much as it could. The color complemented her skin tone. Though Belle longed for sexy, leg-enhancing spiked heels, the shoes were practical. Over the course of a day, she did a lot of walking. Neat, professional, attractive. It was hard to argue with the uniform she donned every day.

However, as Belle slid behind the wheel of her dark blue sedan, she couldn't help but think about the dress that hung in the far corner of her closet. The one she had purchased on a whim last week. Wouldn't it be nice if she were wearing it right now? It was just before eight o'clock and already the temperature was well past seventy.

First thing, Belle promised herself. Before she went to see her mother, she would come home and change. Wearing her uniform during business hours was one thing. Once she clocked out, her wardrobe choices were blissfully her own. Let her mother's eyeball rolling begin.

SITTING IN HER father's office, Belle made a conscious effort not to wipe her palms on her skirt. They were damp, but not excessively so. The last thing she needed was for her father to see how nervous she was. Nerves equaled weakness. If she believed in herself and what she was selling, he expected to see supreme confidence. Otherwise, don't bother.

Elias Richards was a handsome man who carried his years well. At sixty-two, he had been genetically blessed with a full head of hair shot judiciously with silver. Tall, with a fit, slender frame, he believed in a healthy lifestyle. Regular exercise. A balanced diet. He never overindulged his enjoyment of tobacco or alcohol. One whiskey before dinner. A brandy and cigar after. As far as Belle knew, he had followed the same routine his entire adult life. He was a good father. Not demonstrative with his affections, but there was no doubt that he loved his children.

However, in the office, Belle was not his daughter. She was an employee. She had never been given special consideration. The Vice President plaque on her door was there because she worked her ass off to get it. There was no guarantee Elias would agree to her pet project. He would have to be sold on the idea first.

"It makes sense, Dad. Short and long term."

"Are these figures up to date?"

"As of this morning."

"Hmm."

Belle waited. She had worked for her father long enough to understand how he did things. She handed him a proposal. He gave it a quick once over. Asked a few questions before sending her away so he could read it thoroughly. Elias Richards believed in God, family, and the almighty dollar. The order changed depending on the situation.

"*Strive* is a simple concept," Belle said, the name—the entire project—filling her with excitement and pride. "We provide these women with the materials. They provide the skill and labor. The crafts are sold online only. The overhead is almost nothing."

"So is the profit." Elias Richards set Belle's proposal aside. "According to your projections, we won't see a substantial payback for years. If ever."

"The profit margin grows on a yearly basis. It will never rival our other interests regarding dollars in the bank. What we get is the knowledge that we've helped low-income single mothers get on their feet. Provide for their families. That can't be measured in graphs or charts."

Belle had practiced this speech over and over for weeks. In the shower. On her way to work. Before she drifted off to sleep. She knew it backward and forward. What she hadn't been able to rehearse was the passion that came through in her voice. Her body language. It surprised her. *And* her father, if the look on his face was any indication.

Surprised or not, sentiment was never enough to sway Elias Richards. Charity began at home. It wasn't an original motto, but for generations, her family had been a firm believer in the concept. Knowing this, Belle had anticipated her father's reaction.

"The bottom line is this. Our company could use some good will, Dad. The strike you busted last fall. The recall of our not-so-organic bath products. Not to mention the—"

"I get the point, Belle."

"With this project, you will show that *Richards* has a heart." Her father snorted derisively. "Don't discount what some good PR will do. Free PR. Which equals free publicity. We couldn't buy the buzz this will create. And as the program becomes more and more successful, the buzz will grow. Year after year."

That got her father's attention just as Belle knew it would. Free was good. A whole heaping pile of perpetually generated free was even better. She knew from the beginning her idea had no chance unless she could sell this final pitch. Elias wasn't interested in helping single mothers. But he was interested in making his company as high profile as possible. He was too good a businessman to dismiss her idea without a lot of thought.

"I will look this over and get back to you."

Which meant Elias would have his best people look it over and get back to him. Music to Belle's ears. She hadn't thrown that proposal together overnight. The figures were solid. Indisputable. After all the years of working under her father, she knew how such things were done. If they turned her down... Belle wouldn't think about that. She had a contingency plan. Hopefully, she wouldn't have to implement it.

"Enough about business."

Those weren't words she heard from her father very often. Especially while they were at the office. Leery, Belle waited for the punchline. Though she doubted she would find much to laugh about.

"When is this marriage going to happen?"

"The invitations say September fifth. That's a Saturday. I'll be the one in the outrageously expensive dress. Mark your calendar."

"I have. Three times."

"Theo was the one who postponed, Dad. Not me."

"Do you know what your mother would have done if I postponed our wedding—twice?"

It was one of those questions that required no answer. They both knew what Belle's mother would have done. She would have bowed to what Elias wanted and thanked the Lord that he wasn't calling things off permanently.

"I can't hogtie Theo and force him to say *I do*." The image made Belle's lips twitch. Wisely, she didn't let it develop into a full smile.

"You aren't bothered by his behavior?"

Again, it wasn't a question Belle was expected to answer. Elias wasn't privy to her innermost thoughts, but he knew his daughter well enough to figure out when she was overly upset. After the first postponement, Belle shrugged it off as a little blip in their plans. No big deal. The second time she knew what was expected, but she couldn't garner a single tear or tantrum. Her parents knew why she had agreed to marry Theo. From day one, nobody called it a love match. It would be the culmination of a plan years in the making. The Richards family and the Schneider family. The power and money made stronger by more power and money. Belle and Theo were unlucky enough to be born within a few years of each other. Perfect. For everybody but them.

They were friends. Since lust often faded and love could be an illusion, some would say that friendship was a good foundation on which to start a marriage. Belle didn't agree. It was obvious from the beginning that Theo felt the same.

Take the way Theo proposed. It wasn't exactly the stuff of dreams. *"I'm thirty. It's time I made the big move toward matrimony. And it would make our families happy. What do you say?"* In what Belle would later consider temporary insanity, she said yes. Ever since she had tried to think of a way out. Luckily, Theo—in his passive/aggressive roundabout way—was taking care of it for her.

It was obvious her father wanted some kind of assurance. Belle couldn't give him one unless she lied. Or blurted out the truth. Desperately, she searched for something in between.

"Theo is Theo." Belle had no idea what that meant, but it was all she had.

"How is your sex life?"

Okay. Line officially crossed. Belle rolled to her feet. "Time for me to get back to work."

"Women don't always realize how important sex is to men, Belle. If Theo—"

41

"Check your calendar, Dad. This is the twenty-first century. Sex is just as important to women." Belle paused at the door. "And an extra head's up? We are allowed full participation *and* enjoyment."

Belle had the satisfaction of seeing her father's look of discomfiture just before she turned toward her office. The fact that he brought up the subject of sex told her just how worried he was that the wedding was not going to happen. The Richards family did not talk about intimacy of any kind. Belle learned about the birds and the bees from a woefully outdated book that magically appeared in her bedroom one morning. No, it had to be a true emergency for her father to use the S-word.

Time was not on her side. September fifth was less than six weeks away. Belle could hope that Theo would find another reason to back out. If her father was at the end of his patience rope, Theo's must be tearing his hair out. And Milo Schneider didn't have much left. He couldn't afford the loss of another follicle.

In deference to their fathers, Belle decided it was time to put a stop to the madness. She knew what she wanted to say. The problem was getting Theo to listen. Picking up her phone, she dialed his number.

"Belle. To what do I owe the pleasure?"

Theo sounded genuinely happy to hear from her. That wouldn't last long.

"We are having dinner. Tonight."

"Okay." A trace of wariness trickled into Theo's voice. "There is a new place just down the street from my place. I'll make reservations. Does seven work for you?"

"Seven is fine, but not at a restaurant. Come to my place. I'll make lasagna."

"You want to be alone?"

There was actual panic in Theo's voice. Just what every fiancée wanted to hear. Since she wasn't the typical fiancée, Belle wasn't offended.

"We need to settle this wedding debacle once and for all, Theo."

"Don't worry. There won't be another delay."

"My place. Seven o'clock. Don't be late."

Damn straight there won't be another delay, Belle said to herself as she hung up. *Because there won't be a wedding.* Part of her felt guilty for letting the craziness go on for so long. She shouldn't have let it start. Two years they had stayed on this merry-go-round. Belle was sick of it.

Resting her head on the back of her chair, Belle closed her eyes. Unbidden, Ashe's face popped into her head. Not an unusual occurrence. The past month had been riddled with unexpected sightings. He would be a hard man to forget under normal circumstances. To top it off, Ashe was the best sex she ever had. Sadly, he was the best sex she was ever likely to have. One day the longing would end. Or diminish. That's what she kept telling herself. Instead, it seemed to be getting worse.

It was her own fault. Belle had wanted to make a memory. Now she had to deal with the consequences.

One thing was certain. Ashe Mathison was *not* the reason she planned on breaking her engagement. Belle would never change the course of her life because of one night. No matter *how* mind blowing the sex. If she took Ashe out of the equation altogether, the facts remained the same. She and Theo were doomed from the beginning.

CHAPTER FOUR

TEN YEARS WAS a long time—and a blink of the eye.

Ashe maneuvered the rental car through the streets of Boston with ease. This wasn't the first time he had been back. *The Ryder Hart Band* played here last October to a sold-out crowd of enthusiastic fans. It was always an odd feeling knowing his parents and siblings were only minutes away. Regarding accessibility, they might as well have been on the moon.

Ashe made certain Georgia knew when he was in town. All she had to do was ask, and he would have left tickets at the box office. She let him know how much she appreciated the gesture but couldn't attend because of a previous engagement. He wanted to believe Georgia's excuse was genuine. However, it wouldn't have surprised him to find out differently.

Keeping emails and texts a secret was one thing. At one of his concerts, Georgia might be seen by someone she knew. If she wanted to stay on their father's good side—and in the will—she had to play by his rules. The day Ashe walked out the door Randall Mathison made it clear. His oldest son no longer existed. Not just to him, to every member of the family

Yet here Ashe was, winding his way through the Beacon Hill area. Toward his old home. Toward his father. There was no way in hell Georgia would spring it on the old man at the last second. Unless she had a sudden desire to watch the old mansion burn to the ground sparked by the cinders of their father's exploded head.

Ashe pulled onto the street he used to know so well. In the summer, he and his friends would run from each other's houses to play and swim and eat. Then repeat the process the next day. As they grew older, the games changed, but the friends stayed the same.

Funny, he hadn't thought of the old gang in years. Ashe knew he should have stayed in touch. But at first, he was too busy. Between numerous jobs and finding his foothold in the music business, it didn't occur to him. By the time he stopped long enough to catch a breath, too much water had passed under the bridge. The break from his old life had been clean. Ashe was able to admit to himself that it was simply easier to keep it that way.

The homes along the street were old. Most were built well before the turn of the twentieth century. They were immaculately maintained. It was like stepping back in time. That didn't mean the houses were stuck in another time. Renovations happened all the time. The swimming pool was put in when he was ten. The kitchen got a complete overhaul a few years later. And the year before Ashe left, his parents added a bathroom and updated the others. It would be interesting to see how the old place had changed in his absence.

There was plenty of space to park his car in the driveway. The four-car garage was to the side, leaving ample room for visitors. Ashe pulled to a halt, shut off the engine, and waited to work up the nerve to leave the safety of the rented BMW for the uncertainty that waited for him through those mahogany-stained double doors.

Move. Ashe urged himself. *Get off your ass and ring the bell.* There was another option. He could take the chicken shit way out and head the car back to the airport. He could text Georgia that something had come up, and he wouldn't be able to make it. Who would know the difference?

You would. Sometimes Ashe hated the voice in his head. The voice of reason. His conscience. Whatever the name, it could be a royal pain in his ass. Heaving a sigh, he found his balls and left his sanctuary.

As Ashe grabbed his bags from the trunk, including the guitar that he never left home without, his gaze landed on the house next door. The space between the mansions was substantial but from his angle, he could see the window to what was once Belle's room. She didn't live at home—that much he knew. Before he left Los Angeles, Colleen informed him that Belle was still in Boston. Somewhere. Finding her wouldn't be difficult. When he wasn't looking, Quinn programed Belle's number into his phone. His only problem was the fact that Quinn knew how to contact her, and he didn't. *What the hell was that all about?*

Quinn's answer had been simple and straight to the point. She asked for Belle's number. Belle gave it to her. It was difficult to explain his frustration to his friends since he hadn't told them about the one-night stand. Out of embarrassment for himself or deference to Belle, it seemed right to keep the intimate details to himself.

Did he want to call Belle? Without a doubt. *Would* he? That was tougher to answer. After a month, his ego still smarted. He knew how it sounded, but Ashe felt as though Belle had used him as a little vacation fun. Easily picked up. Easily discarded. Easily forgotten.

That was the crux of the matter. Belle left him a short, no-frills note. A definitive period on a very brief encounter. He was better off concentrating on the reason for his trip and leaving Belle alone.

"Ashe!"

Turning, Ashe saw a woman with long dark hair running toward him. Tall and slender, a cream-colored dress swirled around her legs. She looked so happy, he felt his heart lighten. Before she reached him, she stopped, looking hesitant. Uncertain. With a slow smile, Ashe opened his arms. A second later, he caught her close.

"Hello, Georgia." Ashe lifted his sister off her feet, spinning in a circle. "You grew up."

Laughing, Georgia hugged him tight before standing back. Her gaze took him in, her smile widening.

"So did you. I still can't believe my brother is *the* Ashe Mathison." It was said with a definite twinkle in her blue eyes. "I didn't tell my friends you were coming for fear the neighborhood would be stampeded by screaming women who are old enough to know better—but prove time and time again that they aren't."

Walking to the house, Ashe put an arm around Georgia's shoulders. "Thank you," he said with feeling. "From the bottom of my heart." The elbow to his ribs caught Ashe unaware. "Hey." Frowning, he rubbed the spot. "What was that for?"

"You could have *tried* to sound humble."

"About all the screaming women?" Hiding his smile in her hair, Ashe shrugged. "Facts are facts. I can't argue with the truth."

Georgia shook her head, but her laugh was light and easy. "Honestly, you were bad enough before you were a famous rock star. I don't know if your head will fit through the door."

Somehow, it felt as though no time had passed. This was the sister he had known. The one he never stopped loving. Ashe knew it wouldn't be as easy with the rest of the family, but at least he had Georgia.

Suddenly, Ashe didn't feel like laughing. He took Georgia's hand, stopping her from turning the polished brass knob.

"He knows I'm coming. Right?"

Georgia touched Ashe's cheek. Her eyes met his, not wavering. "He knows."

"Did Dad ask you to invite me?"

Opening the door, Georgia tugged Ashe into the house. "I asked, he didn't object." Seeing the disappointment he couldn't quite conceal, she smiled. "For Dad, that was practically a declaration of how much he wants to see you. He isn't here by the way. That isn't a statement about you. It's business. As usual."

"Sounds familiar." Ashe set his bags near the grand staircase. Looking around, he was surprised at how familiar the room felt. "I thought childhood homes were supposed to feel smaller. This one seems to have grown."

"Less clutter. Mom went on a minimalist kick last fall just before the holidays."

"That's right." Ashe turned in a slow circle. "There used to be a huge credenza on that wall and a table with tiny chairs over there. Weren't they antiques?"

"Come on." Georgia took Ashe's small bag. "Your old room has been redecorated." As they started up the stairs, she lowered her voice. "Those pieces were family heirlooms. I don't know how Mom had the nerve to sell them. Dad did something to tick her off. I think it was her idea of punishment."

"What did Dad say?" It had been a long time since Ashe had participated in Mathison family gossip. He enjoyed the moment.

"I was out. According to Sadie, the upstairs maid, Dad went ballistic—at first. Mom waited out his tirade before saying something nobody in the staff could hear. After that, Dad stormed to his office and nothing more was said on the matter."

His parents' marriage had always been a mystery to Ashe. There were rare moments when they seemed to share a genuine affection. Not hearts and flowers love or hot-for-you passion. *Affection.* Other times—most of the time—they exuded a cool tolerance. Ashe knew they had married to please their families. Four children and close to forty years later, they had found the recipe to make it last. Whether either was happy, Ashe couldn't say.

"I know what you're thinking." At the top of the second stairwell, Georgia turned right, stopping at the third door.

"I'm barely through the door, and already you're reading my mind?" Ashe and Georgia had always been close. When Ashe decided to break out on his own, she knew almost before he did. As much as he loved his older sister, he had always found her ability to get inside his head disconcerting.

Georgia laughed, leading the way into Ashe's old room. "How great is that? I was afraid we might have lost the connection."

"Mm." Ashe wasn't sure it was great, but he liked to see Georgia smile.

"As I was saying, you're thinking how sad it would be to spend so many years with someone you never loved—probably never liked. Though I think Mom's feelings were always more deeply engaged than Dad's."

Ashe dropped his bags. Between the odd feeling of coming home and Georgia's assessment of their parents' marriage, he felt strangely unsettled. Though it wasn't exactly like walking back through time. Saying his room had been redecorated was putting it mildly. Ruthlessly gutted would have been a better description. Nothing was the same. It used to look like a place inhabited by a teenage boy. Posters. Sports trophies. A few X-rated magazines hidden away for his eyes only. Whoever was in charge of cleaning the space must have gotten a shock when they came across those.

"It looks like the Chintz fairy suffered from a case of projectile vomiting." Everywhere he looked there were flowers. Big, ugly flowers. "Was this Mom's idea of retribution?"

"This is Mom's idea of fashion." Georgia teasingly fluffed one of what looked like dozens of accent pillows carefully arranged on the bed. "I'll leave you to unpack."

"Thanks, Georgia." Ashe gathered her close. "It's good to be here. I think."

"You can decide for certain at dinner. The whole gang will be there. Dad's edict. Actually, don't bother to unpack. One of the maids will take care of it."

When Ashe was alone, he wandered to the window. It was funny how his memories were slightly off. The downstairs foyer seemed bigger than he remembered. The space between the Mathison house and the Richards seemed larger. In his mind, he had pictured Belle's window much closer. The yard on his side of the dividing fence went on for at least twenty feet. His guess was the distance was close to that on her side. Still, it wouldn't have been difficult to open the window and toss out a wave or a hello.

Teenage Ashe hadn't known Belle was so close. He hadn't thought about it. More fool he.

Catching movement in Belle's window, Ashe moved closer. He knew the chance it was her was slim to none. He hadn't learned a lot about her, but he knew she no longer lived at home. However, that didn't stop him from opening the window for a better look. Just in case.

"I HEARD YOU the first time, Mom." When dealing with her mother, there were times when Belle understood how someone could be *driven to drink*.

"Don't take that tone with me, Belle Millicent Richards." Belle barely controlled a shudder. *Millicent*. Lord, she hated that name. "I want you to try on your wedding dress. I swear you've lost weight. Now is the time to get any necessary alterations taken care of."

"What if I chunk up in the next month and a half? Isn't it better the dress be too big than too small?"

"You aren't pregnant?" With a gasp of distress, Penelope Richards clasped her hands to her chest. "With all three of you children I lost weight the first few weeks. After that, I blew up like a float in the Macy's Thanksgiving Day Parade."

"Something to look forward to."

"Then you are pregnant! Belle, how could you? In a pinch, I suppose we can increase the size of your bouquet."

"Relax, Mom. I'm not pregnant. It was just a joke."

"Goodness." Penelope fanned herself vigorously. "I will never understand your sense of humor."

"I know." Contrite, Belle squeezed her mother's hand. "But you love me anyway."

"True." For the first time since Belle arrived, Penelope smiled. "And you love me."

"Without reservation." They were as different as different could be, but there was a soft spot in Belle's heart reserved just for her mother. No matter how much frustration the woman caused her, that would never change.

"Then do me a favor and try on the dress. For my peace of mind."

"Fine. For you."

Belle trudged up the stairs to her old room. Except for a fresh coat of paint and new curtains, it looked exactly as she had left it when she moved out. She remembered begging her parents for the canopy bed. It seemed so romantic. Now it looked like what it was—a thirteen-year-old girl's skewed fantasy of what romantic really was.

Pink gauze. With a shake of her head, Belle thanked the Lord her tastes had changed.

The walk-in closet was mostly empty. One side stored a few of her mother's winter coats that would soon be swapped out for the lighter fare she wore when the weather was warm. In the back was Belle's wedding dress. Unzipping the garment bag, she pulled it from the padded hanger. Speaking of changing taste. Around the time of the canopy fiasco, this was exactly what her thirteen-year-old self would have wanted.

Belle moved to the floor-length mirror, holding up the reams of stark-white ruffled tulle. The caption could read, *Psychotic Ballerina.*

Reexamining the color of her dress and what it represented, she added delusional. This was her mother's dream dress—not hers. If white was meant to represent purity, her mother had missed that boat by almost a decade. It was another sign—in flashing neon—that she shouldn't have let things get this far.

Removing her clothes, Belle felt a wave of guilt. It seemed wrong to go through the motions. However, she consoled herself with the knowledge that after tonight, she would no longer need to play along with this charade. Belle would happily donate the dress to a needy bride with a tulle fetish.

The low-cut back made it easy for Belle to zip herself in. Hmm. Pinching the side of the fitted gown, she noticed it *was* a bit loose. Maybe five or six pounds worth. She didn't know how it had happened. Certainly not on purpose. Between her busy schedule and worrying about the marriage that wouldn't be, Belle supposed she might have missed a meal or two.

Unconcerned, Belle slipped on the three-inch lace pumps before adjusting the matching headdress. *In for a penny*, she decided. Since it was the last time she planned on ever putting it on, Belle left the closet, planning on calling her mother. That was when she allowed her gaze to fall on the window. *The window*. How many times had she sat there hoping for a single glimpse of Ashe? Then crawled under the Pepto-Bismol canopy, falling to sleep, hoping to dream of her crush?

Convincing herself it wasn't nostalgia that propelled her across the room—the room was stuffy—Belle opened the window and leaned out. Then with a yelp, jumped back in. *It couldn't be*. Her head was filled with thoughts of Ashe. That was why she thought she saw him. He was in Los Angeles living his exciting life. Making music. Bedding beautiful supermodels and movie stars.

Calm down, girl, Belle chided herself, rubbing her churning stomach. Take a deep breath. Calm down. Now, look again. He won't be there. He *can't* be there. Just as she reached for the curtain, ready to peek, a familiar voice called out.

"I know you're still there, Belle. It won't do any good to hide."

There was a time when Belle would have given almost anything to hear Ashe call out to her from his window. She dreamed of morphing

51

into a self-confident flirt who would dazzle him with her smile. Now, all she wanted to do was dissolve into vapor, escaping unseen.

"Are you going to keep me waiting?"

You kept me waiting all through my adolescence. The thought popped into Belle's head, reminding her that she was no longer a gawky girl—unsure and inexperienced. A woman didn't cower in her childhood bedroom. Straightening her shoulders, Belle pushed her head through the drawn-back curtains.

"Hello, Ashe. This is a surprise." Good. Cool, calm, and collected. Very mature.

"I was thinking the same thing." Ashe's eyes narrowed. "Are you wearing a wedding dress?"

A piece of tulle fell over Belle's right eye. *Well, crap.* How could she have forgotten Ballerina Barbie? With as much dignity as she could muster, Belle pushed the fabric aside.

"Yes," she nodded, causing another swatch of the ridiculous material to fall over her face.

"Costume party?" Ashe inquired lightly.

"No." Belle wished mightily that he would let it go. No such luck.

"Wedding?"

"That's right."

"Yours?" Ashe's smile had disappeared, a tightness entering his tone.

"September fifth." Now, why had she said that? Belle meant to correct herself, but Ashe didn't give her a chance.

"Son of a bitch, Belle. Either it was a whirlwind courtship, or you were engaged when we—"

"Quiet," Belle gave a whispered hiss, craning her neck out the window. He wouldn't dare shout to the world that they had slept together. Would he? "My mother might be in the garden. She has the hearing of a bat."

"You should have thought of that before you let me go down—"

52

"Enough!" Sex was bad enough. Oral sex? Belle's mother would have a coronary in the middle of her marigolds. Realizing Ashe was not in the mood for discretion, she decided to end this wedding-themed farce. "Welcome home, Ashe. Bye."

"Belle!" Ashe shouted. "Don't you dare shut that—"

The word window was muffled but distinct. It was followed by a string of curse words. Belle didn't care if the entire neighborhood heard Ashe's foul-mouthed tirade. As long as he didn't drag her name back into it, he could yell obscenities until the cows came home.

"Belle?" Her mother opened the bedroom door. "How does the dress look?"

Like the designer dropped acid and went on a bad trip to end all bad trips, Belle wished she could respond. Instead, she muttered, "Fine. Good. Great," while reaching for the zipper.

"Careful. You'll rip it." Penelope rushed to help. "What is the hurry?"

"I'm cooking dinner for Theo, and I have to stop at the market." Until that moment, Belle had forgotten all about Theo but wasn't above using him as a plausible excuse. Getting out of here in case Ashe got it into his head to finish their argument—at closer quarters—was all Belle cared about.

"That's nice." Treating the gown with more care than Belle would have, Penelope laid it on the bed. "I know it's an old-fashioned notion, but a man's heart and his stomach *are* closely linked."

And the only reason Belle took gourmet cooking classes was to hook a man. The words hadn't come out of her mother's mouth. However, Belle knew it was what she thought. It was old fashioned. Harking back to Donna Reed preparing a meal in a crinoline-lined dress, high heels, and a string of pearls. In many ways, Penelope Richards was a woman of the twenty-first century. But Belle suspected—deep inside—her heart belonged in the nineteen fifties.

"I think you're right, Belle. The dress doesn't need altering."

"Okay." Pulling on her jacket, Belle brushed her lips across her mother's cheek. "I have to run."

Penelope followed Belle down the stairs. "Drive safe."

Belle waved. Rushing to her car, she had just buckled her seatbelt when her phone rang. If it was Theo telling her he couldn't make it, she was going to tear him a new one.

"There is no excuse good enough."

"My thoughts exactly," Ashe said.

Silently, Belle groaned. "How did you get my number?"

"You have more to worry about than that, Belle. Are you still in your room?"

"No. I'm on my way home." Which was the truth.

"We need to talk. Should I come to your place?"

Absolutely not. Belle took a deep, calming breath. "There isn't anything to say, Ashe."

"I don't agree. Should I ask your mother her opinion?"

"I thought you were a nice guy," Belle grumbled.

"I'm a pissed-off guy. Where and when, Belle?"

Quickly, Belle ran through her options. They weren't sizable. Meet with Ashe or take the chance that he wouldn't spill the beans about their brief—but memorable—encounter. Normally, Belle would tell him to go to hell and spill away. Unfortunately, the little problem of her soon-to-be broken engagement stood in her way. She couldn't help it. Disappointing her parents once was inevitable. Belle couldn't face doing it twice.

"Are you busy tomorrow?"

"I'll make the time."

Mentally, Belle went over her schedule. There wasn't anything after lunch that couldn't be moved to another day. She didn't want to fit Ashe in, but he gave her no choice.

"Two o'clock. My apartment." Belle rattled off the address. "And Ashe?"

"Yes."

"Thank you."

There was a pause. When Ashe answered, he did so hesitantly. "What for?"

"I've been crushing on you since I was twelve years old. Now that you've shown your true colors as a blackmailing asshole, I can honestly say that is no longer a problem."

CHAPTER FIVE

BELLE CHECKED THE lasagna. It was bubbling nicely. Removing the blue casserole dish from the oven, she set it aside to rest. At least fifteen minutes or the cheese and sauce would run all over the plates. A loaf of crusty bread was buttered, waiting in a foil packet to heat as soon as Theo arrived. Along with a tossed green salad, it was Belle's go-to meal when she didn't have a lot of time. Tasty and filling, the spicy aroma filled the apartment, making her mouth water. Tonight wasn't going to be pleasant, but at least the food would be good.

What a day. Belle poured herself a glass of wine, taking a grateful sip. The hot shower she jumped into almost as soon as she walked in the door had helped. Donning a pair of loose-fitting pale-blue linen pants and silk t-shirt in a contrasting darker blue didn't hurt either. Makeup free, her hair held back by a glittery clip, Belle padded barefoot around her kitchen.

This was her happy place. Belle could forget about everything when her mind was occupied with spice blends and caramelizing onions. Her best friend, Tracy Drake, once asked why Belle didn't open her own restaurant. Cooking was her passion, not helping to run a multi-million-dollar corporation. The world was filled with brown-nosing would-be vice presidents. But how many people could make a lemon cheesecake scrumptious enough to bring a sane person to tears? Belle simply shook her head. Cooking would cease to be fun if she were out to make a profit.

Looking at the clock, Belle sighed. Quarter after seven. Theo was notoriously late. His mother loved to joke that he made her wait an extra seven days to be born. Since it was expected, Belle always laughed. For the life of her, she didn't get the joke. Babies came when they came. An adult who didn't have the good grace to be on time made a choice—a bad one.

With a sigh, Belle took another drink of the crisp white wine. The problem with extra time was it gave her time to mull certain matters over. Specifically, Ashe. The big jerk. Why couldn't he have looked out that window a few minutes later? Or earlier? Why was he in Boston?

Boosting herself onto one of the red leather-covered retro bar stools that lined the small island in her kitchen, Belle put her elbow on the black granite, resting her chin on her cupped palm. As far as she was concerned, Ashe had broken an unspoken agreement. Los Angeles was his. Boston hers. Or at least this part of the city.

How dare he...? What? Visit his family? Alone with her musings, Belle had the good grace to chide herself. She was glad Ashe had ended his ten-year estrangement. For his sake as well as the rest of the Mathison clan. But why, oh why, had he chosen the exact moment to look out his old window? Any other day, Belle would have looked like... well, she would have looked like Belle. Instead, he found a slightly disheveled marshmallow.

Draining the last of the wine, Belle set the glass down with a firm click. Embarrassment aside, what she had told Ashe was true. Her crush was history. A thing of the past. Just the thought of him used to make her stomach turn over, and her palms dampen. Turning her hand over, Belle rubbed the surface, her lips curving with satisfaction. Dry as a bone. Take that, Ashe Mathison. The crush has been crushed.

Contemplating re-popping the cork on the excellent Chablis, Belle had just decided one solo glass was enough when the doorbell rang. Theo. Finally! And only thirty-five minutes late. For him, that was practically on time.

"I know." Theo walked through the open door, kissing the air in Belle's direction. "I'm late."

"Stating the obvious doesn't help, Theo."

"I was held up."

"At gun point? Tonight, that is the only explanation that will fly."

"Work."

Belle took in Theo's Hawaiian-print cotton shirt and bright green fashionably baggy shorts. Add the flip-flops and the fact that his tan was deeper than the last time she saw him and Belle felt her temper rise. Late she expected. But a bald-faced lie? No matter their problems, she thought they were friends. Now, she wasn't so sure.

"Is that how you're dressing for the office these days?"

"Fine. I took the afternoon off." Theo flushed, but there was a defiant set to his chin. "I work hard. Don't I deserve a few hours of downtime?"

"I'm not your father, Theo." *Or your wife*, Belle could have added. "Save your half-assed excuses for him."

"Belle—"

"Did you get the tips of your hair frosted?" Theo's natural color ran toward dirty blond. No matter how much time he spent in the sun, those highlights did not come from Mother Nature.

"What do you think?" Theo moved to the mirror by the door, turning his head from side to side.

"I don't know. Do *you* like it?"

Theo paused, almost posing, before shaking his head. "I wasn't certain at first. But now, I think it suits me."

Had Theo always been this vain? Tall and athletically slim, he had the kind of good looks that her mother called patrician. He always wore his hair short, but lately started growing it out. Something had changed, and Belle had a good idea what it was. His primping simply solidified her suspicions.

"Theo." Belle rolled her eyes. It was like trying to distract Narcissus from his reflection. "Dinner is ready. Would you like a glass of wine?"

"Just water for me." Theo patted his flat stomach. "Do you know how many calories there are in alcohol?"

Belle poured herself a glass, deliberately filling it to the rim.

"Is that lasagna?" Theo watched her put the casserole on the table. "Carbs galore. I'm cutting *way* back."

"I told you what I was making. Why didn't you say something then?"

"Sorry. I had my mind on a dozen different things."

"Obviously one of them wasn't me." Belle dished herself an extra-large helping. Taking a bite, she had the satisfaction of seeing him track the movement with an envious gaze. Nodding toward the refrigerator, she tore off a chunk of warm bread. "There's green salad. Undressed. Help yourself."

"Belle…"

"Let's save each other another moment of aggravation, Theo. I know there's somebody else."

"You do?" Theo flopped into his seat, lettuce flying from his plate as he dropped the plate onto the table. "How? When? I—"

"I wasn't one hundred percent certain until now."

"Oh, God." Theo covered his face with his hands. "I'm sorry, Belle. I didn't mean for it to happen."

"Are you in love?"

"Yes. Maybe. I think so."

"As long as you're certain." For the first time in hours, Belle felt like laughing. In deference to Theo's distress, she settled for a slight smile. "I think that's great."

"You do?" Theo spread his fingers, peeking at her. "I dreaded telling you."

"Relax. It makes things simpler."

"The hell it does." Jumping to his feet, Theo almost overturned the table. Somehow, Belle was able to save her wine and prevent the plate of lasagna from landing in her lap. "I am stuck. In love with one person, engaged to another. Do you know what my father would say?"

"*Will* say." Belle felt it important that Theo got his tenses straight.

"What?"

"What your father *will* say, Theo. You have to tell him." Belle started to slide the seven-karat diamond off her finger. "This engagement is officially over."

"No!" Theo fell to his knees, frantically pushing the ring back onto Belle's finger. "Please. I think we should go through with the wedding."

"I don't." Belle and Theo played tug of war for a few seconds before she gave up, knowing how ridiculous they must look. If brute force wouldn't work, she decided to try reason. "Don't you want to be with the woman you love? What's her name?"

Theo looked away before swallowing.

"You can tell me, Theo. Unless it's Mona. Anybody but her." Belle's adversarial relationship with Mona Workman began the first day of elementary school and continued to this day.

"Not Mona. Blaine."

"Blaine?" It took a moment for the implications to sink in. "Blaine? As in testicles instead of ovaries Blaine?"

Still not meeting Belle's gaze, Theo stood, nodding.

"Holy shit, Theo. You're gay?"

"No! Maybe." With a deep sigh, Theo ran a hand through his blond-tipped hair. "There's a chance that may be the case."

Belle's thoughts bounced in every direction like an out-of-control pinball. This revelation explained a lot. For instance, their lack of a sex life—a handful of times and lukewarm at best. It didn't excuse Theo's behavior.

"There is so much wrong with this situation." Belle tried to gather her jumbled thoughts. "I don't care that you're gay, Theo."

"No?" Theo's expression brightened.

"Of course not. I *do* care that you put us in an untenable situation."

"Would it help if you knew I thought I was straight—until I met Blaine last summer?"

Just before the first time he postponed their marriage. Mystery number one solved.

"Why not just call off the wedding?"

"I didn't think the whole gay thing would stick."

"I won't purport to be an expert on the subject, but I don't think it works that way, Theo."

"I've been with other women." Theo puffed out his chest in what Belle supposed was a manly fashion. "Lots and lots of other women. It was good, too. Until you."

60

"Careful," Belle warned, eyes narrowing. If Theo accused her of turning him gay, he would get a punch in the nose. Or a kick in the balls. Maybe both.

"Don't get me wrong. You're a very sexy woman. All of my friends think so," Theo assured her. "But it's like sleeping with my sister."

"Jesus, Theo. Really?" Just when Belle thought it couldn't get worse, Theo threw creepy pseudo-incest at her. "All you had to say was that you weren't attracted to me. You should have kept the rest to yourself. To the grave and beyond."

Theo nodded. "Look. I can't tell my father. He would die on the spot."

"That would solve your problem." Belle ignored Theo's dirty look. She was entitled to a few snarky comments.

"The solution is simple. We get married."

This was the least funny situation Belle had ever been a part of. However, if she thought for one second that Theo was joking, she might have conjured up a half-hearted laugh. Unfortunately, she could tell he was serious. Rather than explode with a five-minute verbal tirade, Belle kept it simple and straight to the point.

"No."

"But, Belle—"

"What does Blaine think about all of this? I assume you've told him your plans?"

"Blaine isn't thrilled with the idea. However, he's known he was gay practically from birth." Theo sank onto the sofa. "How can I come out of the closet when I just discovered I'm in it?"

Belle felt her first wave of sympathy. She couldn't imagine what it was like to discover something this life changing. It was hard to get past the way Theo handled it, but they had been friends most of their lives. The least she could do was stand back and look at it from his perspective.

Joining Theo, Belle took his hand, squeezing warmly. "I will support you every step of the way. I have your back. If you want me to go with you when you tell your parents, say the word. I'll be there."

Theo leaned close, his head resting on top of hers. Belle felt a closeness to him she had never felt before. Then he had to ruin the moment by opening his mouth.

"If you marry me, I promise to divorce you after a year. Two at the most."

"Sure," Belle scoffed. "It will be the perfect solution. You can assuage your father and fool around with Blaine on the side. I know." Her words dripped with sarcasm. "To round things off, why don't we have a baby? No way better to prove your manhood than fathering a child."

"Now that you mention it—"

"You're certifiable!" Belle pushed Theo away. "I see a straitjacket and padded cell in your very near future."

"Belle—"

"For the past year, you have lied, wheedled, and wimped out. Be a man, Theo. Admit to the world that you're gay."

"It's not the world I'm worried about."

Belle knew what it was like to live with a domineering father. Things were expected to be done a certain way. For Theo—as the only son—those expectations were through the roof. Belle refused to cave. However, in spite of her better judgment, she did bend. A little.

"I will give you two weeks reprieve, Theo."

"A month."

The man thought he was in a position to bargain? Unbelievable.

"Two weeks, Theo."

"Three?"

"I can end this right now if you want." Belle picked up her phone. "Say the word and I will call my father. Do you want him to be the one to break the news to your parents?"

"God, no." The skin under Theo's newly acquired tan turned a sickly shade of gray. With the end of his shirt, he wiped the sweat from his upper lip. "I'll figure out a way to tell him. If push comes to shove, at least I have the money I inherited from my grandmother."

Once again, it turned out that money was the root of... everything. At least in Theo's world. Rich. Pampered. Spoiled beyond reason, Belle was amazed he wasn't a complete waste of space. He was just so damn likable. She wanted them to stay friends. If Theo did as he promised, that wouldn't be a problem.

"You won't take off the ring?" Theo asked as she walked him to the door. Neither of them was interested in trying to finish dinner. "It would raise a lot of questions."

Belle glanced at the diamond. She had never cared for the design. Too traditional for her taste. But she had lived with it this long. Two more weeks wouldn't kill her.

"I know how this will sound." Theo hesitated.

"I don't think I can handle another bombshell, Theo. If we are twins separated at birth, keep it to yourself."

"Nothing like that," Theo smiled, shaking his head. "I would like you to meet Blaine."

"That's it?" Slowly, Belle released the breath she hadn't realized she was holding. "Name the time and place."

"Thank you, Belle." Theo hugged her. This time, when he went in for a kiss, his lips touched her cheek. "You could have crucified me. Justifiably."

"I would have. *If* I were in love with you. And *if* I had really wanted to marry you."

"I guess I did you a favor."

"Don't press your luck." Shaking her head, Belle pushed him out the door. Serious as a heart attack, she pinned Theo with her gaze. "Remember. Two weeks."

"You have my word."

Belle leaned against the closed door. Glancing at the clock, she was amazed to see how early it was. The drama with Theo had played out in less than an hour. Not wanting to spend the evening rehashing the events over and over, she picked up her phone and dialed the one person Belle knew who could be counted on for a distraction.

"Hey," Tracy answered after the second ring. "That was fast. I thought it would take most of the evening to give Theo the heave-ho. Were there less begging and tears than expected?"

"The evening ended early, but the story is epic. Want to come over?"

"Should I stop at the liquor store?"

Belle grinned. This was why she and Tracy were best friends. The woman knew exactly the right question to ask.

"I'm fully stocked."

"Start pouring. I'll see you in ten."

CHAPTER SIX

ASHE DIDN'T KNOW a lot about reunions. About a year ago he had received an invitation to the get-together marking the ten-year anniversary of his high school graduation. Work kept him away—though he doubted he would have gone. Too much muss and fuss. Ego aside, chances were it would have become more about him and his celebrity than reminiscing with the rest of the attendees.

However, Ashe didn't need to be an expert on the subject to know his reunion with his family was less than warm and fuzzy—Georgia being one of the few exceptions. Not that he had expected tears and sentimentality, but these were his blood relatives. What he expected was… more. Instead, the reactions ranged from cool, to uninterested, to thinly masked hostility.

By the end of the afternoon, Ashe was reminded why walking away ten years ago had been more of a relief than a hardship.

It began as Ashe descended the staircase just after his phone call to Belle. Not certain how he felt—about the woman *or* their exchange—he was brought up short by the sight of his mother. Somehow, Bonita Mathison hadn't changed a bit. Slender, her dark hair was fashioned into a ruthless French twist. Her earrings were simple diamond studs, her shoes sported tasteful heels—never higher than two inches. She wore an elegant shift in a neutral color. Sometimes she donned a matching jacket—depending on the season. She stood as she often had during his childhood, by the small accent table in the foyer fluffing a perfectly arranged vase of flowers.

A feeling of déjà vu rushed over Ashe. When his mother looked up at him, sending her familiar benign smile, he could have been seventeen, rushing with no time to spare, late to meet friends. It was ten years since the last time they were in the same room, yet there was no surprise in Bonita's expression. Not delight or anger or—anything. Ashe couldn't think of a time when she raised her voice or showed excessive emotion—no matter the occasion. Nothing dented that New England blueblood cool. Not even the return of her eldest son.

"Ashe. How nice to see you, dear."

Bonita held out her hand. Ashe took it in his. Slender and bordering on icy, if she were anybody else, he would have been concerned. For his mother, this was normal. He brushed his lips over her proffered cheek.

"How have you been, Mother?"

"Fine. I had a club meeting this morning. A charity luncheon this afternoon." Lightly, she patted his hand before continuing her inspection of the flowers. "Cook is fixing prime rib for dinner. I hope that's fine. You still eat meat?"

It was the first time Bonita acknowledged Ashe's absence. Until that moment, he wondered if she realized he had been gone.

"Still an enthusiastic carnivore."

"Lovely. Then I will see you later. Seven o'clock. Don't be late."

Calmly, she glided from the room.

"Cool as a meat locker," Georgia said, entering from the opposite direction. "Some things never change. Need a jacket?"

Ashe winked at his sister, telling her that though surprised, he was unaffected by their mother's less-than-emotional greeting. "I used to wonder if we were really related."

"Genetically, there is no doubt."

"Really?" Surprised, Ashe shook his head. He didn't see it.

"The eyes. The slope of your nose. The color of your hair. Mom left her stamp. But the rest of you is all Dad. Physically." When Georgia took his hand, Ashe was struck by the difference between her warmth and their mother's coolness. Between that and his sister's smile, he felt some of the chill begin to dissipate from the room.

Unable to help himself, Ashe asked teasingly, "Mom *was* informed when I left, wasn't she?"

"I told her. She may have blinked, but she was late for her flower club so it was hard to tell." Stopping on the last step, Georgia met his gaze straight on. "Don't take this the wrong way. Dad just called. He had to fly to New York. From the sound of it, he won't make it back until the day of his party."

Ashe frowned at the news. "I came home to see Dad—with his blessing. How can I not take his absence personally?"

"I don't think Dad is deliberately avoiding you."

"If you say so." Ashe wasn't convinced.

"Come with me." Georgia pulled him toward the garden. "I know two members of the family who are dying to welcome you home."

"Vivian and Bradley?" Knowing they lived at home, Ashe had expected to see his siblings. Georgia's reaction to his question—a loud snort of laughter—quickly clued him in.

"Sorry." Georgia wiped a bit of spittle from her chin. "Vivian is too self-involved to care about much outside her narrow interests. And Bradley? He is Dad's right-hand man. You, my friend, are the competition."

It was Ashe's turn to laugh, thinking Georgia must be joking. But she simply shrugged.

"If I were the least bit interested in Dad's company—which I'm not—when does Brad think I would find the time?"

"In our brother's world, nothing trumps the family business. He assumes you would drop your little music career in a heartbeat if Dad asked you to. And it's Bradley. The last time somebody called him Brad, I swore steam came out of his ears."

To Ashe, that felt like a challenge. From the twitch of Georgia's lips, it didn't take much to realize that was the point.

As they walked along the rose-lined path, Ashe wondered why he hadn't connected with his brother? There was only a year separating them. But for some reason, Bradley came out of their mother's womb with a huge chip on his shoulder. Ashe was older. A better student. A better athlete. He had a ton of friends—male and female. At least, that was how Bradley saw it. Ashe had no idea how his brother felt until one day he lashed out with a bitter rant. It seemed the girl Bradley liked only had eyes for Ashe.

It was news to Ashe—all of it. Bradley's bitter resentment came as a shock. Ashe had no chance to mend fences—if that were possible. He was gone the next week.

As for Vivian. Two years older, she had no use for Ashe. Or—as Georgia reminded him—anybody else. If it wasn't about her, she wasn't interested.

"I sound like a bitch." Georgia sighed as a white gazebo came into view. "Isn't there an unwritten rule against slinging crap at your family?"

"To outsiders? Hell, yes." Lightly, Ashe tapped Georgia on the chin. "To each other? Sling away. You've given me a heads up on what to expect from Vivian and *Bradley*." Georgia smiled when Ashe rolled his eyes. "Maybe they won't strike me that way."

"When our siblings strike, they never do it head on. Sneak attacks all the way. So watch your back."

Ashe started to laugh until he got a look at Georgia's face. "Seriously?"

"Seriously."

So much for a week of familial togetherness. Ashe hadn't expected them to slaughter the fatted calf. However, he had hoped more than one person would be happy to see him. His hopes for reconciling with his father were fading fast.

"What about you, Georgie?" Ashe used the nickname automatically, glad it slipped out when he saw his sister's face light with pleasure. "Is Josh still the man of your dreams? Are my nieces mostly sugar with just the right amount of spice?"

"I'm a lucky woman, Ashe." Georgia sighed, happily. "I have a secret. Can I trust you?"

Growing up, Ashe and Georgia were each other's confidants. She would tell him about her boyfriends or fallings out she had with friends. Ashe shared his dreams—a career in music. It felt nice to fall back into old patterns.

"Have I ever ratted you out?"

When Georgia looked right and left—and left again—Ashe raised his eyebrows.

"The bushes have ears," Georgia explained. "Unlike you, the rest of our clan does not believe that discretion is the better part of valor."

"Is it really that bad?" Georgia nodded. "Why do you stay?"

"That's my secret." Taking Ashe's arm, they continued across the lawn. "Josh has a job offer in Los Angeles. We've kept it on the QT until everything was finalized. We move a week after Dad's birthday party."

"That's fantastic, Georgie. We can see each other whenever we want."

"I know." There was an added bounce to Georgia's step.

Which brought Ashe to a topic he hadn't planned on broaching. However, knowing that Georgia would be a big part of his life from now on, he felt the need to clear the air.

"I don't know how to ask this without sounding like a whiny little twit. But here goes. Why didn't you come to see me the last time the band played in Boston? Or anytime we were in the area?"

"Ashe—"

"I understand wanting to stay in Dad's good graces. But—"

"We did come."

"You did?" Confused, Ashe pulled to a stop. He turned, looking Georgia in the eyes.

"That was the fifth time I've been to one of your shows."

"I don't understand. Why didn't you tell me? Why not take the tickets I offered you?"

"Massive paranoia and no backbone." With a sigh, Georgia shook her head, her eyes sad. "Do you know how much I've always envied you? You got out. I stayed. I married a man who worked for my father. We live in his home. He pays for the private school my daughters attend. It may not be a perfect life, but it's comfortable."

"Don't beat yourself up for that." Ashe left home because it was the only way. However, he didn't blame Georgia for staying with what she knew. "I'm sorry we missed out on seeing each other." Wanting to lighten the mood, he adopted his best cocky smile. "So you've seen *The Ryder Hart Band* five times. We put on a damn fine show, don't you think?"

"I don't have the words." Georgia grasped Ashe's arm. "I knew you were talented, but... oh, Ashe. The first time, I had to keep reminding myself that it was my baby brother up there. I couldn't take my eyes off you. I cried when you played the saxophone solo on *Missing*

You. I didn't let go of Josh's hand during the entire concert." She chuckled. "It took a week for the circulation to return in his fingers."

"I wrote that song for you."

"Oh, Ashe." Tears welled up in Georgia's eyes. "I'm sorry. I've been a horrible sister. Can you forgive me?"

"Love means never having to say you're sorry."

Georgia froze in the middle of wiping her cheeks. "You did not just say that."

"What?" Lips twitching, Ashe batted his eyes. "You quoted Shakespeare. I can't quote Ali McGraw?"

"Yes, if it weren't perhaps the worst movie line *ever*."

"But memorable." Happy with the results, Ashe brushed the last tear from the corner of Georgia's eye. "And true. I can forgive you for two very important reasons. First, I want to."

"Easy as that?" For the second time that day, Georgia walked into Ashe's open arms.

"Easy because of the second reason. I love you, Georgie. Always have. Always will."

"I've missed you so much."

"Never again." Holding Georgia close, Ashe kissed her temple.

"It was almost six."

Ashe let out a confused laugh. "Six what?"

"Times I saw you in concert." Moving back, Georgia smoothed out the material on Ashe's shirt, wiping the wet spot left by her tears. "I went with Josh to Los Angeles last month—he had a final interview. He was going to be busy, so I wrangled a ticket to the show you did at the Hollywood Bowl. It turned out I couldn't go. I knew a friend was in town on business, so as a treat, I gave the ticket to her."

"A friend?" Ashe hoped he sounded nonchalant. He didn't feel that way.

"Belle Richards? You probably don't remember her. She lived next door."

Ashe nodded. He remembered. And if he hadn't, Belle made certain he would never forget her again. "I didn't realize you were friends."

"We weren't." Georgia shrugged. "We volunteer at the same women's shelter. The point is, when I couldn't make the concert, I thought of Belle. She loved it, by the way."

"Did she?" Luckily, Georgia seemed to miss the sarcasm dripping from Ashe's voice.

"When she called to thank me for the ticket, Belle couldn't stop raving. I think her exact words were, *best concert ever*. She was particularly impressed by your performance."

Ashe covered his laugh with a cough. "She said that?"

"Maybe not those exact words. Come on. Those people I said wanted to meet you are waiting for us in the gazebo. Have you guessed who they are?"

Georgia walked on. For her, the subject was closed. Ashe didn't mind letting it go—until his meeting with Belle. The list of things he wanted to discuss with the lady kept on growing.

"Let's see." Ashe raised his voice, pretending to contemplate Georgia's question. A spate of giggles filled the air, followed by a very loud, *quiet, he'll hear us*. "Could it be pixies?"

"No." Georgia smiled.

The giggles grew in volume.

"Leprechauns?" Ashe tiptoed up the wooden steps. He spied two dark heads, huddled together by a table set for afternoon tea, their ponytails bobbing furiously from the joyous violence of their laughter.

"I don't think so."

"I know." Ashe grasped the girls around their waists, lifting them high. "These must be Nadia and Naomi." He looked from one identical face to the other. His nieces squealed, wiggling with excitement. "But which is which?"

"Guess," they chimed simultaneously.

Georgia had written about her girls. Alike in almost every way. However, one liked pink. The other purple. Ashe searched his memory, hoping he remembered right.

71

"Naomi." Ashe kissed the top of the little girl's head, right above the purple bow. Then turned, repeating the kiss, near a bow of pink. "And Nadia. Am I right?"

Big, blue eyes wide with awe, the matching nods. "How did you know, Uncle Ashe?"

Ashe leaned close to the five-year-old girls, breathing in the scent of bubble gum and lilacs, and whispered, "Magic."

Nodding in complete belief, they wrapped their arms trustingly around his neck.

"What do you think?" Georgia asked.

Ashe sent his sister a bemused smile. "For the first time in my life, I believe in love at first sight."

CHAPTER SEVEN

"THEO IS A no-good cheating bastard. More please." From her place sprawled on the sofa, Tracy blindly held out her empty glass in Belle's general direction.

Happily, Belle obliged her best friend. She and Tracy met when they were twelve. A scholarship student, Tracy entered Lawndale Academy with a massive chip on her shoulder. The Drake family didn't have money, and their blood was working-man red—not upper-crust blue. But she couldn't hold out against a persistent Belle who—despite all signs to the contrary—saw Tracy as a kindred spirit. By the second week, they were inseparable. In all the years that passed, through separate colleges and one failed marriage—on Tracy's side—that hadn't changed.

Tracy brushed her long, dark blond hair from her face. She had a nice face. Even features and expressive brown eyes. However, it was her body that stopped traffic. Forget what the fashion magazines tried to sell a woman. It was Tracy's perfectly placed curves that made the world sit up and notice. In her entire adult life, she had never paid for her own drinks. Men loved Tracy. As for Tracy? She was indulgently realistic. Fun. That was what she wanted—at least for the time being. And fun was what she got.

Tonight was no exception. After an hour with Tracy, Belle felt lighter. It helped that she could tell her friend *anything*. If there was one person Belle could spill her guts to, it was the one person who knew *all* of her secrets. Every last one.

"I cheated on Theo before I knew he was cheating on me," Belle reminded Tracy. She was angry with Theo, but with him out of hearing range, she tried to be fair.

In Tracy's book, fairness went one way. Belle's way. "He cheated with another man."

"That makes us even."

"For a *year*."

"Fine." Belle raised her glass. "Theo wins the bigger asshole prize. Our engagement was a mistake from day one. *That* falls on both of

73

us. I didn't care about sleeping with him, Tracy. Look up going through the motions, insert picture of me."

"If I were sober, I would be too big a person to say *I told you so*." Tracy drained the vodka from her glass. "However..."

"You're halfway to being drunk off your ass." Belle wasn't far behind. "You are the only person I will let get away with it. Go on. Get it out of your system."

"I. Told. You. So. With a big red ribbon attached. My only consolation through this entire debacle was the knowledge that you never would have walked down that aisle."

Belle frowned into her glass. "I wish I was that certain."

"I had a plan. Kidnapping might have been involved."

"Might have?" Because things hadn't reached that point, Belle could laugh. "I hope to hell you aren't joking. If I had been stupid enough to get myself in that god-awful dress and in the church—poised to make the biggest mistake of my life—I need to know that you would have saved my ass."

"Remember Linus?"

"The cross-country truck driver you dated last year?" Belle sighed when she thought of the tattooed gentle giant. "I was sorry when you dumped him."

"It was mutual. We are better as friends. And *that* friend was going to help *this* friend whisk you away before we reached the church."

"And *that* is why I love you." Belle turned a blurry, considering look Tracy's way. "Maybe we should become lesbians."

"Wishing gets you many things, my sweet. This body," Tracy made a drunken gyration, "isn't one of them."

"My loss." Belle sighed dramatically.

"You have no idea." Tracy closed her eyes, riding the heady wave of alcohol rushing through her blood. "Enough about the five-second blunder."

"Theo lasted longer than five seconds." On this subject, Belle had no desire to defend her soon-to-be ex-fiancé. "Ten was about his average."

The friends had a good laugh at Theo's expense. Or was *she* the real joke, Belle wondered. She lay under a man while neither of them enjoyed the experience. Theoretically, she was old enough and smart enough to know better. Yet it happened. Multiple times.

"I am sad and pathetic."

"Wrong. You *were* sad and pathetic. That changed when you did the deed with Ashe Mathison. You are now my hero."

"It was a one-night stand, Tracy." A *really, really* good one night stand.

"I thought you were okay with that. A memory to warm the cockles when you're old and gray."

"I will *never* be gray." Belle and Tracy shuddered at the thought. Aging gracefully was one thing, but there were limits. "As for my cockles, Ashe threw a big bucket of cold water on them."

"I know, I know." Tracy waved a hand dismissively. "He broke your agreement. The one he didn't know about."

"It was implied," Belle mumbled belligerently.

"Fine. Let's put that aside for a moment. Ashe Mathison lived up to your fantasies. Correction, from your glowing review, he surpassed them. Blew them out of the water. How many times did you orgasm?"

"Multiple times." *Five* to be exact. "I left Los Angeles surrounded by an afterglow to beat all afterglows. *That* is why I resent Ashe. He showed up a month later and popped my lingering bubble of sexual contentment."

"Lingering bubble of—" Tracy shook her head. "If you can think that, let alone say it, you need more booze."

"Blame Ashe. I was pleasantly schnockered until you mentioned his name. That makes him a buzz kill—on every level."

"I think you should sleep with him again."

"Me too."

"What?" Tracy tried to sit up. Instead, she crashed onto the floor. Luckily, the area rug cushioned her fall. With great effort, she pulled herself up enough to peek over the coffee table. "Repeat that."

"Let me rephrase that. I'm ninety percent certain I *want* to sleep with Ashe again. However—"

"Ugh." Tracy flopped onto her back. "Why does there have to be a *however*?"

"Because this is real life. That night in Los Angeles wasn't. Ashe has proven himself to be a blackmailing jerk. At least I liked Theo when I slept with him."

"You can't judge Ashe on what happened earlier today. Damn. My buzz is wearing off, too. Where's the bottle?" Belle grabbed Tracy's weaving glass-clasping hand, steadying it long enough to pour a few fingers of vodka. "Ashe couldn't have known you would be there. In a wedding dress—purchased for your wedding. He slept with an engaged woman. That bit of information would throw anybody for a loop."

Belle snorted, dismissing Tracy's argument. "Women constantly throw themselves at Ashe." In her mind, Belle glossed over the fact that she could add herself to the list. "I doubt I'm the first engaged woman he's slept with."

"You might be the first to announce it after the fact—in such a dramatic fashion."

"None of that matters. Tonight, I'm drunk enough to think about making the same mistake twice. Tomorrow, when I'm stone-cold sober, that won't be a problem."

"That's exactly why you shouldn't wait. Invite him over now."

Belle laughed. So hard she almost ended up on the floor with Tracy. "Not going to happen," she announced emphatically as soon as she was able to catch her breath.

"Oops," Tracy snickered.

"Oops?" Belle sat up too fast. Grasping the side of the chair, she tried blinking away her blurred vision. "What does oops mean?"

"The last time I took a toilet break, I texted Ashe. He should be here in…" Tracy squinted at her watch, before giving up. "Soon."

"Are you crazy?"

Belle weaved her way to the apartment's balcony doors, throwing them open. In and out, she tried to breathe away her drunk. Instead of clearing her head, the cooling air almost knocked her on her butt. Grasping the frame, she steadied herself.

"Crazy like a fox. Ah, my ride is here." Tracy announced when her phone beeped. "I called a taxi just after I contacted lover boy."

"You can barely walk straight. How are you going to get downstairs?"

"Thank God for elevators. And vomiting." Her skin going an interesting shade of green, Tracy stumbled toward the bathroom.

"If you get any of that on my floor, you're cleaning it up."

A few minutes later, admirably steady on her feet, Tracy returned. "Not to worry. When it comes to throwing up, I have excellent aiming skills."

"I know. In high school, you hit Jimmy Gordon's feet with the precision of a bombardier."

"The bastard deserved it for deserting me at the dance to make out with what's her name. After catching him with his hands up her skirt, he's lucky all I hit were his feet."

"Tracy." Leaving the door open, Belle sent her friend a pleading gaze. "Please tell me you were kidding? Ashe is *not* coming here tonight?"

With a noncommittal smile, Tracy slid into the shoes she tossed off when she arrived. Just as she was reaching for her purse, the doorbell rang.

"That should be him now."

Following behind, Belle shook her head.

"How would Ashe have gotten through security at the front of the building? He didn't buzz me."

"You've seen Ashe Mathison—close up. All it would take was one smile and every woman—and half the men—in this complex would let him in. No questions asked."

Belle knew Tracy was right. "What does that say about the state of the world?"

"Pretty people rule—unless you are otherworldly smart. I know it isn't fair." Before Belle could remind her to check the peephole, Tracy threw open the door, literally falling into a surprised Ashe's arms. "Ashe Mathison. Long time no see."

To Ashe's credit, he didn't hesitate to catch Tracy—and continue to hold her upright. "I'm sorry. Have we met?"

"Only in my dreams," Tracy sighed, patting his chest. Smiling, she patted him again, her hand lingering. "Oh, my. Somebody works out."

"Ashe, this is my best friend, Tracy Drake. Though I might need to reconsider. Would you please make certain she gets to her taxi in one piece?"

"Sure." Ashe hooked his arm around Tracy's waist. "Do you promise to buzz me in?"

"Yes," Belle nodded. "What would be the point of refusing? You made it this far without my help."

Ashe grinned. "I lucked out. Mrs. Birch on the third floor needed help with her groceries."

At a spry ninety-one, Mrs. Birch was the biggest flirt in the building. *And* a hopeless romantic. Never a fan of Theo, if the woman thought Ashe was a possible substitute, she would let him into the building day or night.

Tracy waved as Ashe helped her into the elevator. "Bye."

"Call me as soon as you get home."

"Will do."

Belle closed the door, trying to gather her thoughts. Knowing she had to meet with Ashe was one thing. But this wasn't how she planned it.

Standing straight, she closed her eyes, attempting to touch her nose with her fingertips. To her relief, she hit a bullseye every time. Maybe Ashe had scared the alcohol out of her system. Circling the room, Belle cleaned up as she went. More likely was the fact Belle hadn't drunk as much as Tracy.

The vodka bottle—her friend's favorite—had a big dent in the contents. When serious, Belle preferred whiskey. Tonight, she stuck with wine. A few glasses on an empty stomach made her fuzzy. But the effects had worn off quickly.

Telling herself it was a matter of pride, not that she cared what Ashe thought, Belle walked through her bedroom to the attached bathroom, stopping in front of the vanity. Considering the day's events—and a few libations to dull the senses—Belle looked pretty good. Removing the clip, she ran a comb through her hair before splashing some water onto her face. Nice natural color in her cheeks and lips.

"Not bad for a night at home and an uninvited guest," Belle declared. Thinking for a second, Belle gave herself a definitive nod. "I don't care what anybody says, Tracy's invitation does not count."

True to her word, Belle released the security door seconds after Ashe buzzed. Though it wasn't possible, it seemed as if her doorbell rang a few seconds later. Impulsively, Belle hit play as she passed her iPod. Hooked up to a built-in speaker system, music—low and a little bluesy—filled the room.

"Mission accomplished." His body lightly brushing Belle's as he passed, Ashe didn't wait to be asked in. "I slipped the cabby a few bucks. He'll make certain she gets into her apartment safely."

"Thank you."

It felt odd, searching for something to say. In Los Angeles, Belle felt so at ease. Now? Not so much. So she fell back on an oldie but goodie. Playing the good hostess.

"Can I get you something? A drink?" Joking, she added, "Lasagna?"

"Really?" Ashe's eyes lit up. "I'm starving."

"Okay." Briefly thrown by the unexpected answer, Belle moved to the kitchen. "Did Tracy's text keep you from dinner with your family?"

"No." Ashe took a seat on a stool. "I—Wait. *Tracy's* text? It wasn't from you?"

"My friend's idea of being helpful. Sorry." Belle filled a plate. "Is that too much?"

"Cleaning my plate won't be a problem. But let's backtrack. Tell me about the text."

Belle shrugged. Setting the microwave, she took a glass from the cupboard. She set it, and a bottle of water, in front of Ashe. "I didn't send it. What did it say, by the way?"

Ashe took out his phone, hit a couple of buttons, handing it to Belle.

I'm free. How about you? Come on over so we can... talk. If you know what I mean.

"For crying out loud."

Shaking her head, Belle set down the phone. It was classic Tracy. Stir the pot and see how things settle. Belle loved the woman with all her heart, but there were times when she wished her friend would leave well enough alone.

"I didn't come over here expecting sex," Ashe informed her.

"Good thing, because that boat sailed in Los Angeles and you aren't getting a return ticket."

As she removed the plate from the microwave, her back to Ashe, she rolled her eyes. Not the best metaphor ever constructed, but it would have to do. It made her point. That was what mattered.

"That smells amazing."

Ashe's eyes honed in on the steaming lasagna with a look of anticipation. Considering Theo's reaction, it was a nice balm to Belle's ego. She was about to serve the meal—all happy homemaker—when she remembered why this scenario shouldn't be happening. A second before Ashe could chow down, Belle snatched the plate away.

"Hey," Ashe protested, his face falling like an under-baked cake.

"I appreciate what you did for Tracy. Big kudos for playing the gentleman."

"Who said I was playing?"

Ignoring Ashe's teasing tone, Belle's eyes narrowed with renewed resolve.

"I'm pissed off at you. Remember this afternoon? Blackmail is an ugly business, and it doesn't get rewarded with a helping of my exemplary lasagna."

"*You're* pissed off? If either of us is entitled to a case of self-righteous indignation, it's me."

Seeing what she was about to do, Ashe hustled around the island, retrieving the plate before Belle could dump the contents down the garbage disposal. Blocking her with his body, he took a bite. Belle had to admit, she enjoyed the way his eyes closed. The sigh of pleasure wasn't bad either. Seeing how much Ashe enjoyed her cooking was a boost to her ego, but it didn't erase his actions.

"You're the injured party? I don't think so. You were going to rat me out to my mother. Hardly the *gentlemanly* thing to do."

"I wouldn't have told her," Ashe assured Belle, taking another bite.

Belle snorted, unconvinced. "You threw the threat out there fast enough."

Ashe shrugged, walking back to his seat. "Tell me about the ring. It wasn't on your finger when we met in Los Angeles. Is that your thing? Playing around on the fiancé when you're out of town?"

Just in time, Belle stopped herself from hiding her hand behind her back. It would have been a pointless gesture. Ashe had seen the ring—and the wedding dress. Out of sight, out of mind might work in some cases. This was not one of them.

"If you are worried about such things, why didn't you ask me if I was engaged before we—?"

"Fucked like rabbits?"

It wasn't Belle's tendency to blush. However, Ashe's crude interpretation of their night together brought her close. The words bothered her. In spite of everything, she remembered it as beautifully passionate. Discovering Ashe didn't feel the same, hurt. Belle lifted her chin. Not that she would let him know how his words affected her.

"The point is, if sleeping with an engaged woman bothers you so much, you should have used your tongue to ask questions before sticking it down my throat."

Though she wasn't comfortable in the role, Belle could play the crude game. If Ashe's frown was any indication, she was better at it than she would have thought.

"It wasn't like that," Ashe admitted hesitantly. "You're right. I should have asked questions. That was my plan." His warm gray eyes—void of animosity—met hers. "If you remember? You kissed me first."

Belle felt her shoulders relax, her anger dissipated. This was the Ashe she found irresistible. *Oh, boy.* A little more of this and her resolve to never sleep with him again would be in serious jeopardy.

"It shouldn't have happened." Intellectually, Belle knew it was true. That didn't change the facts. She had no regrets. It shouldn't matter, but she couldn't help asking. "Are you sorry it did?"

"No." Ashe started to smile but at the last second, his lips flattened. "Until I thought you were using me as a last fling. It tainted the experience."

"I didn't plan on sleeping with you, Ashe. It just... happened."

Straight faced, Ashe nodded. "I've been told I'm pretty damn irresistible."

Belle laughed. By the twinkle in Ashe's eyes, that had been his intention.

"I won't flatter your ego by agreeing."

"It isn't necessary. Your actions spoke louder than words."

"Insufferable," Belle muttered, opening the refrigerator. But her lips twitched, blooming into a full-fledged smile. *Insufferably charming.* "There's more lasagna if you want it."

"I better stop." Ashe pushed the cleared plate away. "Belle?"

"Hmm?" Turning, Belle held one of her famous cheesecakes. She baked it the other day—just because—and planned to serve it to

Theo. That hadn't worked out—to put it mildly. Since Ashe enjoyed her lasagna so much, she hoped he had room for dessert.

"Is that homemade?" Whatever Ashe was about to say was lost the second he spied the confection.

Belle nodded. "I love to bake. Want a piece?"

"Yes." Ashe's nod was enthusiastic. "Is this a regular thing?"

"Baking?" Belle measured a small piece, making it bigger when Ashe sent her an, *are you kidding me* look. He spread his fingers wide. "It relaxes me. When I'm at home, I am usually in the kitchen."

"Mm. This is what I hope they serve in heaven." Ashe closed his eyes, savoring the first bite. "Why don't you weigh three hundred pounds?"

"I'm smart enough to give most of the baked goods away. And yoga. Lots of yoga."

"Hot?" Deliberately, Ashe held her gaze, slowly licking his fork.

The man was evil. Refusing to jump, Belle took his question at face value.

"I do all kinds. Hot yoga. Power. ISHTA is a current favorite. The choices are endless."

"Must make you very flexible."

Unoffended by Ashe's teasing, Belle cut herself a piece of cheesecake—about a third of the size she served him.

"Down, boy," she laughed, sitting next to him. "My flexibility is none of your concern."

"I suppose you're right." With a sigh, Ashe took another bite. "Is the wedding really a go?"

How to answer that? Outside of Tracy, Belle had no intention of telling anybody about her Theo situation. Two weeks. As much as the delay galled her, Belle promised. There was one bright spot. Ashe believed she was engaged. Soon to be married. Since officially involved women seemed to be an issue for him—call it a no-touch zone—there was no way Belle was going to eliminate that buffer by spilling the Theo beans.

"Theo and I are still engaged." As long as Ashe didn't push, a part of the truth should suffice. "I apologize, Ashe. In Los Angeles, I—"

"Don't." Thoughtfully, Ashe rubbed the back of his neck. "I might have overreacted this afternoon."

"Really?" Belle knew she had no right, but the sarcastic tone slipped out none the less. To her surprise, Ashe let it slide.

"I was surprised to see you."

"It's safe to say we both belong to that club," Belle laughed. "Imagine how I felt. At least you knew I was in the city. I thought you were in Los Angeles. At first, I thought the tulle from my dress made me hallucinate."

"Does that happen often?" Ashe looked amused—and puzzled. "Fabric-induced aberrations? That's one I haven't heard."

"The right elements have to converge. Yards and yards of fluff. A childhood bedroom. The proper state of mind." Belle sipped her water, smiling back. "It might have been one for the medical journals. Since you turned out to be flesh and bone, it's a moot point."

Without asking—on either side—Ashe helped Belle with the brief cleanup. She offered coffee, which he declined.

"I know it's getting late."

"Ten thirty? How is that late for a rock star? Just a second." Belle checked her phone. "Tracy is home, in bed, safe and sound."

"Good. It isn't late," Ashe conceded, continuing. He followed Belle to the living room. "I thought you might need to get up early for work." He shook his head. "That's another of the many things I don't know about you. What do you do for a living, Belle?"

Normally, that question didn't give Belle pause. Vice President. It sounded impressive. And was—in its way. Few people delved further, satisfied with the title. Something told her Ashe would want more. She was right.

"What does Vice President mean? Day to day. What are your responsibilities?"

How to explain? Ashe had it easy. Unless they lived under a rock, everybody knew what he did. And did very well indeed. The world knew who Ashe Mathison was. His face was his calling card.

Belle wondered what it was like to be that famous. She wanted to ask, but Ashe waited for an answer.

"I smooth the waters."

"Come again?"

To Belle, it made perfect sense. However, she understood Ashe's confusion. She rested her arm on the back of the sofa, her body angled toward him.

"My father deals with a lot of people. Daily. Weekly. Yearly. Occasionally, feathers get ruffled. It doesn't take much in this day and age of global business and one-touch emails. Misunderstandings happen. My father's style leans toward abrasive. That's when I step in and—"

"Smooth the waters. Is there really enough of that to keep you busy?"

"You have no idea. Last week, there was a Chinese delegation in town."

Belle went on, telling Ashe the story that in retrospect had him—and her—laughing. At the time, Belle was tearing her hair out.

"I get it. Your father's faux pas keep you hopping. But are you happy, Belle?"

"Happy? I'm..." Belle swallowed. She asked herself that question all the time. Outside of Tracy, nobody else ever did.

"It's okay." Ashe's hand lay on the back of the sofa, inches from Belle's. Closing the distance, he brushed his fingertips against hers in an oddly comforting gesture. "I can hear your answer in the tone of your voice. See it in your eyes."

"I'm not *un*happy, Ashe."

"No?"

Belle sighed. What was the point? Ashe read her too easily. She found it disconcerting and comforting. It was an odd combination. But what was new? Her feelings for Ashe had always been complicated. As a teenager and an adult.

"I have nothing to complain about. Nothing. I'm healthy. My home is comfortable. I have the best friend anybody could ask for. My parents love me. Money has never been a problem."

"Aren't you forgetting something?"

Belle frowned, doing a mental inventory. She drew a blank.

"I don't think so."

"Your fiancé? Shouldn't he be on the list?"

Oh, boy. Leave it to Ashe to pick up on that. As far as Belle was concerned, she hadn't forgotten Theo. How could she? He wasn't an important part of her life. From day one of their engagement, Theo was never more than an afterthought. Sad but true. The usual rush of guilt didn't come. *What a relief.* She and Theo should have cleared the air long ago.

"The importance of my fiancé goes without saying." *Well put.* Belle mentally patted herself on the back.

Ashe seemed to accept her answer, but rather than take the chance he was gearing up to put her through another round of dodge the question, Belle turned the tables. Since she was genuinely interested, it was easy.

"What brought you back to Boston?"

"My father's birthday." Ashe didn't move his hand. Belle didn't ask him to. "The invitation came as a surprise—to say the least."

"It came from your father?"

Ashe shook his head. "Georgia. Which reminds me. You didn't mention that she was the reason you were at the concert."

Unlike before, there was no need for Belle to scramble for her answer. When Georgia offered her the ticket, there were no stipulations about keeping the source a secret. However, when Belle met Ashe, the last thing on her mind was his sister.

86

"It wasn't meant to be a secret, Ashe. It simply didn't occur to me."

Nodding, Ashe tapped Belle's finger again. Lightly, almost absently, as if the connection was subconscious. Belle, on the other hand, was very much aware. It was difficult to be so close. To know what it felt like to hold him —bare flesh to bare flesh—knowing she would never again experience Ashe's touch beyond that little tap.

"I knew I had to come." Ashe circled back to the reason he was in Boston. "Dad is turning sixty. Life doesn't hand us any guarantees. This could be my one and only chance to reconnect."

Though it was hard to imagine an estrangement from her father—especially one that lasted ten years—Belle was sympathetic.

"I admire you for taking the first step. It couldn't have been easy."

"Terrifying. Seeing Georgia was worth it. And her daughters stole my heart. But the rest of the family." Ashe shivered as though an arctic chill had swirled through the room.

"I take it from the way you wolfed down my lasagna, dinner with your family was not a success. Did things flame out with your father?"

"Dad wasn't there. Business is keeping him out of town—according to Georgia."

"You don't buy the explanation?"

Ashe shrugged. "I have no reason not to. I never knew my father to avoid a confrontation. I doubt that's changed."

"Then what happened at dinner? Bad béarnaise? Inferior cut of meat?" Belle lowered her voice conspiratorially. "Mushy vegetables?"

"Nope. From the few bites I was able to enjoy, I would say my mother has herself a superior cook. It was the company that sent my stomach roiling. It didn't settle until I got a whiff of your excellent lasagna."

Belle did a quick mental rundown of Ashe's family. Georgia was a doll. Her husband a sweetheart. And as Ashe already discovered, their twin dynamos were enviably adorable. Bonita Mathison was a chunk of ice. That couldn't have come as a surprise. His sister, Vivian always struck Belle as vain in the extreme. *Me, me, me.* No husband there. That left Bradley. Of all the Mathisons, Belle knew him the least. However, Tracy went out with him about six months ago. It hadn't gone well.

"I'm not a fan of your brother."

Ashe didn't blink at Belle's comment. "What did he do to you?"

"Not me. Tracy." Belle hesitated. Tracy wouldn't mind, but it might not be the kind of information Ashe would appreciate hearing.

"Did he hurt her?" Ashe's voice remained calm, but his fingers tightened on the sofa—white knuckled.

"Not physically. Bradley is more of a verbal abuser. It was great for the first few weeks they went out. Then he began picking away. Criticizing the way Tracy dressed. Her weight. Even the color of her hair. Bradley thought the blond wasn't blond enough."

"I hope Tracy told him to go to hell. And what the hell is wrong with her weight?"

Belle could have kissed Ashe for that one comment alone. Too bad she had sworn off that particular indulgence.

"There is nothing wrong with Tracy. Period. And she knows it. If he hadn't charmed her to start, she would have shown him the door after the first dig. Her mistake was giving him the benefit of the doubt."

"He's an asshole. Where does the doubt come in?"

"One or two insults after a barrage of flattery. Tracy thought it might be an aberration. She was wrong. Bradley somehow knew the exact buttons to push. Where Tracy was the most vulnerable. Tracy is so open she would have given him plenty of ammunition without realizing what he would do with it."

"Please tell me she didn't put up with his shit."

"Not my Tracy. She's a fighter. Bradley tried to leave her in a whimpering heap, but by the time he crawled out the door, he was the one with blood dripping from his ears."

Ashe grinned. "She gave as good as she got?"

"Better." When Tracy recounted the confrontation, Belle wished she could have been a fly on the wall if only to see Bradley reduced to tears.

"He cried? Damn. Time to turn in his man card."

"I don't think he was ever issued one." Belle sighed. "I'd like to believe Bradley learned his lesson. But I doubt it."

"I can attest to that."

"Dinner?" His expression grim, Ashe nodded. "I'm surprised he would do that in front of your family."

"If Dad had been there, he wouldn't have dared." Ashe closed his eyes, rotating his neck. "I hadn't forgotten what my family dynamic was like. However, it had become a hazy memory. Softened by time and distance. The tension. The less-than-veiled insults. My tolerance for that shit has lowered to almost zero."

"What did you do?"

"I could have traded verbal barbs with my brother—and held my own. But Georgia's girls were at the table. They might be too young to understand what was happening. Still..."

Belle smiled gently. "You're a good uncle, Ashe."

"Maybe." Ashe's eyes opened, meeting Belle's. "Leaving in the middle of the meal worked tonight. I can't rely on that method for the rest of my stay. Little brother and I need to come to an understanding."

"Bradley is stubborn. You might have to punch his lights out." Belle batted her eyes innocently. "Just to drive home your point."

Ashe chuckled. "I'll keep it in mind. Though beating Bradley up might not be the best way to foster family harmony."

They fell into an easy silence, the room dimly lit by the accent lamps flanking the sofa. Belle leaned her head back, closing her eyes. This was nice. Relaxed. She was aware of Ashe—that would never change. However, she didn't feel an overriding sense of urgency the way she did in Los Angeles. Sex was off the table. Perhaps they were on their way to being friends. She hoped so.

"That's me."

"Hmm?" Languidly, Belle raised her eyelids. "What's you?"

"Listen."

Doing as Ashe asked, Belle tuned her ear to the music playing softly in the background. This was one of her favorite songs by an artist she recently discovered. She loved the long instrumental section—dominated by a saxophone.

"*That's* you?" Belle sat up, her eyes wide with wonder. "Why didn't I know that?"

"I wrote the song. It wasn't right for *The Ryder Hart Band,* so I put it out there for another artist to pick up. When Jimmy Todd—"

"Slow down, buddy. You wrote *Undercurrent*? And played on the recording?"

"Why so surprised?" Ashe seemed amused by her reaction. "It's what I do, Belle. I play. I write. I sing—a little. Lately—when I find a young artist I like—I've done some producing."

"Jimmy Todd, for example?"

"That's right."

What were the chances? Belle's taste in music was pretty fixed. She had artists she liked. Her iPod was filled with *The Ryder Hart Band*—a bit of information she kept to herself. It was unusual for her to add somebody new. Jimmy Todd was the exception. All because of that one song. Unbelievable.

"When do you find the time?"

"You would be surprised how much downtime we have when we aren't touring or recording. I like the idea of restocking the shelves—so to speak. My friends and I were given a hand up back in the day. It feels good to do the same for somebody I believe in. And on that note, I should be going."

This time, when Belle glanced at the clock, she was amazed to see it was well after twelve o'clock. Time had slipped away. Despite the hour, she was reluctant for the evening to end. She couldn't expect to see Ashe again. He was in Boston to reconnect with his family. Despite the stumble at dinner, that was still his goal. Besides, he thought she was to be married. He had made it clear that fact put her off limits.

90

It was easy to curse Ashe's moral conviction. The problem was, it was one of the things that made him so appealing. It had been easier when she thought he was a blackmailing jerk. Now? Belle wished he had a few more flaws that she could hate. Instead, it seemed Ashe Mathison was practically perfect. Damn him.

"Thank you for one of the best meals I can remember in a long time." At the door, Ashe took her hand. "Part of it was the food. Mostly, the company."

Charming and sweet. Add on sexy. Gorgeous. Belle already knew what he could do to her in bed. *Damn, damn, damn, Ashe Mathison.*

"I hope things work out with your family."

"Time will tell." Ashe didn't get the hint when Belle tugged on her hand. He held fast, his thumb gently rubbing the back, heating her skin. "Would a kiss be out of the question?"

That's an option? Belle wanted to jump into Ashe's arms, cover his mouth with hers, and forget the world outside her door. Would she regret it in the morning? Maybe. But who would they be hurting? Theo was cheating. Why shouldn't she?

"Forget I asked," Ashe said, opening the door. "I don't want you to do anything you would regret."

A conscience was a great thing—until it wasn't. Belle's was on overload. Yes. No. Maybe. Why couldn't she jump one way and be satisfied with her decision? Because, that annoying little voice in her head reminded her, this isn't just any man. It's Ashe. Temptation personified.

"Would you regret it?" The words slipped out, but Belle was glad. If she couldn't have a kiss to enjoy, at least she would have the satisfaction of knowing if Ashe was as conflicted as she was.

Pausing, Ashe shook his head, his lips curving into a half smile.

"After the way you left things in Los Angeles? Finding out you're engaged to be married? I should regret taking you into my bed."

Ashe smoothed a hand over Belle's hair. "But I don't. There's no way in hell I would regret a kiss, Belle. Now. Tomorrow. Ever."

Without another word or a backward glance, Ashe walked away. Slowly, slightly dazed, Belle stepped into her apartment, shutting the door. She pressed her back against the surface, sliding to the floor with a sigh.

One thing hadn't changed. Belle *was* over her crush. Unfortunately, those girlhood feelings had been replaced by something far more serious. And infinitely more dangerous. It was only a kernel—more of a notion than a full-fledged emotion. However, Belle knew—given a chance—it would take hold and never let go. She didn't have the guts to say the word.

The little voice in her head had no such problem. Belle's attempt to block it out failed abysmally. The whispered word snuck through her defenses. It echoed through her brain.

Love.

CHAPTER EIGHT

"WHAT ARE YOUR plans?"

"The point of this trip was to see my father. That hasn't changed."

Ashe had called Los Angeles to check in—a common occurrence when one of the bandmates was out of town. It was early, and he knew that like him, Zoe was usually up with the sun. Besides, Ryder and Dalton shared their beds these days. Ashe didn't want to disturb them or their ladies.

Ashe listened to the sound of strings being plucked. Not an unfamiliar occurrence. Zoe never went anyplace without one of her many guitars. Ashe had two best friends. *Male* best friends. He was just as close to Zoe. However, as a woman, the dynamic was different. Not that he would tell her that. From the beginning, she insisted they treat her as they would any other member of the band. Forget her sex.

Easier said than done. Zoe was Ryder's little sister. Ashe had met her years before she joined the band. By then, she was his sister too. She was a strong, independent woman who could take care of herself. However, when they first met, she was a quiet, vulnerable fifteen-year-old girl. Zoe didn't let that part of her show very often. When she did, Ashe wanted to wrap her in cotton and protect her from the world. Of course, if he attempted such a foolish mission, she would have his balls on a plate.

Zoe *was* their equal in all things. She was also the best guitar player Ashe had ever known. Bar none. Ryder couldn't hold a candle to her. Neither could Ashe. A fact they weren't shy about admitting. And her voice. Ashe sighed thinking about it. She refused to step up and sing lead, but her voice was the stuff to make the angels weep.

"Daddy is AWOL. Brother dear is an asshole. Sister number two is a waste of space. At least you have Georgia and her brood."

Count on Zoe to reduce matters to basics. She was the most pragmatic member of the band, and Ashe loved her for it.

"Today I get to spend the day spoiling my nieces."

"You sound happy about that," Zoe said, her voice as dry as the Sahara.

Ashe smiled. He could almost see Zoe's shudder. She was tolerant of children but had little use for them. All those years in foster homes made her lose her taste for sticky, smelly, whiny little tykes. She had her fill, thank you very much.

"Naomi and Nadia are sweethearts. And they love their Uncle Ashe."

"That explains it. You are a sucker for an adoring woman—no matter her age."

"True." An image of Belle popped into Ashe's head. The one woman he *wished* adored him was out of his reach. The irony wasn't lost on him.

"A whole day?" Zoe sounded skeptical. "What are they? Four? Five?"

"Five. I can handle them." That's what Ashe kept telling himself. He had a doubt or two. But he refused to admit it to Zoe. "Besides, the beauty of being an uncle is that I get to rev them up on parks, toy stores, and copious amounts of sugar then—"

"Dump them in Mommy's lap." Zoe's chuckle made Ashe's grin widen. "The perfect plan. Your sister might question welcoming you with open arms."

"I have carte blanche—for one day and one day only."

"You won't spoil the little darlings after this?"

Zoe knew him well. "I didn't say that. From here on, I'll temper my spoiling. However, since this is our first solo outing, I want it to be memorable."

"Dolls," Zoe said emphatically. "The big ones with long, shiny hair and ruffled dresses. That's what I wanted when I was that age."

Ashe swallowed. There was nobody to buy Zoe a doll. Or presents of any kind. She didn't talk about it often, but she and Ryder had hellish childhoods. If she told him to buy his nieces big, fancy dolls, that was what Ashe would do.

"Thanks for the tip," Ashe answered with deliberate lightness. Then, because he knew Zoe just as well, changed the subject. "What's on your agenda?"

"Avoiding Smith Carson." Zoe growled the name as if spitting out the filthiest curse words imaginable. "Ryder is giving him a tour of the studio this afternoon. Dalton plans to join them. I don't."

Ashe couldn't understand Zoe's animosity toward Smith Carson. It seemed to come out of nowhere. For the first time since the idea of combining the two tours arose, Ashe hesitated. Up until now, they had treated Zoe's negativity as a joke. If there was more involved, Ashe wanted to know.

"Has Smith Carson tried something with you?"

"Tried something? As in made a pass?" Zoe laughed. Hard. "What would you do if I said yes?"

"Kick the pretty boy's ass."

Ashe expected more laughter. Zoe was notoriously fierce about fighting her own battles. When she replied, her tone was sober as a judge.

"Thank you for the thought. It means a lot to know you have my back, Ashe." It sounded as if Zoe cleared her throat. "But it isn't necessary."

"You're sure?" Zoe's uncharacteristic show of emotion made Ashe's throat tighten. "I have a mean right hook."

"According to his bio, Smith Carson is a martial arts expert. Are you sure you want to take that on?"

That gave Ashe pause. "How expert?"

"Beats me. The point is, you, my would-be hero, are not. If Carson messes with my virtue, I'll deal with him the good old-fashioned way."

"Knee to the nuts?"

Zoe simply laughed. "Have a good time with the tiny terrors. And call back soon."

"Say hi to Smith," Ashe teased.

"Up yours, Mathison."

"I love you, too, kid."

Ashe grinned, ending the call. It was a good feeling knowing he had people who cared—worried. Friends who wanted him around. He loved Georgia. He was looking forward to getting to know her little girls. As for his father? He was a wild card Ashe couldn't count on. Not yet. But one thing would always be constant. His family—the family of his heart—waited for him in Los Angeles.

Whistling, Ashe headed down the stairs. He needed three things to start his day. A long run. A hot shower. Followed by a big breakfast. In the driveway, he bent to tie his shoe. He adjusted the baseball cap and sunglasses. Ashe didn't expect to be recognized at this hour, but donning a little camouflage had become second nature. Ready, he started out along the familiar streets at an easy jog.

Taking the corner, Ashe increased his speed as his body warmed and his muscles loosened. Suddenly, he realized there was one more thing he needed. The name of a toy store that sold big dolls with long, shiny hair and ruffled dresses. He could ask Georgia, but that would take away the fun of surprising her as well as her little girls.

Ashe was a good three miles into his run, feet pounding the pavement, his heart beating fast when the answer came to him. Who better to ask than someone who had lived in the city her entire life?

Belle Richards. It gave him the perfect excuse to get in touch with her. Ashe knew it wasn't a good idea. But what the hell, he told himself, heading back the way he came. It was only a phone call. It wasn't as though anything was going to happen.

Always ready to call somebody out on a bullshit statement—even himself—Ashe laughed. The truth was, for all his moral high-ground rhetoric and resolve, if Belle gave him any indication she was willing, he didn't think that ring on her finger would mean much.

Ashe wanted her in Los Angeles. He wanted her when he woke the next morning—alone. He wanted her now.

Last night hadn't helped. Time alone with Belle—just talking—reinforced his feelings. It was one thing to desire her. But now there was an added element. He liked her. A lot. It moved her to a new category. One Ashe had never dealt with before now.

There were scores of women Ashe had wanted. Belle was the first one he could grow to need.

CHAPTER NINE

BELLE HUNG UP the phone. It was barely nine o'clock, and that already was the third mini blowup she had averted since arriving at work. Even with the world's multitudes of time differences, she didn't understand how people wound themselves up so tight, so early.

With a sigh, Belle sipped her second cup of coffee. Last night when she told Ashe her job was to smooth things over, she hadn't exaggerated. Luckily, it wasn't all she did. Her pet project was coming along nicely. When her father approved the budget—Belle refused to consider him turning her down—everything was in place to start moving forward.

As Belle clicked on the computer file for *Strive*, she felt a surge of excitement. Everything was meticulously documented and researched. Her plan to help single mothers earn an income that would allow them to stay at home and provide a good life for them and their children wasn't just a pipe dream. It was doable.

The applications—a distressingly large amount—had been processed and screened. At this stage, Belle's handpicked staff spent most of their time making certain the women they chose were legitimately in need. It was vital that no scam artists slipped through. Money would be tight at first, and Belle was determined not to waste a penny. She put her trust in those under her to make certain every applicant they accepted was legitimate.

However, Belle was in charge of the bottom line. *Never turn your back on the money.* It was one of the first—and most important—lessons her father taught her. She followed it religiously in her professional *and* personal life. Every check, every bank transfer, every spreadsheet was checked and approved by her. No exceptions.

As Belle scanned today's updates, she felt a glow of satisfaction. One day, she promised herself, the fledgling company would grow. Expand to include not just women, but others who were looking for a hand up—not a handout.

"Belle?"

"Yes, Pru?"

From Belle's first day as Vice President, Pru Craddock had been her assistant. Though Pru was almost ten years older, Belle thought of them as starting out together. Vividly, she remembered interviewing the other woman—it was a toss-up which of them had been more nervous.

At the time, Pru had been a single mother getting back into the workforce after staying home through her late teens and early twenties to raise her two children. One divorce and a deadbeat dad later, she was desperate to find a job. Though her father had advised going with somebody more qualified, Belle had never regretted her decision. Pru was the inspiration for *Strive*. In fact, her assistant sat on the advisory board. Her input had already proved invaluable.

"Ashe Mathison is on line three."

Belle stared at the blinking light on the communications console as if she had never seen it before.

"Belle? Are you there?"

Realizing she wasn't breathing, Belle took several deep breaths. *Stop acting like you've never received a phone call from the opposite sex*, she chastised herself. *He's just a man*. Belle had almost convinced herself it was true when Pru blew her argument out of the water.

"Is it *the* Ashe Mathison?" Normally, Pru's voice was calm and professional. As she said Ashe's name, it quivered with barely suppressed excitement. "I mean, how many could there be?"

"Ashe is definitely an original," Belle admitted, her mouth twisted. Part smile. Part consternation.

"Then it is him. Oh, my," Pru gasped. "Oh, my. My girls and I *love The Ryder Hart Band*. I can't believe I am this close to a certified rock star."

Dealing with Pru's overheated reaction calmed Belle's nerves.

"I don't think he's that close, Pru. A few miles, at least."

"But it's as though he breathed in my ear." There was a pause before Pru burst out laughing. "Did I just say that? I'm sorry, Belle. I can't imagine what's wrong with me."

Belle understood as was well as anybody. "Ashe Mathison tends to have that effect on women. Even from a distance."

"You've met him?" In spite of her recovery, Pru sounded slightly breathless.

"When I was in Los Angeles. And before you ask. Yes, I met all of the band members."

Pru gasped. "I was going to ask if he is as sexy in person as he was in music videos. I can't believe you met *The Ryder Hart Band.* Ryder *and* Dalton?"

"And Zoe," Belle confirmed, amused by Pru's reaction.

"I—"

Before Pru could spout one more *oh, my*, Belle interrupted.

"Did Ashe say what he wanted?"

"Oh, no. I can't believe I've left him on hold. He didn't give a reason for calling, and I was too flummoxed to ask. Should I put him through?"

"Sure." *What was the harm? It was only a phone call*? "Hello, Ashe," Belle cringed at her overly bright tone. "How are you this morning?"

"Good."

Belle heard Ashe clear his throat. Was he nervous? That didn't seem likely. However, the idea that she might have put a dent in his easy confidence smoothed out Belle's nerves.

"Is there something I can do for you?"

"I need some help."

Belle relaxed. Help was her specialty. "Shoot."

"First." The lowered timbre of Ashe's voice made Belle's blood warm. *Just the sound of his voice*. For God's sake, how many times did she need to remind herself that she was a grown woman, not a hormonally challenged teenager? "Did you get enough sleep?"

Sweet *and* sexy. And funny. And smart. And— Belle put a halt to her thoughts. Listing Ashe's assets could take all day, driving herself crazy in the process. It was getting harder and harder to remember—or care—that he was off limits.

"I had plenty of sleep. Thank you. How are you doing?" Since Ashe asked, it was only polite for her to do the same. The fact that Belle wanted to keep him talking as long as possible had nothing to do with it.

"Great. I had a long run. Breakfast was stellar—sans family." Ashe sounded relaxed and happy. "I anticipate the rest of my day will be even better."

"Really?" Finding Ashe's enthusiasm contagious, Belle smiled. "Why is that?"

"I get to spend the day with two beautiful women."

"I see." Belle knew her words dripped with ice. Her reaction had been automatic. Jealousy. It wasn't a familiar emotion. However, she had no problem recognizing it.

"My nieces," Ashe qualified. Belle felt herself relax until he added, "The only adult woman I want to spend time with isn't available."

Was it wrong that Belle wanted to do cartwheels all over her office? Was she worried that her emotions were more up and down than a yo-yo riding a rollercoaster? Yes, on both counts. For the sake of her sanity, Belle moved the conversation back to where they started.

"You said you need help?"

Thankfully, Ashe followed her lead.

"Where can I buy a doll? Two dolls, to be exact."

"For Nadia and Naomi?" Belle knew it was a ridiculous question. Unless Ashe had some peculiar tastes—that she didn't want to know about—why else would he ask her about buying dolls?

"That's right," Ashe chuckled as if reading her thoughts. "They need to be big. With long, shiny hair and frilly dresses. Or was it ruffled dresses? Is there a difference? I should have written down Zoe's instructions."

Ashe sounded slightly bemused—which made sense. Belle doubted he spent a lot of time contemplating ruffles versus frills. That he cared so much about making his nieces happy made her lips curve and her heart sigh.

"Frills and ruffles can exist separately or together. Does that help?"

"Not even a little. I'm sunk."

"You weren't planning on going to the store yourself?"

"I was before the whole ruffle/frills debate. You think I'll screw it up?"

"It isn't that," Belle assured Ashe. "Any salesperson could guide you to a perfect purchase. It's just…"

"What?"

"When was the last time you went shopping in a store?"

"I honestly have no idea." Ashe took a few moments. "Now that you mention it, I shop online. Or my assistant takes care of it."

"Because…" Belle enjoyed leading Ashe to his ultimate revelation. He was a smart man. It didn't take long.

"Fine. I'm famous. However, you would be surprised how often I move around without anybody recognizing me."

"I'll bite. How often?"

"It happens." Ashe sounded defensive.

"I'm sure," Belle said, placating him. "I just thought it would be easier if you let me buy the dolls. I can have them delivered. No muss. No fuss."

"You wouldn't mind?" The relief was evident in Ashe's voice.

"It will be fun. No matter how old a woman gets, the little girl in her never goes away completely."

"Well, *Grandma*, I appreciate it."

"My pleasure."

"Just one thing. Would you mind if I picked the dolls up at your place?"

Bad idea, Belle, her little voice cautioned. As much as she hated to admit it, the little voice had a point. "I'm sure the store can get them to you this afternoon."

"It isn't that. I will be with the girls all afternoon, and I want the dolls to be a surprise. If they arrive while we're out, the cat might be let out of the bag."

Belle had no problem saying no. Most of the time. When she agreed to Theo's proposal, it had been a huge mistake—and the reason she shouldn't say yes to Ashe. About anything. Not that it mattered. She couldn't seem to help herself.

"Okay. Have your day out with the girls. I'll hit the store this afternoon. Drop by my place around six o'clock."

"Oh. I almost forgot. If possible, one doll should be dressed in pink, the other purple."

Just to be safe, Belle jotted the colors down—though she couldn't imagine forgetting.

"Got it."

"I can't thank you enough, Belle."

"Give your nieces a day to remember. That will be all the thanks I need. And Ashe?"

"Don't worry. We're taking a picnic—and some kites—to the park. Followed by ice cream. In a hat and sunglasses, I'm unrecognizable."

Belle doubted that. But she knew Ashe wouldn't put those little girls in the path of stampeding fans. A weekday in the park was the perfect place for them to blend in and bond.

"See you at six."

"I won't be late," Ashe promised.

There was nothing she could do, Belle thought, hanging up the phone. The man got to her—on every level. With a resigned sigh, she swiveled around in her chair until she faced the small office window that brightened the room with a sliver of sunlight. She could admit to herself that Ashe Mathison tempted her resolve. The secret to holding her convictions firm was not admitting them to him.

That decided, Belle checked her schedule. The toy store she had in mind was only a few blocks away. She could use her lunch hour to shop, spending the rest of the afternoon to clear up what looked like a bunch of not-so-important busy work.

Belle felt a surge of anticipation. It had been a long time since she had visited a toy store. Though married, her siblings had yet to reproduce—much to her mother's increasing dismay. There were no children in her immediate family to spoil with ridiculously impractical gifts. Having a reason to wander through the aisles was a treat she hadn't expected but would thoroughly enjoy.

Lunch time fluctuated greatly. Somedays, Belle had Pru order in something that more often than not wasn't worth the time it took to unwrap and toss in the garbage. Today, things fell perfectly into place, and she was able to leave the office at twelve thirty sharp.

The walk to the toy store gave Belle a chance to stretch her legs and breathe in the surprisingly mild mid-August air. As her heels clicked briskly along the pavement, she hummed a random song. Or not so random, as it turned out. *You Bring Me Trouble* had been a big hit for *The Ryder Hart Band*. A song she knew for a fact who wrote it. Ashe. Belle's peal of laughter drew admiring glances from a few suited passersby, but she didn't notice. If she had, it wouldn't have mattered. For now, there was only room for one man—and his songs—in her thoughts. Whether she liked it or not.

There was something about a toy store. The way it smelled. The sense of wonder. There weren't many children at this time of day, but those Belle could see were wide eyed with endless possibilities. Sensory overload. Belle imagined every parent came through the doors with a plan—determined not to waver. She admired their fortitude. Those big, pleading looks would be hard to ignore. Then again, she didn't have years of experience. Saying no—no matter how cute the kid—had to become easier over time.

"May I help you?" a smiling young woman asked Belle. Her name tag, shaped like a bundle of colorful balloons, spelled out Willa in sparkly purple letters.

"Thank goodness," Belle smiled back. "I could have happily wandered for hours. I've passed this store dozens of times wishing I had an excuse to come in. Your selection is amazing."

"If we don't have it, nobody does." Willa pointed to the sign on the wall. "It's a good slogan. And true. Special orders usually arrive within a day."

Belle knew the importance of keeping clients happy. It could be the difference between a business flourishing or floundering.

"I need two dolls. Big ones." Belle spread her hands wide as if describing the fish that got away. "Pink and purple. Is that doable?"

"Come this way." Willa led Belle down an aisle. "Doll Land is one of our largest—and most popular—areas."

"Wow," Belle said, her eyes as big as any child's.

"You look the way I felt my first day working here." Willa flipped her long, dark braid over her shoulder. "I had a blast learning the inventory. I could play with the dolls with the pretext of doing my job."

"I would have done the same." Belle turned in a slow circle, trying to take it all in. Halfway around, she spied exactly what she was looking for. Raising her hand, she pointed at a shelf toward the back. "There."

"The twins. Good choice." Willa retrieved a step ladder, climbed the rungs, before carefully retrieving one of the dolls. "Except for the color of their dresses, Millie and Jilly are identical."

Almost three feet tall, Millie was dressed in yards and yards of pale pink lace. Dark haired, the tresses hung down her back in long curls. Her face was sweet. Welcoming. Somehow, the manufacturer managed to avoid the vapid doll expression that—in Belle's opinion—sometimes boarded on creepy.

"Jilly is exactly the same?"

Willa handed over Millie's twin. The lace was a pale lilac. Otherwise, there were no visible differences.

"They are perfect," Belle declared.

"Are you sure you don't want to look around before making your final decision?"

"Positive."

As easy as her shopping expedition had been, by the time Willa retrieved a set of boxed dolls, elaborately wrapped them in velvet paper and curly bows, Belle's lunch hour was almost over.

"Do you want to take them with you, or would you like them delivered?"

Belle frowned. She thought about the size of the boxes. Wrapped and beribboned, they were huge. "I walked from my office. Otherwise, I would put them in the trunk of my car."

"If it isn't too far, I can have one of our stock boys carry them for you."

Impressed by the personalized service, Belle accepted. Ten minutes later, she and Zeke, a gangly young man who carried a large shopping bag in each hand, were in the elevator, heading to her building's underground parking garage.

"I'm right over here."

Stepping through the open doors, Belle led the way to her car, a happy bounce in her step. She wished she could see Naomi and Nadia's faces when they opened their presents, but that was a small blip in her good mood. The important part was helping Uncle Ashe spoil them just this side of rotten.

"Holy cow." Zeke came to a halt in front of Belle's car. "You must have pissed off somebody good."

Belle felt her level of happy drop—considerably. All four of her brand new radial tires were flat. Slashed to pieces, by the looks of it. Damn it. The point of paying an exorbitant monthly fee for parking— besides the convenience—was the supposed high level of security. Belle always felt safe walking to her car alone no matter how late the hour. Looking at her car, she would have to rethink that.

"I didn't piss anybody off good," Belle sighed. "It's vandalism. I doubt I'm the only car they hit."

"You don't want me to stay until the police get here. Right?"

Zeke's gaze shot around the garage as if he expected the cops to pop out of the shadows. Belle didn't know if his jumpiness was because of personal reasons or a general distrust of law enforcement. At the moment, she didn't care.

"I'll call them from my office." Belle popped the trunk lid. Not trusting Zeke, she carefully laid the packages flat, careful not to squish the bows. "There's no reason for you to stick around."

"Thanks, Ms. Richards." Zeke breathed a sigh of relief.

As soon as they entered the elevator, Zeke pushed the button for the lobby. The doors were still opening when he scampered away, clutching his generous tip. He *had* done his job, and Belle appreciated it. Considering the way he turned squirrely, she gave him bonus points for not dropping her packages and running. Not leaving her alone in the parking garage when it was obvious he wished he could be anyplace else, was worth a few extra bucks in Belle's estimation.

Thoughts raced through Belle's head. She was certain the slashed tires had to be random vandalism. There was no other logical explanation. She didn't make enemies. It wasn't her style to bully her way to what she wanted. Not wanting to make a scene, she calmly returned to her office, asking Pru to join her. Closing the door behind them, Belle told her assistant what had occurred.

"That's horrible," Pru gasped. "All four tires?"

"Unfortunately. Why couldn't this have happened last week when the old ones were still on?"

"I admire your attempt at a joke, but this is serious, Belle."

Belle considered it the perfect time to toss out a mood lightener. However, Pru was just processing the disturbing news. When Belle first found her car, she hadn't been in the mood to laugh.

"I need you to contact the police. Then call my insurance agency. And Pru," Belle said as Pru made notes, "do not mention this to anybody. Especially not my father."

"He's bound to find out." Elias Richards had eyes and ears everywhere. "Don't you think you should be the one to tell him?"

"I will. After I've spoken to the police."

Belle didn't want her father to overreact. She would fill him in *after* the police confirmed that her car was simply in the wrong the place at the wrong time. It turned out, the police were not convinced that was the case.

"We can't be certain this was an act of simple vandalism, Ms. Richards."

"I don't understand." Puzzled, Belle frowned at the uniformed officer sitting across from her. "Are you saying somebody deliberately targeted me?"

"At the moment, we aren't saying anything." Officer Clarke's gaze was cool and steady. "Your car seems to be the only one targeted. Did you notice the words scratched into the paint?"

"No." Belle felt a chill race up her spine. "What did it say?"

"Die, Bitch, die." He watched Belle closely. "Are you certain you can't think of anybody who would have a reason to do this?"

"Slash my tires and wish me dead? I'm happy to say I can't think of a single person."

Belle knew her sarcasm wasn't helping. But Officer Clarke's tone made it sound like he didn't believe her. The whole thing had freaked her out. The policeman was pissing her off. Belle did not consider it a good combination.

"We have the security footage from the garage." Standing, the officer handed her his card. "If you think of anything, give me a call. Whether you think this is a threat or not, Ms. Richards, I suggest you take it seriously. Don't walk to your car alone. Always lock your doors."

"Are you trying to scare me?" Because he was doing a good job.

"Yes." Officer Clarke didn't smile, but his expression softened. "I tell the same thing to my wife. Taking precautions is smart, Ms. Richards. No matter the situation."

"You're right, Officer Clarke." Belle shook his hand. "Thank you for coming so promptly. I promise to take your advice."

"Well?" Pru entered almost immediately after Officer Clarke's exit. She brought Belle a cup of tea and one for herself. "What did he say?"

"The world is either paranoid, or I'm screwed." Filling Pru in, Belle sipped the hot drink. The chill had moved from her spine through

108

her entire body. "I can't for the life of me think who would do such a thing."

"Everybody loves you." Belle snorted, almost spitting her tea across the surface of her desk. Pru laughed. Just as quickly, she sobered. "That's how *I* see it. It makes no sense. I suppose you could have picked up a weirdo stalker."

"*That's* a lovely thought." One Belle hadn't considered. "Whatever the answer, Officer Clarke had a point. We—and I'm including you—need to rethink our personal habits. Just because we are strong, independent women, it doesn't mean we're invincible."

"There's a self-defense course I've been thinking about taking. The first class is next week. I'm certain I can get us in. Want to go?"

Pru's enthusiasm was contagious. So much so, Belle decided to expand their circle.

"That's a great idea, Pru. Ask around the office to see if anybody else wants to join. But—"

"I know. Don't tell them about your car." Pru shook her head. "Everybody saw the police officer, Belle. The speculation has started."

"Nip it in the bud. Casually mention that I'm donating money. That should slow the gossip for now."

"And your father?"

Belle sighed. "I'm on my way to his office."

They walked out together, Pru detouring to her desk. Belle continued down the hall. Guarding the entrance to the office with the fierceness of a Doberman, was her father's longtime assistant.

"Is my father free, Connie?" It might have been cowardly, but for once, Belle hoped the answer was no.

Connie Bernard, an attractive woman of indeterminate age, looked at Belle over the rims of her no-nonsense glasses.

"He has a conference call in twenty minutes." Without a flicker of expression, Connie pressed a button. "Belle is here to see you, Mr. Richards."

"Send her in."

Girding herself, Belle entered the office. She expected her father to blow up. Instead, he was calm. And completely unreasonable.

"You should move back home."

"Dad—"

"It's safer. The security on your building is a joke. I don't know why I didn't say something before now."

"Because I'm a grown woman capable of taking care of myself." This over-protective father mode needed nipping in the bud. "I will be cautious, but I won't change my life, Dad."

"It will only be for a month. Once you and Theo are married, I won't have to worry about you living alone."

"Theo can barely protect himself. If somebody broke into our home, his first instinct would be to hide in the closet." Considering Theo's recent sexuality admission, that probably wasn't the best example.

"Do you think this is funny?"

Belle hadn't meant to smile. Since she couldn't share the joke with her father—not that he would find it funny—she bit the inside of her cheek.

"I love you, Dad. And I appreciate your concern. However—"

"Dinner."

Belle was used to her father's interruptions. Not that it made them more palatable.

"What about dinner?"

"If you won't agree to move home, I insist you come to dinner. Tonight. No arguments, Belle. I won't take no for an answer."

"Fine. It's been awhile since we've all sat down for a meal."

It wasn't difficult to figure out her father's strategy. He would enlist her mother to guilt Belle into moving home. It was an old tactic. One that hadn't worked since she reached puberty. However, Belle had to give him props for pulling the old chestnut out of his bag of tricks.

"With your car out of commission, you can catch a ride with me."

"The insurance adjuster has come and gone. Pru called the tire store, and they are sending somebody to replace the old ones. There's no reason I can't take my car."

"What about the other damage? Die, Bitch, die? Do you really want to drive around with that for everybody to see?"

Her father had a point, Belle admitted reluctantly. Her car was drivable. But she didn't want to deal with the questions raised by the all-too-obvious vandalism. She had planned on dropping her car at the body shop on the way to work in the morning. Now, it seemed like a better idea to take care of it today.

"I'll ride with you." Belle knew it would placate her father if she gave him something to do. "Can you get somebody to take care of my car? I'll have Pru send Connie the name of the shop."

"You look tired." Elias walked her to the door where he gave her a warm hug. "A nice relaxing evening with your family is exactly what you need."

Hugging him back, Belle gave herself a moment to rest in her father's strong, loving arms. "I'll be in my office. Let me know when you're ready to leave."

Belle was halfway down the hall when she remembered the dolls in the trunk. If she were the type to believe in fate, Belle would blame this afternoon's drama on her mixed feelings about seeing Ashe again. She had waffled between thinking it was no big deal and the worst thing she could do. Fate stepped in and took the choice from her. It was a drastic way to eliminate temptation. However, it *was* effective.

Flopping onto her chair, Belle tried to decide the best way to get the dolls to Ashe when her phone rang. *Tracy*. Why hadn't she thought of her right away?"

"Hello, my favorite best friend."

Belle laughed. "How many best friends do you have?"

"One. And she's my favorite." Tracy made it sound perfectly logical. "I wanted to call sooner, but I was under a deadline."

Tracy was a freelance artist. The pay was great, and it gave her time to paint. Next month, a very prestigious New York gallery was hosting a night of her work. The world had finally discovered what Belle had always known. Her friend was wildly talented. From now on, the sky was the limit.

111

"Deadlines are your drug of choice. Your blood wouldn't pump quite as vigorously without them."

"How sad it is that?" Tracy quipped. "I need deadlines, and you need..."

"Don't say it," Belle warned.

"Ashe Mathison."

"You said it." The truth didn't hurt, but hearing it from her best friend made it impossible for Belle to ignore.

"Damn straight. It's a good thing, Belle. One of us should get our jollies from good old-fashioned sex."

"There was nothing old fashioned about it."

"Yes! Something *did* happen last night. You can't see, but I'm doing a happy dance."

"Halt the boogie, Ginger Rogers." Tracy needed to find a man. Her friend was *way* too invested in Belle's sex life. "I was talking about what happened in Los Angeles. Last night, Ashe and I talked. Nothing more."

"Oh, come on! You had no problem jumping his bones when that stupid engagement was a real thing. Why deny yourself now that it's caput?"

"I promised to keep that under wraps. Remember?"

"Belle." Tracy heaved a huge, frustrated sigh. "You told me."

"Theo knew I would tell you because I can trust you to keep the news to yourself."

"Ashe isn't likely to blab it around town. You are using it as an excuse to make him keep his clothes on. I groped that chest, Belle. It's almost criminal to have so much fine male flesh at your disposal when you aren't willing to enjoy it."

"Speaking of criminal." Not the best segue she had ever made, but Belle jumped when she saw the chance to change the subject. "My car was vandalized."

112

"At work?" Any hint that Belle was in trouble shifted Tracy to all business. "What happened?"

Belle filled Tracy in. She didn't try to gloss over the unsettling part.

"Pru is right. Everybody loves you. I can't imagine who would do this."

"As much as I love to hear my friend's high opinion of me, I have to face the facts. The odds that I inadvertently pissed somebody off are growing higher as we speak."

"Or it's random. That's still an option, Belle."

The bottom line was simple. Belle would hope the vandalism wasn't personal, but she would stay vigilant in case it wasn't. That was all she could do short of locking herself in her parents' house, armed guards patrolling the perimeter. On no account would she let that suggestion slip to her father—even in jest.

"I'll be fine," Belle assured Tracy—and herself. "However, I have a problem. Would you mind delivering a couple of dolls?"

"Is that code for something kinky? If it is, I'm all in."

Chuckling, Belle shook her head. "I'll remember that if the situation arises. Sometimes, my dear, a doll is just a doll. Two of which are waiting in the trunk of my car to make a couple of little girls very happy."

Tracy listened in silence as Belle told her about the favor Ashe had asked her to perform.

"Honey, do you have a fever? I love your parents, but dinner with them does not compare to naked Ashe Mathison."

"He won't be naked, Tracy."

"I can dream, can't I?" When Belle didn't answer, Tracy jumped on the pause. In a sing-song voice, she said, "*I know what you're thinking*. Is Ashe as beautiful without his clothes as I imagine?"

Rather than deny where her mind had wandered, Belle smiled. "As good as you think he looks, take my word for it. Your fantasies can't come close to the truth."

"I hate you."

"No, you don't."

"Fine," Tracy conceded. "I hate the fact that you could have him in a snap but won't."

"You may be overestimating Ashe's interest."

"We both know I'm not."

"It's a moot point. I'm having dinner with my parents. And before you argue." Belle knew her friend well. "Dad was pretty shaken by what happened today. Under that world-beater, tough-as-nails exterior is somebody's daddy. Mine."

"Since my father is the same way, I can't tear down your reasoning. Tell me what you need."

After arranging for Tracy to pick up the dolls, Belle texted Ashe, alerting him to the change of plans. Though she didn't give him the specifics as to why she couldn't make their meeting. To her surprise, he answered immediately.

"*Instead of Tracy bringing them to me*," Ashe texted, "*would she mind if I picked them up at her place?*

A quick call to Tracy, followed by a few more texts, and the plan was finalized. Ashe would be at Tracy's apartment at six o'clock. He thanked Belle again but didn't ask any prying questions.

Belle wasn't surprised that Ashe's lack of interest bothered her. Part of her was grateful she didn't have to explain. Another part wondered why he didn't care enough to find out.

Sitting back in her chair, Belle sighed. All the feelings she had for Ashe seemed to be contradictory. Why should these be any different?

CHAPTER TEN

ASHE STOPPED HIS car in front of an old brownstone conversion. Built before the turn of the last century, it was at one time a single-family dwelling, each floor was now a separate apartment. According to Belle's directions, Tracy's place was at the top.

This was not the way he pictured his day ending. The start had been stellar. Talking to Belle could easily become one of his favorite ways to pass the time. She made him smile. And think. And want.

The middle part of his day hadn't been what he expected. It had been better. Little girls—he soon learned—were a force to be reckoned with. Naomi and Nadia challenged his preconceived notions at every turn. One second girly, the next fearless warriors. Then out of the blue, they were so sweet it made his heart ache with joy.

Ashe was not too proud to admit his nieces had worn him out. However, getting his second wind had been easy when he remembered the treat he had waiting for him. Another evening with Belle. Or at least, that was his plan. When he arranged to pick the dolls up at her apartment, he did so with an ulterior motive. If he could wheedle a few more hours of her time, Ashe would declare the day damn near perfect.

Seducing Belle into bed would have been *the* perfect ending. Ashe was tempted to find out if he could do it. His instincts said yes. His ego said it wouldn't take more than a kiss—or two—and some well-placed caresses. Tempted or not, he didn't want to put Belle in the position of lying to her fiancé. He believed Los Angeles had been a convergence of circumstances. A bit of nostalgia, a little alcohol, and an old crush had led Belle to give in to temptation. For Ashe, it had been a simple case of lust.

That was then. Now, his feelings for Belle had deepened. Given time, Ashe thought, she could become someone special.

Walking up the brownstone steps, Ashe wondered about timing. In music, it was everything. It could mean the difference between a hit and a dud. When he sat down to write a song, Ashe had the benefit of three other sets of ears to help him set the right tone. With Belle, he didn't have his bandmates to back him up. When he made a move—right or wrong—he was on his own. It was a scary thought knowing he could screw things up so easily. Even worse? Because Belle was engaged to marry another man, there wasn't much to screw up. He had found a tiny little pathway into her life. Now that he was there, what the hell was he going to do?

Tracy buzzed him in with a chipper, "Hey, gorgeous. Come on up."

Shaking his head, Ashe jogged up the three flights. Something told him he was going to like Tracy. Her humor appealed to him. And she was Belle's best friend. That was a pretty good recommendation in his book.

The door to the apartment was open, music blaring. The smell of paint filled the air. Not the kind one put on walls. The kind an artist used on canvas. Ashe's first thought when he walked into the room was color. One word. It fit since there wasn't a space that wasn't covered with it. Everywhere he looked. Reds, blues, greens, yellows. Pink, gray, orange, lavender. There wasn't any reason for the kaleidoscope to work—yet it did.

"What do you think?"

Tracy, dressed in paint-splattered overalls, walked toward him holding out a glass of red wine. Her lips wore a smile; her feet wore nothing. Her dark hair was pushed into a pile on top of her head. And on the tip of her nose sat a tiny smudge of magenta.

"I think I should be blind." He sipped the excellent Bordeaux, looking around. "Yet somehow, I can see. You have a unique style, Tracy. I salute you."

"That may be the best reaction I've ever gotten."

"Better than Belle's?"

"Interesting that you would mention her."

"Why wouldn't I?" Ashe didn't like the speculative light in Tracy's eyes. She saw too much. "Belle is the reason I'm here. Our common denominator."

116

"Common denominator." Tracy tapped her glass against his. "Well said. Not that I'm surprised. Your songs are like poetry set to some damn hot music. I'm a fan, by the way."

"I can say the same." Ashe moved to get a closer look at a painting on the far wall. "Is this yours?"

"I should have known you would be drawn to that one." Tracy stood at his side, watching him closely.

The subject was in shadow except for the back of her head and just a sliver of her profile, the slight curve of her lips, which were gently touched by the glow of the setting sun. She stood in a forest, her hair glossy, her skin gleaming. It made Ashe wish he was there to find out if the rest of her was as bare as her shoulders.

"It's Belle."

"When I painted that, I finally felt like an artist." Tracy looked at Ashe, not the painting. "Belle has always been my fiercest supporter. When I didn't believe in myself, she did. Somehow she always knows what I need to keep me going. A pep talk. A kick in the ass. I love that woman."

"The painting is amazing, Tracy." Ashe made a conscious effort not to reach out. He longed to touch Belle's image. He longed to—*Jesus*. Ashe simply longed. For Belle. "I would like to buy it. Name your price."

"That's a dangerous sentence, Ashe." Tracy smiled, shaking her head. "A greedy woman might try to gouge you. However, it's not for sale."

Feeling a deep sense of disappointment, Ashe made himself turn away. Not that he was ready to give up.

"Is there any way I can change your mind?"

"Don't hurt her."

Genuinely surprised, Ashe frowned. "Why would you say such a thing? Belle and I don't have that kind of relationship. I don't have the power to hurt her."

"Yes, you do."

Confused, Ashe searched for meaning in Tracy's words. He could think of only one plausible reason.

"Is this about my brother?"

"Bradley, *don't call me Brad*, Mathison? Hardly." There was contempt in Tracy's tone, but not heat.

"Belle told me what my brother did to you. I wish I had the power to apologize for him."

"That's sweet," Tracy said, briefly squeezing Ashe's hand. She looked him in the eyes, nodding as if coming to a decision. "Belle said you were one of the good guys. I think she's right. So I'll repeat myself— which I rarely do. Do not hurt her."

"She's engaged." It seemed important for him to remind Tracy— and himself—of that fact.

"Theo?" Tracy scoffed. "He's the least of your problems."

"What does that mean?" With a mysterious shrug, Tracy walked away. Ashe was right on her heels. "Tracy—"

"Here are the dolls." She pointed toward two large bags. "Since they are wrapped, Belle took pictures. She wanted you to see what you were getting—in case you didn't like what she picked out."

Ashe wasn't thinking about the dolls. He was still trying to decipher Tracy's *don't hurt Belle*. And, *Theo is the least of your worries*. He wanted Belle. Badly. It seemed to him the only thing standing in his way was her fiancé. Tracy's cryptic words suggested otherwise.

"This kind of thing was never my style, but they are beautiful." Tracy handed him her phone. "Are they what you had in mind?"

The dolls sat side by side, reminding him of Naomi and Nadia— when they were girly cute, not mini-hellions. They seemed perfect. However, since he had absolutely no experience on the subject, he would trust that Belle's choice was the right one.

"Great." Ashe handed Tracy her phone.

118

"I'll text Belle. I know she's anxious to find out your reaction. After the day she's had, she deserves a little pat on the back for a job well done."

Ashe tensed at Tracy's words. "Did something happen to Belle?"

"Relax. She's fine. Just a bit of an upset."

Waiting for Tracy to elaborate, Ashe finished off his wine in one gulp. "Well?" he demanded when she didn't elaborate.

"Belle's car was vandalized. Slashed tires. Scratched paint. It happened in what she thought was a safe place."

"I can see why that would be unsettling." Ashe's shoulders relaxed until he saw the expression in Tracy's eyes. "There's more?"

"You know a little. I'm trying to decide if I should spill it all." To Ashe's growing annoyance, Tracy thoughtfully tapped her chin. "There is something I think Belle should have told you. But because she didn't, I can't. Understand?"

Ashe understood very well. He and his friends kept each other's secrets in a death grip. They felt free to tell each other everything and anything because there was complete trust in their small, but rock-solid circle. As much as he wanted to know what Belle was keeping from him, he couldn't ask Tracy to betray her best friend's confidences.

"If I pushed Belle to tell me, would she?"

"No." Tracy didn't hesitate. "If it were just her secret, I think she would. But she made a promise."

"Does this concern what happened to her car, or her engagement?" Ashe felt like he was playing an elaborate game of twenty questions.

"Ask her all you want about the vandalism. She'll tell you. Theo is what's hanging her up." Tracy set her glass down with a definitive click. "Screw this. I want Belle to be happy so I'm going to push the best friend confidentiality envelope."

Ashe almost shouted a hallelujah. At this point, he would take anything he could get.

"I don't know if I have the power to hurt Belle. I can promise you I would never consciously do so."

"I believe you," Tracy nodded. Then her eyes narrowed. "You understand that if you go back on that promise, your balls are mine." She made a quick chopping motion.

As a man, Ashe was particularly fond of those appendages. He was certain he would keep his word. However, he took Tracy's not-so-subtle threat seriously.

Ashe met her gaze, his nod solemn. "What can you tell me?"

"Theo is not a problem."

That was it? Ashe wondered. After the buildup, *Theo is not a problem*, was all he was getting?

"Tracy—"

Grabbing him by the arms, Tracy gave Ashe a shake, her eyes boring into his. "Listen to my words. Theo. Is. Not. A. Problem. Understand?"

Slowly, as Tracy's meaning sunk in, Ashe smiled. *Damn straight, he understood*. The subtleties didn't matter. Belle could fill those in at a later date. Right now, *Theo is not a problem*, was the sweetest phrase he had heard in a long, long time.

"I love you, Tracy." Ashe gave her an exuberant kiss before rushing toward the door.

"Hey, Hot Lips. Don't forget the dolls."

Rolling his eyes, Ashe made a quick detour, scooping up the bags.

"Thanks."

"One more thing." Tracy blocked his path. "Give me your phone."

At that point, Ashe wasn't in the mood to argue. Before handing it over, he punched in the password, then watched as Tracy's fingers flew over the keys.

"What's this?" he asked, looking at the screen.

"That is where you will find Belle. In an hour or two, she'll need a taxi to take her home. Do I need to tell you what to do?"

Ashe shook his head, grinning. "No, ma'am. You do not."

"YOUR FATHER MAKES a very good point, Belle."

"He always does. He's a god!" Belle mumbled under her breath.

"What did you say, dear?" her mother inquired from the other end of the dining room table.

"She said—oomph." Belle's younger brother Marshall rubbed his side, sending her a narrowed look. "I won't forget that," he whispered.

"Good," Belle spoke through gritted teeth. "Maybe you'll finally learn to keep your mouth shut."

"Must the two of you always devolve into childish patterns? We are adults. Act accordingly."

As the oldest—and a certified clinical psychiatrist—Dinah carried an air of superiority that should have driven Belle crazy. Where Belle and Marshall had their father's looks, Dinah was the spitting image of their mother. Brown hair streaked with gold and a slender build. When Belle was younger, she tried to copy her sister's regal carriage. Eventually, she gave up. On Dinah, it looked natural—right. On Belle, not so much.

The only thing that saved Dinah from coming off as a snotty-nosed bitch was the twinkle in her coffee-colored eyes. They weren't as close as some sisters, but the bond was strong and the love undeniable.

"Belle can take care of herself, Mom." Marsh loaded his plate with another helping of mashed potatoes. "Besides, the police don't have any proof that the vandal had a personal agenda. Right, Dad?"

"I spoke to the police commissioner just before we sat down."

Belle wiped her mouth, hiding her smile. It wasn't that her father was a name dropper. But she wondered if he realized how unusual it was to have a powerful city official on speed dial. Since he was friends with everybody from the head of the city council to the mayor, she doubted it.

121

"I must call Miriam. It's been ages." And Penelope Richards knew all the wives. "What did Herbert say, dear?"

"The officers assigned to the case are still going over the security footage. He promised to call as soon as they know anything."

"Until then, I plan on living my life as I always have." Belle's stance on this was firm. For her family's—and her own—peace of mind, she added, "With increased caution and awareness."

"The chances are slim to none that this was personal," Dinah said, delicately taking a tiny piece of chicken Kiev into her mouth.

"Is this your personal or professional opinion?" Marsh asked with mock seriousness.

"Professional, smartass. Personally, I would prefer Belle stay with Mom and Dad. However, it would be impractical on every level. She's a grown woman with her own life. More important, living in fear is not living."

"Amen, sister." Belle applauded Dinah. "What was the point of providing your daughter with an expensive Ivy League education if you refuse to heed her learned opinion?"

"I'm not refusing, Belle." Her father wasn't used to having the minority opinion. "I want you safe. End of discussion."

"I don't think so." With her father, Belle knew when to pick her fights. On this one, she was entrenched to the bitter end.

"Dinah is correct, Elias." Bertram Cornwall, Dinah's husband, calmly interjected his opinion. Also a psychologist, he was a respected profiler for the FBI. Belle had always thought he was handsome in a professorial kind of way. "Slashing tires and keying cars is the behavior of a conflicted person. It is a way for him to vent his frustration on an inanimate object. The fact that it belongs to Belle was probably an unfortunate coincidence."

"And the message he left?" Elias spared his wife by not repeating the words. "It seemed very specific."

122

"I disagree." Bertram loved a good debate. In his enthusiasm, he missed his wife's look of warning. "Die, Belle, die, would be a specific message. Bitch connotes the man's displeasure with females in general."

"Oh, dear," Penelope gasped.

"Bertram," Dinah laid a hand over his. "That's enough."

It took a moment, but Penelope's distress finally penetrated Bertram's clinical mind.

"I'm sorry. My words were meant to comfort."

"I understand." Penelope pulled herself together. She might look like a puff of wind could blow her over, but when she wanted, her spine was like a steel rod. "Are you certain you feel safe on your own, Belle?"

"I am." Belle stood, moving to her mother's side. Brushing her lips across Penelope's cheek, she said, "Thank you."

"Just a minute, Penny." Elias didn't like the turn the evening had taken.

"Dad." Facing her father, Belle rested her hands on her mother's shoulders. "I love you for caring. I love you, period. You need to trust me."

"I do."

"Then let's drop the serious talk for tonight."

When her father simply nodded, Belle took her seat with a satisfied sigh. It wasn't often Elias Richards let anybody have the last word. She planned on savoring the moment.

"What's for dessert?" Marshall inquired, still tackling the huge amount of food remaining on his plate.

"Strawberry shortcake," Penelope said with a mother's indulgent smile.

And that was that. The conversation turned away from Belle—much to her relief. Marsh wasn't finished with dinner, but she was. On the pretext of using the bathroom, she assured everybody that she would be right back.

Belle slipped into the library and onto the balcony. The truth was, she was dying to find out what Ashe thought of the dolls. By now, Tracy would have texted her with his reaction. Several new texts. The first was the one she wanted.

Ashe is very happy with your choices. He asked me to thank you. Great job.

It was nice, but Belle wished she had heard the words from the man himself. Then she noticed that the last text was from Ashe. With a tingle of anticipation, she opened it.

Don't bother with the taxi. Call me when you are ready to go home.

Warmth spread across Belle's skin when she thought about Ashe picking her up. She didn't blame Tracy for masterminding his text. If the situation were reversed, Belle would have done the same. Her friend was simply giving Belle what she couldn't ask for on her own. That said, the answer had to be no. After a few keystrokes, she read what she had written.

No. Thank you, but no. Glad you liked the dolls.

Before she could vacillate, Belle hit send. Satisfied, if not exactly happy, she was about to put her phone away when she received an answer from Ashe.

The dolls are perfect. I won't take no for an answer, Belle.

Ashe Mathison had some nerve. He *had* to take no for an answer.

You don't have a choice. Belle's fingers hit the keys with undo force. *No means no.*

Belle didn't have long to wait for his reply.

The next time I kiss you, if you say no, I'll stop. You always get to say no. However, I am picking you up. If you don't agree, I will show up at your parents' door. In case you've forgotten, I'm just next door. Do you want to explain me to them?

Belle stared at the text, her heart racing. *The next time I kiss you.* It left little doubt there would be a next time. And soon, unless she missed her guess. Belle wouldn't say no—she wanted his lips on hers.

However, she wasn't going to roll over. At least not immediately. This time, when she typed, there was a smile on her face.

Blackmail? Again? Not cool, Ashe.

In her mind, Belle could see Ashe's face as he read her words. Like her, he was smiling.

It isn't blackmail when you want it as much as I do. What time, Belle?"

On the one hand, Ashe didn't have much of a case. He *was* guilty of blackmail. On the other hand, he was right. She wanted it. *At least* as much as he did. Ready to concede the fact, Belle sent a final text.

Ten o'clock. Send me a head's up when you arrive.

Instead of words, Ashe sent the most lascivious smiley face Belle had ever seen. Leave it to him to find a sex-themed emoji. Laughing, she left the balcony.

Entering the dining room, Belle took her seat. She was a big fan of strawberry shortcake. But it wasn't the dessert she was looking forward to. Glancing at her watch, she did the math. One hour, thirty-six minutes and... twelve seconds to wait. Not long in the scheme of things. Tonight, it seemed like an eternity.

CHAPTER ELEVEN

ASHE TAPPED THE steering wheel, the curved surface acting as the saxophone he played in his head. It was a song, more of a riff. Improvisational. Jazz, not rock and roll. When he wanted to let his brain sail free, Ashe liked the untethered feeling this kind of music gave him.

Parked—waiting impatiently for Belle—Ashe felt the notes flowing through him. When it came right down to it, music had no boundaries. Rock, country, jazz. They borrowed from each other, melding into something better—stronger—than the original.

When Ashe, Ryder, and Dalton started their band, they were determined to embrace an open-minded attitude toward their craft. It allowed them to grow artistically. They were rock stars, but nobody could pigeonhole their sound. It was a combination of their backgrounds, their influences, their strengths, and weaknesses. It was what made them so popular today, tomorrow, and forever. Timeless.

That wasn't Ashe's ego talking. It was a fact. Pure and simple.

Opening one eye, Ashe checked the time. He had parked at the end of the Richards' long, cobbled driveway. His text to Belle was acknowledged with a, *be right there,* response. Had it only been five minutes?

Chuckling at himself, Ashe wondered why he was acting like a teenager on the cusp of his first sexual conquest. Was time supposed to quiet a man's raging libido? Thirty was staring him down hard, for Christ's sake. Yet Belle made him feel ten years younger. Thankfully without the sweaty palms. Just to be certain, he rubbed his hands together. Nope, not a drop of moisture.

With his eyes trained on the house, Ashe saw the front door open. Belle waved at whoever was just out of sight, before slipping off her shoes, running down the driveway. Ashe wanted to think she was as impatient as he was.

Sliding from his seat, he walked around the car, timing his arrival at the passenger side to coincide with Belle's.

"Hello," Belle said, a bit breathless. "I don't know if I should thank you for the ride or kick you in the shins."

"Kicking is a bad idea. Unless you want to break those pretty toes."

Ashe maneuvered Belle until her back was to the car. He didn't crowd her. He didn't touch. But he could feel the warmth of her body. See her smile. It was enough. If he made his move now, there was no telling what would happen. Whatever he did, he wasn't doing it where the world—and Belle's family—could watch.

"I'll save my retaliation for later." Belle's gaze went from his eyes to his mouth, before raising back to his eyes. "How was your day?"

"Better than yours."

"Tracy told you?" Belle didn't sound upset.

"Some." Ashe helped her into the car, before making his way to the driver's seat. "I hope you'll fill in the blanks."

"I don't know if I can tell it again." With a sigh, Belle buckled her seatbelt. "What exactly did Tracy tell you?"

"Car. Slashed tires. Scratched paint. Your turn."

"Okay. Die, bitch, die. Maybe personal, maybe not."

Ashe felt a jolt of concern. "Holy shit, Belle. That is not what I was expecting."

"Join the club. Though I warn you, it is not an exclusive membership."

Starting the car, Ashe pulled away from the curb. His mind raced. He listened as Belle told him everything, her voice weary. He wasn't surprised. Compared to what she had been through, a couple of rambunctious little girls was nothing.

"Can we talk about something else? Anything else?" Belle stretched, her mouth covering a yawn. "For some reason, the more I repeat the same words over and over, the more it wears me out. Reinvigorate my brain."

"How?" Ashe let the subject slide. But tomorrow, he was going to call in a few favors. Belle's father wasn't the only one with connections. Being a famous rock star had its perks.

"Sing me a song."

"That I can do. Any requests?"

"*Night Angel*," Belle answered without hesitation.

Ashe felt a jolt of pride. His songs were his babies, but *Night Angel* was special. Its birth hadn't been easy but worth every ounce of sweat and frustration.

"Close your eyes."

When Belle had done as he asked, Ashe began to hum the opening bars. Singing lead wasn't his strength. His voice was meant to blend with others—a part of a whole. For the first time in his life, Ashe wished the notes he made with his voice were as perfect as the ones he made when he played an instrument. However, he knew that Belle didn't care. She needed comfort. So he put his ego aside and sang.

Ashe's strong baritone was deep and true. It filled the car, crooning to Belle about a beautiful woman who was trapped in a world of pain and punishment until the sun went down and she was free to give herself to the man she loved. Those few hours made the rest of her existence bearable.

More than once, Ashe had been asked if the song was about a special woman. Had he loved and lost? Was it a true story? Ashe never gave a straight answer because he knew the mystery of the song's origins was part of its power. The true story wasn't sensational or terribly interesting. *Night Angel* came from where most songs came from— Ashe's imagination.

None of that mattered. Not tonight. Not to Belle. Ashe knew the second she drifted into sleep by the rhythm of her breathing. The way her body lay boneless—relaxed and trusting.

Ashe finished the song, believing that even in slumber, Belle could hear his voice.

Belle's vulnerability touched him. Ashe considered himself an evolved person, sensitive to a woman's strength and independence. No amount of evolution would eliminate a man's instinct to protect what was his.

Jesus. When had he started thinking about Belle that way? She was his? The sparkling rock on her finger said otherwise. *Belle* said otherwise. As for Ashe? Like it or not, the caveman that lurked inside him had decided she belonged to him.

Wouldn't his friends have a laugh if they could hear what was going on inside Ashe's head? Happy go lucky. That was his well-earned reputation. He always assumed when he finally fell, it would be a gentle journey. No drama. No angst. Certainly no fiancé standing in his way. Belle certainly came with all of the above. Was she worth the effort? Did he have a choice?

Ashe couldn't laugh at the situation, but he had no problem chuckling at himself. So many questions when there was only one that mattered. Did he love Belle?

Struggling for an answer, Ashe breathed a sigh of relief when Belle stirred, opening her eyes, saving him from his thoughts.

"I dozed off." Belle stretched her arms over her head. "I'm sorry I missed the end of your song. What I heard was beautiful. Why don't you ever sing lead?"

It was taking longer to get to Belle's apartment than Ashe anticipated. This time of night, he expected less traffic. Stopping at a red light, Ashe placed a hand on Belle's forehead, certain she must have a fever. Nope, cool as a cucumber. He snorted. There was no accounting for taste.

"It was decided long ago that Ryder would take the lead. Acoustically speaking, the world should thank us."

"That's something I've always wondered about." Belle shifted, facing him as much as her seatbelt would allow. "Why did you go with *The Ryder Hart Band*? I know Ryder is the front man but aren't all of you equal?"

"We are." Ashe signaled a right turn, heading down Belle's street. "Dalton and I were the ones who suggested the name. We liked the idea of making Ryder the face of the band. He could be the one recognized in public while we enjoyed the perks of a successful band while maintaining our anonymity. Ryder was opposed."

"He didn't want the fame either?"

"Are you kidding?" Ashe grinned. "Ryder revels in that stuff. He's an adulation junkie. Always has been. No, he wanted a name for the band that reflected all of us. That's Ryder. He loves the spotlight, but believes there's room enough for all of us to bask in the glow."

"You love him, don't you? I can hear it in your voice."

"He and Dalton are my brothers. Zoe my sister. We're best friends. As tight as any family."

"They gave you what you needed when you needed it most. What?" Belle asked when he sent her a surprised look.

"Most people don't understand our connection."

"You don't tell many people what you've told me." Belle rested her hand on Ashe's thigh. "I'm glad you feel you can trust me enough to open up—even a little."

"Trust is a big issue with all my friends." Ashe had the fewest reasons for keeping outsiders at arm's length. Over the years, he had adopted his friends' wariness. "It's easy to talk to you, Belle."

"I'm glad." Belle squeezed his leg. "Finish your story. Ryder didn't want you to name the band after him. Is that it? He gave in?"

"Not exactly." Ashe pulled into a parking spot across the street from Belle's building. Turning off the ignition, he took her hand in his— just because he liked the way it felt. "After much debate, we decided to put five names that we all agreed upon into a hat."

"*The Ryder Hard Band* included?"

"Yes." Shaking his head, Ashe chuckled. "What Ryder didn't know until much, much later, was that Dalton and I made certain *The Ryder Hart Band* was the only choice."

"That's wicked. And brilliant." Belle looked impressed.

"You should have seen the look on Ryder's face when he pulled out his name. You would have thought his puppy had died. Before he could insist on best two out of three, Dalton whisked the hat away."

"Hence, the world knows you all as *The Ryder Hart Band*."

"Hence," Ashe said with a wink.

"And when Ryder finally found out?"

"He was pissed. However, it was too late to do anything about it. We had our first gold record. Our concerts were selling out. Ryder stewed for about five minutes, then joined us for a good laugh." That was how things usually went with Ashe and his bandmates. They didn't let things stew. That was why, ten years and counting, they were a tight-knit group. Super glue had nothing on the bond that held them together.

Belle laughed, the sound warming Ashe's blood. It drew him in, making him want to hear it again. And again.

"I was just thinking." Belle grinned. "After all the trouble you went through to make Ryder the face of the band?"

"Yes?"

"How did that work out for you?"

"Not great," Ashe admitted with a fatalistic shrug.

From the beginning, the band's fans had looked beyond Ryder, embracing Ashe, Dalton, and Zoe with near-equal fervor. While Ryder couldn't show his face without creating a stampede, Ashe could still go unnoticed when he was out and about. But it was a rare occurrence.

The band's manager, Alden Christopher once summed it up best. *The Ryder Hart Band* had four stars. Talent and personality—something each of them had in abundance—had a way of making their way to the forefront. No matter the best-laid plans of mice and men. Or Ashe Mathison and Dalton Shaw.

"Are you coming up?"

Ashe couldn't decide if it was hope or nerves he saw in Belle's eyes. Hopeful nervousness? That seemed about right.

"It would be ungallant not to—considering the mess with your car."

"The feminist in me needs to remind you that women can take care of themselves."

"I hear you loud and clear." Ashe jumped from the car. Belle's door was open in a snap. He held out his hand. "Ready?"

"As a feminist." Belle let Ashe help her from the car. "I understand that it isn't a weakness to ask for help. I'm strong—not stupid."

"Does that mean you'll let me check every room and under the bed?"

Belle laced her fingers with his as they crossed the street. It was a move Ashe approved of—wholeheartedly.

"It means I appreciate having you near. No matter the circumstances."

Belle punched in the security code, letting them into the building. Ashe had to admit, his senses were on high alert. He was used to bodyguards and security experts keeping him safe while the band toured. Being on the other side—keeping somebody safe—was a different experience.

Ashe had no formal training. However, he had seen enough movies to have a good idea how it worked. Watch the shadows for lurking figures. Get Belle from the car to the building as quickly as possible. Be aware at all times.

"What are you doing?" Belle asked when he checked the elevator before hustling her inside.

"Vigilance has become my middle name. At least for tonight." Much more would be exhausting, Ashe decided. Mentally and physically. He was smart enough to realize he was not up to the job.

First thing tomorrow, Ashe was getting his assistant to check out bodyguards in the Boston area. It might not be necessary, but he wanted to be prepared. Talking Belle into the idea could come later.

"Do you realize how ridiculous that sounds?"

"Yes." Not that he cared. Guiding Belle down the hall, he turned his back to her as she opened the door. "Get inside. You can laugh at me once the locks are in place."

"I thought you were going to check under my bed?"

So much for waiting to laugh, Ashe thought when he heard the amused tone of Belle's voice.

"I am. After."

Smiling, Belle tossed her keys onto the small accent table.

"After what?"

"This."

The kiss wasn't planned. Often, spontaneous was better. Not better, Ashe thought as he took Belle's mouth with his. Freaking amazing.

132

Belle tasted like strawberries. Fresh and ripe. Ashe couldn't get enough, his tongue delving deep, tasting again and again. It had been too long. It felt like forever.

Wrapping one arm around Belle's waist, Ashe anchored her to him. Body to body. His fingers threaded through her soft, fragrant hair, cupping the back of her head, drawing her closer. It only took a second for Belle to become a full participant. Taking. Giving. Everything felt so damn good. Every touch. Every brush of the lips. Every sigh. God, the way Belle sighed. The sound turned up the heat on an already raging fire.

"Is this going to happen?" Belle tipped her head, giving Ashe better access to her sweet neck. "It shouldn't happen, Ashe."

"Yes, it should."

Ashe backed Belle toward the bedroom, his mouth never leaving hers. Frustrated by the slow progress, he scooped her into his arms. True to his word, he stopped in every room, examining closets, behind the shower curtain. If anybody the size of your average three-year-old could fit, Ashe checked.

"Talk about a mood killer," Belle teased, twining her arms around his neck.

A scorching kiss was Ashe's response, leaving Belle boneless.

"You were saying?"

Belle sighed, licking her lips. "I have no idea. Carry on. I'm enjoying the ride."

Satisfied by her answer, Ashe finished the tour in a few long strides. He would have laid Belle on the bed, yet he had promised to look underneath. However, she wouldn't release him.

"The frame goes all the way to floor." Belle breathed the words into Ashe's ear, her tongue bathing the lobe before her teeth gently bit down. "Drawers," she explained, biting again. "Extra storage."

Ashe couldn't have cared less. All he wanted was for Belle to keep doing what she was doing.

"Ashe?"

"Hmm?" Since Belle raised her mouth of her own accord, Ashe took the break in the action to toss her onto the bed.

"What did Tracy tell you?"

Belle looked so appealing, propped up on her elbow, her expression earnest. Ashe could have teased. Or prevaricated. Instead, he told her the truth.

"Tracy's exact words were *Theo is not a problem*." Ashe watched Belle's reaction closely. "Is he?"

"I made a promise." Belle toyed with her engagement ring. Meeting Ashe's gaze, she took it off. Rolling to her feet, she opened a box on the dresser, placing the ring inside. A second later, she was in his arms. "Do you want the whole story?"

"After." Ashe slid a hand under the hem of Belle's shirt.

A grin broke across Belle's face. "After what?"

Belle's shirt hit the floor, followed closely by the rest of her clothing.

"After I've had my fill of you." Ashe couldn't stop looking. Belle made his mouth water.

"When will that be?" Belle gasped, then moaned, when Ashe placed his hand on her breast.

"An hour." Ashe kissed her lightly. "A day?" The kiss deepened. "A month?"

"A year?" Belle sighed the words when Ashe raised his head.

Pulling Belle close, Ashe lowered her to the bed. A year? Ten. Ashe knew it was too soon, but he couldn't help it. He was damn close to asking for a lifetime.

"Save the story." He touched Belle's knee, opening her legs. "This is going to take a while."

CHAPTER TWELVE

"PANCAKES? FROM SCRATCH?"

"Do you use a mix?"

Belle gave Ashe a horrified look as she handed him a plate. Four perfectly fluffy pancakes sat in the middle, a pat of butter melting over them. Ashe poured a generous amount of heated maple syrup—the real stuff—breathing in the heady aroma.

"No." Picking up his fork, Ashe made the first cut. Tender as the first flowers in spring. "I get mine the old-fashioned way. I buy them in a restaurant."

"Most of those restaurants use a mix," Belle informed him as she pulled herself onto the stool next to his. "Mine are better. Trust me."

"I don't have to." Ashe took a bite, his eyes closing with pleasure. "Bliss, Belle. Pure bliss."

On top of the night spent in Belle's arms, Ashe didn't know how things could get much better. Wait. He paused halfway to his next bite. Yes, he did.

"You need to return the ring, Belle."

"I will."

"Today would be good."

"I agreed to give Theo two weeks." Belle went to the griddle, flipping a perfectly golden cake. "It wouldn't be fair to go back on my word."

"Do you honestly believe the man will come out to his parents? After a year of hiding his affair, why would two weeks make it any easier?"

"It won't." Without asking, Belle slid another stack onto Ashe's plate. "Chances are good that he won't do it. However—"

"You made a promise."

"That's right. Would you like some orange juice? Fresh squeezed."

"When did you have time?"

"While you were in the shower." Belle handed Ashe a filled glass.

"*We* were in the shower. I know that for a fact. See?" Ashe leaned closer. "I'm still wearing a ridiculously satisfied grin."

"Not so ridiculous." Belle gave him a quick kiss. "I slipped out while you were shaving."

"Unbelievable." It wasn't a criticism. Ashe was genuinely impressed. "Where do you get the energy? I'm refueling for a run. Though thanks to you, I could skip it. I received a fine workout last night. Mighty fine."

"Thank you."

"Are you blushing?" Ashe tipped Belle's chin up. "After the things we did? I didn't think that would be possible."

"Some of us aren't as jaded as others." Belle swatted his hand away. "You and your groupies having rock star orgies every night. I may not be a dew-fresh rose, but I'm not a perverted degenerate either."

"Isn't that a little redundant?" Ashe tried to hide his smile, but it was difficult. "Pervert and degenerate are pretty much the same things."

"*That's* what you took from my mini tirade?"

"What did you want me to say?"

"That I exaggerated. Your sexual survival is not predicated on a constant diet of groupie-filled orgies."

Belle waved her arms, the metal spatula coming dangerously close to knocking the bowl of batter onto the floor. Taking pity, Ashe gave in and smiled.

"No to orgies. Ever. I don't know where I would find one if I *were* interested."

"You could always host your own." The twinkle was back in Belle's eyes. "The potential participants would show up in droves."

Ashe cringed. "I don't want to think about where people like that come from. Or what kind of STDs they pass back and forth." Ashe shuddered. Belle right with him. "As for groupies?"

"Yes?" Belle crossed her arms, waiting.

"I've had sex with fans. I don't know if they could be called groupies. How many men have you slept with?"

Belle's eyes widened. Grabbing a sponge, she lowered her head, wiping the already clean counter. "What kind of question is that?"

"It's the same kind of thing you asked me."

"No." Belle loaded the dishwasher. She looked anyplace but at him. "I asked about your kinky rock star lifestyle. Not once did I inquire about the number of notches on your bedpost."

"Proverbially speaking."

"Naturally. Your bed is brass. It would be a crime to dent the surface."

Belle looked around for something else to clean. Before she could swipe his plate and half-eaten pancakes, Ashe took her hand, pulling her around the island. Swiveling his chair around, Ashe spread his legs, positioning Belle between them.

"Why the freak out?" he asked.

Expelling a deep sigh, the energy seemed to seep from Belle along with the air. She sank into Ashe's arms, resting her head on his shoulder.

"Your level of sexual expertise exceeds mine. By quite a bit."

"Tell me. Just so we're on the same page. Is that a bad thing? Am I a slut or are you a prude?"

"I don't want to disappoint you."

"Disappoint me? Belle." Ashe gently rubbed her back, his other arm holding her close. "Do you honestly believe I would spend hours— hours mind you—in your bed out of what? Pity? Does that make sense?"

"I didn't say my thoughts were logical. Only human."

"You are a natural, Belle. If you hadn't confessed, I would have taken you for a professional. Semi-pro at the very least."

"Are you making fun of me?" Belle laughed, burrowing as close as possible. It was a sound Ashe craved. Like air. Or her pancakes.

"Only a little. Would you like me to prove I mean what I say? I'm pretty sure I have another round or two in me."

Ashe expected Belle to laugh off his suggestion. It was getting late, and he knew she was expected at the office. He should have known not to expect the expected. Taking his hand, Belle headed toward the bedroom.

"Another round?" She whipped Ashe's shirt over his head. "Two would make me late for work."

"Twenty minutes?" Ashe asked, shucking off the rest of his clothes.

Belle was right with him. Together, they fell onto the bed. Looping her arms around his neck, she nodded.

"That sounds perfect."

TEN YEARS SINCE Ashe had spoken to his father and their first communication came via text. The world had changed, and Randall Mathison with it. His father used to scoff at the idea of sending a message with a few taps of a keyboard. Email was bad enough, he used to say.

It seemed—unless someone was doing it for him—Randall had given in to the siren call of technology.

Was it odd that Ashe had to wipe his hands before opening a message from his father? Under the circumstances, he was willing to give himself—and his nerves—a pass. He had never stopped loving his father. Leaving and not caring were two different things. If Ashe had stayed, his soul would have died. Not all at once. Bit by bit. Working behind a desk was never going to be for him. Just the thought of his buttoned-up shirt and conservative tie choking the life out of him had Ashe rubbing his neck and breathing deeply.

However, the business was his father's life. It must have seemed natural to expect his eldest son to feel the same. Ashe's training to someday take over had started before he could walk. There was such pride in his father's voice when he would introduce Ashe to his friends and colleagues.

"Watch out," Randall used to say. "Ashe is my best and brightest. He will take this company further than I ever dreamed. Work with him or he'll beggar you all."

Ashe could remember a time when those words made him proud. When had that changed? When did they start to feel more like the crack of doom instead of a father's praise? The answer was easy. It changed when Ashe's dreams solidified. When he realized that music was the only thing that mattered. When going to the office had morphed from fun to torture.

Teenagers may be the most self-involved creatures on Earth. Ashe had been. All he could think about was what he wanted. How to make himself happy. Not once had he considered it from his father's point of view. If he had, he might have handled things differently.

When Ashe left, it ended his father's dreams—and broke his heart. *That* was something his teenage self hadn't realized. It had taken a long time and a lot of thought to come to that realization.

Nothing would have kept Ashe in Boston. However, if he could go back and do things again, he would have told his father he loved him. That he respected the business and the man who ran it. He would have tried harder to explain—everything.

This was Ashe's second chance. He didn't want to blow it. Taking a deep breath, he shook his head. If this was his reaction to a freaking text, how would he act when he met his father face to face? An image of himself, stiff and formal, shaking Randall's hand, flashed through his mind. Maybe a stilted, *Hello, Father*. Ashe smiled. When had he ever used the word father? Dad. A teasing Pops. But never father. Leave it to his vivid imagination to make things worse than they already were.

Ashe gave himself a figurative kick in the ass and opened the text. What he read put to rest the majority of his fears—and made his eyes sting with emotion.

"Welcome home, son. Welcome home. I say it twice because I want you to know that is what it is. Your home. No matter what a stubborn fool once told you, it always was and always will be. I have so much to say. I hope you forgive me for using this ridiculous method of communication—Ashe grinned—*to break the ice. Call it an old man's nerves.*

I know the office isn't your favorite place, but I would like you to meet me there at three o'clock. As I said, there is so much to say.

139

It sounded like his father, Ashe thought. The father he knew before the rebellious teenage years. Ashe didn't kid himself. The hard-nosed S.O.B. was still there. Going into this reunion expecting a meek milquetoast would be a mistake. And frankly, horrifying. Ashe shuddered at the thought. In his memory, Randall Mathison was larger than life. That was what Ashe wanted to find. Hopefully with a few of the hard edges worn down—on both of them.

Ashe had a definite spring in his step all morning. The text from his father was a nice cherry on an already luscious sundae. *Belle.* Just thinking her name made his heartbeat kick up, and his lips curve into a smile. The woman was a pistol. In and out of bed. Now that her fiancé was out of the picture, all bets were off. He wanted Belle. No. He *needed* Belle. What that meant or where it would lead, Ashe didn't know. His smile widened. He would find the answer—and enjoy every kiss, touch, and conversation along the way.

Jogging down the staircase, Ashe found his mother arranging flowers near the front door. She sent him a benign smile. He felt too much exuberance for anything less than a hug and a kiss. Pulling her close, Ashe brushed his lips across Bonita's powdered cheek.

"It's good to be home, Mom."

Blinking with surprise, Bonita's smile warmed.

"It's good that you're here, darling."

Ashe marveled at how easy it was to change some things. With a different attitude and bit of affection, he felt a small connection to his mother that had never existed before now. *Small* was the operative word. Bonita's expression quickly turned back to placidly cool as she resumed fiddling with her flowers. But it was something.

"That was nice." Georgia squeezed Ashe's hand. She stood in the hall just off the foyer, apparently a witness to his brief moment with their mother. "Mom is a tough nut to crack. I'm never certain if it's because she has no emotions, or doesn't know how to show them. Either way, it was nice of you to make the effort."

"It's different when you're a kid, and you need your parents' approval." Ashe walked with Georgia toward the patio. "I always

140

resented Mom's cool demeanor, certain it was a reflection of her feelings for me."

"I don't think you were wrong, Ashe. Not entirely." Georgia took a seat at a table laid out with a pitcher of iced tea and a plate of cookies. She poured Ashe a glass before doing the same for herself. "She loves us—I think. Who knows what goes on inside her head?"

"My point is that it doesn't matter anymore." Ashe felt as if a burden had lifted from his shoulders—one he hadn't known he carried. "I accept that Mom is who she is. Resentment is gone. It's a good feeling."

"Is that California speak?" Georgia teased, offering him a cookie. Coconut. Since they were his favorites, he took three. "I hadn't pegged you as a New Ager."

"I sat in with a group one time. Between the twang of the Sitar and the secondhand pot high, my headache hung on for two days. It was not for me."

"What kind of rock star are you? I thought drugs were de rigueur."

"Not as much as they used to be. Not in my group at all. I experimented a bit when I tried to break into the scene."

Ashe could laugh now. The truth was, he had been damn lucky. Drugs didn't sit well with him. First, the high was never terribly high. Second, the day after, he was left with a raging hangover—the kind he never had after a night of boozing. If Ashe had liked drugs—and they had liked him—who knew what would have happened? He hoped he would have had the brains to quit before it went further than experimentation. Ashe imagined a lot of people felt that way. People who had ruined their lives. Or worse—had no lives left to ruin.

"Shouldn't the girls be getting home soon?"

Georgia nodded. "Their playdate with their best friend Monica included lunch and swimming. They should be home—and ready for a nap—anytime."

"Swimming? Are you sure it's safe?"

"They were swimming almost before they could walk."

"That's good but—"

"The pool is supervised at all times. I wouldn't let them go otherwise. Two days and you've turned into an overprotective uncle. I wouldn't have guessed you had it in you."

"Me neither," he admitted with a wry smile.

Ashe looked at his watch. He had asked Belle to drop by this afternoon around two o'clock. Since she had purchased the dolls, he thought she would get a kick out of seeing the girls' reactions as they opened the packages. On a selfish note, he wanted to see Belle. The sooner, the better. Perhaps he had an addictive personality after all. He needed a hit of Belle before the withdrawals got any worse.

Ashe had spent part of his morning talking to his contacts at the police department. The video showing vandalism of Belle's car was what they termed inconclusive. The perpetrator kept his back to the camera. They are almost certain it was a man because of his build. Other than that, they had no leads. If it was personal, the perp gave no indication. The act was fast and efficient. From start to finish, less than four minutes expired.

It sounded like a professional job. But what was the point? There was no attempt to break into the car. Though no official word had come down, it seemed the police were chalking it up to a random incident. Nothing more. It sounded good. However, Ashe wasn't ready to forget what had happened. One more hint that somebody was harassing Belle and he would call in a bodyguard. After talking to a friend who knew about these things, he had a candidate on speed dial. Hopefully, it wouldn't be necessary, and Belle would never need to know.

"Why do you keep looking at your watch?"

"Am I?" A glance—five minutes ago—was all Ashe remembered. He would have to take Georgia's word that it occurred more than once. "I'm expecting someone. A friend."

"From high school?" Mind bogglingly efficient, Georgia sent a maid after more glasses. "Would you please bring a fresh pitcher of tea and more cookies, Hilda?"

"Right away."

"Where was she lurking?" Ashe swiveled his head, looking for more undercover servants.

142

"I pushed a button." Georgia pointed under the table. "Mom had them installed a couple of years ago. There's at least one in every room. Including the bedrooms."

"Why does that seem weird?"

"Because it is. It's also convenient in a house this size. It took some adjustment. At first, none of us remembered buttons were there, but now we use them all the time."

Ashe couldn't imagine living in a house this size—or having servants to buzz. Then again, until quite recently, he couldn't imagine needing room beyond his downtown loft. A wife. Children—someday. They changed a man's way of thinking.

"I am getting ahead of myself again," he muttered under his breath.

"Pardon?" Georgia sent him an inquiring smile. "Did you say something?"

"Nothing important." For now, anyway.

"Which friend is stopping by? I don't remember any names. I was too mature and sophisticated to pay attention to my little brother's boring buddies."

"Very alliterative. And they weren't boring." Ashe tossed his napkin at Georgia. It landed on her head, half covering her face. Sticking out her tongue, she flung it back. Ashe laughed. "Very sophisticated."

"Oh, shut up." Georgia sat straight, her face prim. The twitching lips ruined the effect. Under Ashe's unwavering stare, it took no time for her to break down and laugh. "Why can't I stay mad at you?"

"Because you were never mad in the first place. When you are truly angry, you hold on to it just fine."

"As my ever-patient husband can attest to." Georgia took a sip of tea. "Are you going to tell me who is coming or is it a secret?"

"Not a secret. A surprise. One for you and one for my nieces."

"I hope you didn't go overboard, Ashe. The girls love you. Gifts aren't necessary."

"That's what makes it so much fun to give them."

"Fine." Georgia perked up. "What did you get me?"

Ashe loved the look of anticipation on Georgia's face. It made him glad that Belle's visit wasn't the only surprise he had for her. "I thought gifts weren't necessary."

"Not *necessary*. Fun."

"Fair enough." Ashe couldn't argue with Georgia over that one.

"Excuse me, Miss Georgia." Hilda set a filled tray on the table. "There is a woman asking after Mr. Ashe."

"Anybody I know?" Georgia directed the question to Ashe, not the maid.

"I said it was a surprise." Ashe followed Hilda into the house.

"I should have known your friend would be a woman," his sister called after him.

Ashe had many friends. Men and women. However, Belle Richards was in a class all her own. She waited in the foyer, her face lighting up when he walked into the room. It sent his heart racing—he wouldn't be human if it didn't.

The last time he saw her, she was dressed for work, leaving the apartment looking every inch the high-powered business woman. The suit—fitted perfectly to her subtle curves—had him thinking of the zipper at the side of her waist and the sound it would make when he lowered it. Slowly. The image of the skirt pooling at Belle's feet and the tiny lace panties he knew she wore underneath, had stayed with him all day. A wonderful torment.

"You changed. I liked the suit you had on this morning."

"Shh!" Belle's eyes darted around the room. "You are not supposed to know how I was dressed this morning. Or any morning."

"Relax. Hilda veered off to the kitchen. We're alone." Ashe reached for Belle's hand, pulling back when he saw the ring on her left hand. "I hate that thing."

"Honestly?" Using her right hand, Belle threaded her fingers with his. "It feels like a weight on my soul." She shook her head. "That may be a little overly dramatic, but you get my drift."

144

Ashe expelled a resigned sigh. "I'm trying to understand, Belle. It isn't easy."

"Try living the lie." Gently, Belle took back her hand. "Eleven days and counting."

"Theo is a spineless ass."

"A spineless ass that I agreed to marry. What does that make me?"

"Family pressure." Ashe remembered well. "You made a mistake. Thank God you won't have to live with it much longer."

"Amen." When Ashe tried to lean in for a kiss, Belle quickly stepped out of reach. "None of that. I let you lure me here against my better judgment."

"Me?"

"Don't bother with the innocent look. I know better. It's my fault. I could have said no. However, I'm human. Seeing the look on those little girls' faces when they open their presents was too much of a temptation to resist."

Ashe took a step closer, the look in his eyes heated. "Why don't we slip into the linen closet? A little necking amongst the antique lace tablecloths? What do you say?"

"I say you are out of your mind," Belle laughed. "If you don't behave, I'm leaving. Understood?"

"Do you want me to beg?"

That seemed to bring Belle up short. "Of course not." She looked at him for a second, turning her head in a speculative manner. "Would you?"

Ashe teased, but Belle's question made him wonder, and it wasn't a good feeling. *Would* he beg if she asked? It was crazy. He wanted her. That part was simple. The need was strong. But it would take more than a sexual urge to bring him to his knees. It would take… *Well, shit*. Ashe laughed at himself. The answer stood before him. He knew the second her lips moved into a smile. So beautiful. So perfect. Only one thing— one person—could ever bring him to his knees.

"Belle?"

145

Ashe might have told Belle exactly what she did to him, right then and there, if Georgia hadn't chosen that moment to appear. He took a deep breath, letting it out slowly. Was he sorry for his sister's interruption or relieved? As the women embraced, he decided, either way, he was in trouble. Down for the count. Going under for the third time. Pick a metaphor. It added up to the same thing. He was in love. There was no going back.

"Hey." Georgia shook his arm. "Earth to Ashe. I asked you a question."

Ashe frowned. "Sorry. What did you say?"

"Are you okay?" Georgia gave him a bemused smile. "You look a little green around the gills."

Really? Ashe swallowed, trying to dislodge the lump in his throat. He thought love was supposed to be a good thing. So why did he feel slightly nauseous?

"Too many cookies." Ashe picked the most likely excuse he could think of and ran with it.

"He was the same as a little boy," Georgia told Belle. "Sweets were his downfall."

"Fascinating." Belle looked like she enjoyed his discomfort. "I'll alert the tabloids."

"Careful," Georgia warned, her tone light. "Ashe has a phobia about publicity."

"Is that right?" Noting that Georgia's gaze was on Ashe, Belle sent him a wink. "I would think you would be used to it by now."

"Depends on the kind of publicity. Friends who leak information lose that status quickly."

"I'll keep that in mind."

"Honestly, Ashe." Georgia shook her head with a chuckle. "Stop trying to scare Belle. She might leave and never come back."

"Trust me." Ashe looked at Georgia, but his words were meant for Belle. "That's the last thing I would want to do."

"Good." Satisfied, Georgia smiled. "Now that I have your attention, you can answer my question. When did you and Belle meet?"

"You brought us together."

"Me?" Georgia looked genuinely confused.

"The ticket you gave me for the Hollywood Bowl concert?" Belle picked up the story. "By chance, I ran into a friend of Ashe's in the audience. She invited me backstage after I mentioned that our childhood homes were right next to each other."

"What are the chances?" Thank goodness Georgia seemed unaware of the current of awareness flowing between Ashe and Belle. "You didn't mention that you saw Ashe."

"Didn't I?" Belle frowned as if she truly couldn't remember. "I suppose it slipped my mind. We only spoke for a few minutes. Isn't that right, Ashe?"

"That sounds right." Ashe shrugged casually. However, his gaze was locked with Belle's. "Our *conversation* was brief."

Belle's eyes narrowed, warning him. But the flush on her cheeks told Ashe that she remembered the most important part of the evening. The part after they stopped talking.

"I'm sorry, Belle. Where are our manners?" Georgia looped her arm through Belle's. "Let's take this outside on the patio."

Georgia poured more tea, offering cookies all around. Taking one, Belle thanked her. Before looking inquiringly at Ashe.

"Are you certain your stomach can take another one of those?"

Ashe popped the bite-sized treat into his mouth. "When I want something, I don't hesitate."

"What if it isn't good for you?"

There was no need to answer. Ashe simply raised an eyebrow, his look telling Belle what she needed to know. He couldn't resist. The cookies—or her. If they turned his stomach on its side now and then, he was more than willing to live with that.

"I called Belle to ask her a favor." Ashe decided it was time to move the subject back to neutral territory before Georgia did more than send him a puzzled frown. "When I told her I wanted to buy Nadia and Naomi a gift, she agreed to take care of it."

Georgia smiled, handing Belle a napkin. "How kind of you. I hope it wasn't any trouble."

"None at all," Belle assured her. "In fact, it gave me an excuse to wander through rows of toys for the first time since I was a girl. I plan on spending more time there now that my sister is expecting."

Georgia clapped her hands together, her face lit with excitement. "How wonderful."

"Dinah found out this morning. After sharing the news with her husband, she stopped by the office. Dad is thrilled, as you can imagine. His first grandchild. I think he was starting to think that none of his children would reproduce."

Seeing the sparkle in Belle's eyes and the bloom of color in her cheeks as she spoke about her sister made Ashe wonder if the glow of a mother-to-be could rub off on the aunt. Belle looked so happy, it was an image he knew he wouldn't soon forget.

The sound of laughter and excited voices drifted through the screened French doors, drawing their attention.

"There are my little angels." Georgia rolled her eyes, grinning. "Tell Dinah if she needs advice to give me a call. After handling two at once, I'm an expert."

"Uncle Ashe." A pair of ponytailed dynamos barreled onto the patio heading straight for Ashe.

"Fickle. That's what they are. Since Ashe has been here, Mommy has become a second-class citizen."

After basking in a round of exuberant hugs and kisses, Ashe whispered something only the twins could hear. Whatever it was sent them rushing toward their mother, arms open wide.

"We love you, Mommy." The girls climbed on Georgia's lap, snuggling close.

Laughing, Georgia kissed the tops of their heads. "I love you, my little scalawags." The word, a gentle tickle to their ribs, sent Nadia and Naomi into a fit of giggles. "Did you have a good time at Monica's?"

Words, most unintelligible, poured out. The twins finished each other's sentences or spoke at the same time. Georgia seemed to understand every word, nodding as if it was the most important, interesting conversation she ever experienced. It was one more example

148

of what a good mother she was. They might not understand right now, but one day they would. Nadia and Naomi were very lucky little girls.

While all eyes were on the girls, Ashe took the opportunity to slip away. He dashed up the main staircase, retrieving the bags from his bedroom closet and was back on the patio before the twins had wound up recounting their day.

"And Monica has a new puppy," Naomi said with a new level of excitement, the purple ribbon adorning her ponytail bouncing as she spoke.

"He's gold with white paws, and it tickles when he licks my face," Nadia chimed in.

"Uh, oh," Ashe muttered to Belle as he set the packages next to her chair. "I can't wait to see how Georgia handles this one."

An old hand at this kind of thing, Georgia did what mothers have done for generations. She used misdirection to change the subject.

"Look, girls. Uncle Ashe has a surprise for you."

There was a reason mothers used the method to get out of sticky, non-winnable situations. Because it worked. The puppy conversation would rear its ugly head at a later date, but for now, the girls were skillfully distracted.

"What is it?" Naomi slid to a halt in front of the box that was almost as tall as she was.

"Are they really for us?" Nadia breathed, her eyes big with wonder.

"Let's see." Ashe knelt, an arm around each girl. "One box is tied with pink ribbons. The other with purple. What do the cards say?" He turned the sparkly paper so the twins could see. "Nadia on this one. Naomi on the other. I guess they *are* for you."

Reaching with little hands, they stopped before touching, glancing at their mother for permission.

Georgia nodded. "Go on. But first, what do you say?"

"Thank you, Uncle Ashe." The words were sincerely spoken—in stereo—and accompanied by fierce hugs.

"You're welcome." Ashe ran a hand over their heads, ending with a light tug on each ponytail.

After that, it was every present for itself. Ribbon and wrapping paper flew in every direction. How such little creatures could create such contained chaos was a mystery, but Ashe enjoyed every second. Even better were the gasps when they first laid eyes on the twin dolls, followed by tears of happiness, squeals of joy, and another round of hugs and kisses for Uncle Ashe.

"That is officially the best money I have ever spent."

The girls sat on a blanket that their mother had wisely spread on the grass. Each doll went through a thorough examination. Oohs and awes exchanged as they shared each find.

"Thank you for inviting me." Belle hadn't stopped grinning since the girls first caught sight of the presents. "Having you tell me their reactions wouldn't have been the same."

"I know it's crazy." Georgia shook her head, looking a bit sheepish. "I want one."

"I know." Belle laughed, Georgia joining in. "I thought the same thing when I was in the store."

"I love watching them. Happy, sad, angry. My girls are such a joy. Naturally, happy is the best. Thank you for making a memory none of us will ever forget."

Ashe returned Georgia's hug. He had to remember to tell Zoe what a big hit her suggestion of the dolls turned out to be.

"Speaking of presents." Belle took a small box from her purse, giving it to Ashe. "If you don't mind, I think I'll join the girls. I can't resist a closer look."

"What is this?" Georgia asked Ashe when they were alone.

Ashe turned Georgia's hand over, placing the package in her palm, the shiny silver wrapping paper shining in the sunlight.

"A thank you. For staying in touch over the years."

"You mean the very least I could do?"

"I mean," Ashe caught and held Georgia's gaze, "that I would have been too stubborn to make the first move. You kept me tethered to this family—no matter how loose the ties."

"You're my brother. I don't need a thank you for loving you."

"Yes, you do." Ashe made a very good living using words. However, writing a song was easier than telling his sister how he felt. "I love you. Take the gift. Okay?"

"Okay." Georgia laughed, her expression as she tore off the wrapping paper mirroring that of her daughters as they opened *their* presents. "Oh, Ashe."

Belle had picked up the package from the jeweler because it was near her office. But Ashe had chosen the gift. Over the phone, he described what he wanted. The platinum bracelet was perfect. Three charms hung from the delicate loops. Two pink pearls represent Nadia and Naomi. Birthstones for June, the month they were born. The third— an emerald—was for May, Georgia's birth month.

"It's perfect."

"Funny," Ashe grinned, accepting Georgia's hug, "I thought the same thing."

Georgia held out the bracelet for Ashe to put on her wrist.

"Thank you," she said, admiring the way it looked. "You made me and my babies so happy, I almost regret what I'm about to say."

"Almost?" he teased. "What did I do?"

A burst of laughter shifted his attention over Georgia's shoulder, watching with a smile as the twins vied for Belle's attention.

"That." Georgia pointed to where Ashe's gaze had drifted. "You can't keep your eyes off Belle."

"She's a friend. And beautiful. Why wouldn't I look?" Ashe didn't doubt Georgia's observation. He couldn't help watching Belle. A lot. However, now was not the time to admit his weakness. "I'm sure you're exaggerating."

"What about the blatant flirting?"

151

So Georgia had picked up on that. Belle would not be pleased. "I flirt. It comes naturally. I didn't realize what I was doing."

"Only yesterday I bragged you up to my book club. *Ashe is such a gentleman*, I told them. Gentlemen do not seduce engaged women."

"First I'm watching and flirting. Now I'm seducing? That's quite a jump." Ashe hadn't seduced Belle. What happened had been—and still was—consensual on both sides. "If it will put your mind at ease, I can assure you that I do not now, nor have I ever, made a play for a woman if I knew she was in a committed relationship."

"Honestly?" Georgia watched Ashe, looking for any sign he lied.

"Absolutely."

Ashe knew there were a ton of loopholes that conveniently let him off the hook. Belle's situation was the perfect example. To the outside world, she was a happily engaged woman with a wedding on the near horizon. Ashe knew better. He couldn't explain. Even if he could, he didn't know what his sister's reaction would be. In this case, silence truly was golden. What Georgia didn't know wouldn't hurt either of them.

"I can't tell you how relieved I am. If you had your sights set on Belle, tomorrow night might turn awkward."

"Dad's party?" Ashe frowned at Georgia's nod. "What does one have to do with the other?"

"Theo and his family are invited. They R.S.V.P.'d some time ago. I have to assume Belle will come with them."

It was a natural assumption, Ashe thought, emptying his glass of tea. Why then, hadn't Belle mentioned it?

CHAPTER THIRTEEN

"BECAUSE THEO DIDN'T mention it to me."

Ashe had just arrived at Belle's apartment. There had been no opportunity for him to ask before she left his parents' house. Why the question scratched at his brain—a minor irritant in an otherwise great day—he couldn't say. Everything about Theo and the fake engagement annoyed Ashe. This wasn't any different. Except for one thing. Knowing the wedding wasn't going to take place was one thing. Having to spend an evening in the same room with the make-believe couple was another. A man could only be expected to take so much.

Naturally the first thing through the door, Ashe tossed his concerns at Belle. Her surprised expression answered his question before a word left her mouth.

"Won't Theo's parents find it odd if you don't accompany him?"

Belle popped the cork on a bottle of wine, pouring them each a glass. She took a sip, her expression thoughtful.

"I don't have to tell you that it's an odd situation."

"No, you do not." Ashe skirted the kitchen island. "Just a second. I forgot something."

"What?"

Setting down Belle's glass, he took her in his arms. "This."

The kiss was long, hungry, and might have led directly to the bedroom if Ashe had the patience. Instead, he took Belle right there, her underwear in tatters, her back pressed against the refrigerator. It wasn't his smoothest performance. However, when Belle's cry of release filled his ears, Ashe decided a quickie in the kitchen wasn't a bad way to start an evening.

"What was I saying?" Belle sighed happily, resting her head on Ashe's shoulder.

Ashe had carried Belle to the sofa, leaving her just long enough to retrieve their wine.

"Something about Theo's parents?" Ashe was pretty certain that was it.

"Right. Now that Theo is out—at least to me—I can't help wondering if his parents know."

"That he's gay? I thought *he* didn't know until—? What's his name?"

"Blaine." Belle wrapped Ashe's arm around her waist. "Not the gay part. Only that Theo doesn't want to get married. His father is obsessed with Theo carrying on the family line."

"Is that still a thing—outside of royalty?"

"Apparently it is. Bloodlines, and all that crap. Mine seems to be acceptable."

"Naturally." It felt as if Ashe had traveled back in time—to an episode of *Dynasty*.

"You're too young to remember that show," Belle laughed when he shared his thoughts.

"Dalton got hooked while we were recording our first album. He said watching it late at night helped him relax. The rest of us decided, what the hell, and joined him. I don't know if it helped, but the album went multi-platinum, and we won a Grammy."

"Here's to *Dynasty*." They clinked glasses. Belle sighed. "Whatever the explanation, Theo's parents have treated the engagement with kid gloves from day one. They don't push us to be together. They haven't pushed period. Until the last postponement. Theo's father finally put his foot down. Marriage or else."

"Or else what?"

"Loss of Theo's cushy lifestyle. His job is a sham. He goes to work when he wants—which isn't often. Mostly, Theo plays. His father won't disinherit him, but the money will run dry fast unless the wedding happens. A grandchild in the first year wouldn't hurt."

"You were picked as a brood mare? Nice," Ashe sneered. "Do you think the marriage would have lasted a year?"

"That's the scary part. If I had been foolish enough to go through with it, I don't know if I would have divorced Theo. When I commit to

154

something, I tend to dig in until the bitter end. I think that's why Theo wanted to go through with the wedding."

Belle snuggled closer as if looking for comfort. Ashe was happy to oblige. He kissed her forehead. Then her words sank in.

"Theo what?"

"Didn't I mention that?"

"No. I would have remembered that bit of lunacy."

Sitting up, Belle rubbed a hand over her face, taking a healthy drink of wine. With a sigh, she looked at Ashe.

"Theo wanted to get married to placate his father. He said I could divorce him in a year."

Before, Ashe had simply disliked Theo. Hatred was sliding in— quickly.

"Did you kick him in the nuts? Or send him for a mental evaluation? Hopefully both?"

Belle laughed. Not full-fledged. Edgier. Somewhere between a scoff and a chuckle. "I gave him two weeks. Which he tried to turn into a month."

"You held firm."

"Damn straight, I did."

Ashe would have kicked Theo's sorry ass out the door. That was him. Belle's approach was more subtle. However, there was a rod of steel at her core. Anybody thinking Belle was a pushover would be in for a big surprise.

"Come to the party."

"Your father's birthday party?" When Ashe nodded, Belle gave him a half smile. "You want me at the party? With Theo?"

"I want you at the party. With me." Ashe slid his hand through Belle's hair, cupping the back of her neck. "It would be different if you and Theo were a real couple. Lots of people will be there. Nobody will think anything about you mingling without your faux fiancé. Or disappearing for a few minutes."

This time, Belle's laugh had genuine humor in it.

155

"Disappear?" She turned her head, kissing Ashe's wrist. "With you?"

"Not *with* me. If we were to meet—by accident—in an empty room, who would know."

"It's a tempting thought. But I don't know if I should go."

Ashe took out his phone. He hadn't shown his father's text to his sister. If things didn't go well, the disappointment would be his and his alone. Showing Belle felt right. He brought up the message.

"Read this."

Watching Belle's expressions, Ashe waited for her reaction.

"That's wonderful." Belle looked up with a smile. "Something changed in him. Don't you think that's encouraging—for all of us? People can evolve, no matter how old."

"I know it's crazy. But..."

"What?"

Ashe shrugged. "If I go in there with sky-high hopes for a reconciliation, am I asking for him to pull the rug out from under me?"

"You think your father is going to punk you?"

When Belle put it like that, Ashe admitted it did sound ridiculous.

"Not a joke. More of a misunderstanding." Closing his eyes, Ashe dropped his head onto the back of the sofa, pulling Belle into his arms. Having her close helped him think. "What if Dad's new attitude is predicated on the idea that I'm back for good?"

"Your father isn't a fool, Ashe. He has to know what you've done with your life. The success. The money. Why would he think you'd give that up?"

"I don't know. My last memory of my father isn't a good one. We were two stubborn idiots. We weren't interested in a compromise—not that there was one. I'm afraid that hasn't changed. Five minutes alone and we might find ourselves at each other's throats."

"Don't let it happen."

156

"That's it?" Ashe gave Belle a small shake, venting his frustration. "That's your advice? Don't let it happen? Christ. Embroider it on a pillow, why don't you?"

"Mock if you want, but it *is* good advice. You aren't a kid anymore, Ashe. If you don't want to fight with your father, don't. If he says something you don't like, ignore it. Or walk away. You *do* have a choice."

Belle was right. About everything. Ashe's father no longer held all the power. They would never be true equals. That wasn't possible in a parent/child dynamic. However, a lot had changed in ten years. No matter what his father thought, the life Ashe had forged was important. There was no going back—only forward. He simply had to keep that in mind.

Ashe breathed in. Belle. Her natural fragrance brought him another level of calm. She never wore perfume. Or cologne. The lotion that she diligently applied after every shower was silky but unscented. It was a choice he heartily approved of.

"Is that how you handle conflict with your father? Calm and cool."

"At the office, I'm an employee, not a daughter. Dad's word is law. Privately, we do pretty well."

"How often do you walk away?"

Belle chuckled, one shoulder hitching upward. "It happens. Though not as often as it used to." Belle sobered. "I have no idea how he's going to react when I tell him about Theo."

"Theo has a boyfriend. It will be hard for your father to blame you."

"True," Belle nodded slowly. "I don't think Theo's parents will be as understanding. They will search for an excuse. Who turned my son gay? I'll be the perfect whipping girl."

"Do you care?"

"Not at all. My mother might not agree. She and Theo's mother are friendly—if not friends. It will be awkward at first. However, Mom is tougher than she looks. She'll survive. We all will."

Belle wouldn't simply survive. She would flourish. Ashe had no doubts. More than anything, he wanted to be around to see it happen. The logistics had him stumped. Belle was firmly entrenched in Boston. Her family. Her friends. Her work. It wouldn't be fair to ask her to move.

As for Ashe, this hadn't been his home for a long time. If things worked out with his father, he would visit whenever possible. But his life—and the family of his heart—were in Los Angeles.

There had to be a compromise—if they were committed to finding one. That was the problem. Ashe knew how he felt. Belle was another matter. Too soon, he reminded himself. Give her time to drop Theo the Leech, deal with the repercussions, and get used to the idea of having Ashe in her life. No matter how much he would like to rush things, slow would be better—for both of them.

"I think I will come to your father's birthday party."

"Really?" That perked up Ashe's lagging emotions. "I'm glad. But what changed your mind?"

"You." Belle brushed her lips across his. "I've been to so many parties where I wished I could disappear. I never did. Of course, you weren't there to make the idea irresistible."

"Me? Irresistible?" Ashe nuzzled Belle's neck, tasting her smooth, soft skin. "Tell me more. Better yet, show me."

Ashe's hand had just begun to slide under the hem of Belle's dress when a loud buzz filled the room, signaling somebody wanted in the building.

"Ignore it." Ashe grabbed at Belle's hand as she tried to stand up. He had to give her credit, she was fast, easily avoiding his grasp.

Laughing, Belle swatted away Ashe's second attempt to draw her back. "It might be one of my older neighbors. Sometimes they need help with their groceries." She pushed the intercom. "Hello?"

"I have a package for Belle Richards. You have to sign."

"Okay. Give me a few minutes."

"I'll go." Ashe already had his shoes on.

"There's no need. It's a secure building. If the guy looks strange, I won't open the door."

"What constitutes strange in your opinion?"

"I don't know." Belle shrugged. "I'll know when I see it."

"Tell you what." Ashe moved Belle from where she blocked the door. "You think about it. Next time, once you've decided what strange is, you can go."

"There's no need to be condescending."

Ashe pulled Belle close, kissing her breathless. "Not condescending. Protective. Is there anything wrong with caring about your safety?"

Still recovering from his scorching kiss, Belle leaned against the wall, shaking her head. "When you put it like that? I guess not."

"Good. Pour me another glass of wine. I'll be right back."

It turned out that Ashe exaggerated how little time it would take. Exiting the elevator, instead of a delivery man, he found a medium box sitting unattended just outside the apartment building's front door. Preferring to err on the side of caution, Ashe left it where it sat, examining it from inside.

Plain brown and unmarked, Ashe could see Belle's name, but that was it. No address of any kind—to or from. A zip of warning raced up his spine. *Better safe than sorry.* If ever there was a time to heed that old chestnut, this was it. Backing away from the door, Ashe took out his phone. He called his friend at the police department.

"YOU DID THE right thing," Martin Blanton told him. Ashe wasn't sure if that was a relief or not. Part of him was hoping the Deputy Chief of Police would laugh off Ashe's worries as paranoia. Instead, he deployed a bomb squad.

"A bomb? Seriously?" Ashe backed further away from the door.

"It's a precaution. But, yes. We take these things very seriously. Hear that?"

Even over the phone, Martin's ears were attuned to the sound of a siren. It took Ashe a little longer to pick up the distinctive wail A few seconds later, a police car pulled to a stop. Right behind was a black van.

"Listen to what my men have to say and follow their instruction to the letter. Understand?"

"Yes. And thank you, Martin. Anytime you need tickets to a concert, say the word."

"You know I will. I'll check in with you later."

There wasn't much for Ashe to do. The police officer told him to go back to Belle's apartment and prepare to evacuate at a moment's notice. Ashe was just getting off the elevator when his phone rang. *The police?* That was fast.

"All clear, Mr. Mathison. It wasn't a bomb."

"Thank God." Ashe let out a sigh of relief. "What was it?"

"Is Ms. Richards at home?"

"Yes."

"Please let her know that we need to speak with her. We'll be there in a few minutes."

Before Ashe could ask for clarification, the officer hung up.

Belle took the news admirably calm.

"What do you want me to do?" she asked "Tears and hysteria? Not my style. You called the police—which was absolutely the right thing to do. But until we know more, all we can do is wait."

Watching Belle pace, Ashe realized she wasn't as unaffected as he first thought. For some reason, the more wound up she became, the calmer he felt. That would seem to bode well for their future. When one of them lost their cool, the other would stay on an even keel.

"Want to sit down?" Ashe patted the sofa cushion next to him.

"Nope. I'm better if I keep moving." Belle raised her wine glass, then stopped. "Food. We haven't had dinner. The last thing I need is more alcohol on an empty stomach."

Ashe followed Belle to the kitchen. "Can I help?" he asked as she rooted around in the refrigerator. "I'm not a great cook, but I can chop the hell out of your vegetable of choice."

"Eureka!" Triumphantly, Belle emerged, clutching something wrapped in brown butcher paper.

"What do you have there, Archimedes?"

Passing by, Belle batted her eyelashes. "There is nothing hotter than a man who can reference a dead Greek mathematician."

Ashe laughed. The woman was crazy—in the best of all possible ways. "I'll be sure to tuck that information away for later use."

"You do that. In the meantime, grab the salt from the cupboard to your right." Belle unwrapped two of the most beautiful steaks Ashe had ever seen. "The secret is getting the meat to room temperature. And letting it sit with a nice coat of seasoning on both sides. By the time the police leave, these lovelies will be ready to grill."

"I thought we could order in a pizza."

"I told you, working in the kitchen relaxes me. Something tells me I'll be cooking up a storm very soon."

Right on cue, there was a knock at the door.

"I'll get it." Ashe brushed his hand over Belle's as he passed her. Taking a quick check out the peephole, he opened the door. "Please come in, officer."

"Good evening, Ms. Richards."

"Hello, Officer Clarke?" Belle shook his outstretched hand. "I didn't expect to see you."

"I was on duty when the call came in. This is Officer Michaels." He introduced a stocky man of average height, his short dark hair barely visible under his hat.

"Ms. Richards." Officer Michaels nodded. "Mr. Mathison. We met downstairs."

"Would you like to sit down? Can I get you anything to drink? Water? Coffee?"

"No, thank you, Ms. Richards." Clarke took a seat, flipping pages on his notebook. Michaels remained standing, his hands clasped behind his back. "It was smart to call the police, Mr. Mathison. If it had been a bomb... Well, I don't think we need to go into that."

Ashe agreed. Belle stiffened the second Clarke mentioned a bomb. He took her hand, frowning when he found it ice cold. However, when she spoke, her voice was sure and strong.

"What was in the box, officer?"

"A dead cat."

"Mother fucker," Ashe hissed.

"We couldn't tell for certain, but our best guess is that the animal was killed by a car. It was probably found along the side of the road then put in the box."

"Sick is sick." Ashe said a silent prayer of thanks that Belle hadn't opened that box.

"I agree. There was a note."

"Let me guess." Belle squeezed Ashe's hand. "Die, bitch, die?"

Clarke nodded. "Obviously, the two incidents—your car and the dead cat—are linked by the message. I wish I could tell you more. We do have a few questions."

"I'll tell you whatever I can."

"Did you recognize the delivery man's voice?"

"No," Belle shook her head. "I'm certain it wasn't anybody I know."

The rest of the questions were routine. Belle was as baffled as the police. If somebody wanted to scare her, they had succeeded. Why? She had no idea. By the time the officers left, there were no answers, only questions.

"I'm calling in a bodyguard," Ashe announced as he sliced a ripe tomato.

"Okay." Belle turned the first steak, the loud sizzle filling the kitchen. "Remind me again why you need one?"

Ashe stopped chopping. "Don't be cute, Belle. The bodyguard is for you."

"No." Belle plated the steaks, adding a side of crispy fried potatoes and perfectly steamed asparagus. "If you're done, put those on the salad, and we are ready to eat."

"Damn it, Belle." Unconcerned about aesthetics, Ashe dumped the tomatoes in a big heap. "Your car. Now the cat. There's no telling what might come next."

"Bring the bowl. Everything is perfect. You don't want the food to get cold."

With a low growl of frustration, Ashe joined Belle at the table. She looked so calm, her expression annoyingly placid.

"You can't ignore what happened."

"I'm not." Belle loaded Ashe's plate with greens. "I told you, cooking relaxes me. Eat."

"The bodyguard makes sense." When she simply stared at his plate, Ashe speared the salad with undue force, shoving several pieces into his mouth.

"It's scare tactics, Ashe. I don't know why, but I'm not in danger."

"Yet."

Ashe tackled the steak. Juicy and tender, he allowed himself to savor the bite while deciding how to convince Belle to see reason. He could go behind her back. Bring in the hired muscle without her knowledge. Belle would have a fit when she found out. By then, the police would hopefully have found whoever was guilty.

It would be easier if Belle would cooperate. Taking a sip of wine, Ashe prepared for another round of arguments. Taking a deep breath, he opened his mouth. Then he looked at Belle. Really looked. She hadn't taken a bite of food. On each side of her plate sat her hands—balled into a fist. In one she clutched a steak knife, a fork in the other. Eyes closed, she took shallow breaths as if that was all she could manage.

"Belle—" Ashe left his chair, kneeling beside her.

"I'm scared."

"Me too." Carefully, Ashe opened her fingers, removing the utensils. "We'll figure it out. I promise."

"I should have stayed in the kitchen. I could have baked all night. Cakes and cookies. There's a peanut butter fudge recipe I want to try. As soon as I sat down, the nerves crashed down on me."

Ashe rubbed Belle's back in a slow, circular motion until it seemed like she had returned to normal.

"Baking is good. But I'll end up eating most of it. I won't be able to resist." Ashe lifted her into his arms. "The last thing the world needs is to see me waddling around the stage."

"I wouldn't let you over-indulge." Belle wrapped her arms around Ashe's neck, her lips brushing his cheek.

"Just to be safe, why don't we find another way to relax? One that burns off the pounds instead of packing them on."

"Sex?" Ashe could feel Belle's lips curve into a smile.

"You know, I hadn't thought of *that*. I was going to suggest calisthenics or a nice, long run." Ashe stopped by the bed. "If your heart is set on seeing me naked, I guess that's okay."

Belle slid from Ashe's arms. Placing her hand on his chest, she gave him a shove. Grabbing the hem of her dress, she pulled it over her head. "I wouldn't want to make you do anything you found distasteful."

"Oh, boy." Ashe swallowed. Belle stood, hands on hips, in nothing but a lacy pink bra and barely there panties. "If you are the alternative, I may never go running again."

"I'll take that as a compliment."

Slowly, Belle straddled Ashe's hips, sliding her hands under his t-shirt. Her touch was cool against his heated skin. Now, he was the one having trouble breathing, but it had nothing to do with nerves. It was all Belle. Intoxicating. Beautiful. Breathtaking. She left a trail of kisses across his chest, her teeth and tongue making him groan with pleasure.

"Tell me you want me," Belle whispered in his ear. "Tell me *what* you want. Anything. I'm yours. Just say the word."

"Anything?" Ashe's hands slid up Belle's back, unhooking her bra. She let the straps fall down her arms until it landed, a pool of lace on his chest. In a flash, he wrapped it around her wrists. Rolling her over, he held her hands above her head. "This could take all night. Think you can handle it? Handle me?"

Eyes glowing hot, Belle stretched, the hard tips of her breasts brushing against Ashe's chest.

"All night with you? Yes." She sighed with a slow smile as Ashe's mouth hovered over hers. "Please."

"I want you. Are you really mine?"

"Yes."

Ashe sealed her words with a kiss. Belle was his. It wasn't exactly a declaration of love, but it was a start.

CHAPTER FOURTEEN

ASHE HAD INSISTED on driving Belle to work. She hadn't argued—exactly. Instead, she pointed out the obvious. He couldn't deliver and pick her up every day for an indefinite period of time. It wasn't practical—or doable.

"If you would agree to a bodyguard, he would drive you."

"Or she."

Ashe chuckled, shaking his head. "I am too tired to have a discussion about the equality of women in the workforce."

"No discussion necessary. There *are* women bodyguards. Either way, I refuse to have one. You can dot that with a big, fat, emphatic period."

"Which is why I'm behind the wheel, dropping you at work. Dot that with a *bigger, fatter* period."

"And tomorrow?"

"I'll do the same."

"Tonight is your father's birthday party. Aren't you planning on heading back to Los Angeles right away?"

Belle didn't like to think about it, but there wasn't much choice. This thing they had going—whatever it was—had a very short shelf life. It had progressed beyond fun and games. However, expecting more would be the worst kind of fool's errand. She was already looking at probable heartache. Not a broken heart. Just a long, wide, gaping crack. The last thing she needed to do was imagine that Ashe wanted more. *That* would be a fast track to a heart smashed into a million pieces.

"I thought I might stick around a day or two."

"Oh." Belle licked her suddenly dry lips. "I'm sure your father will be happy to hear that."

Belle waited for Ashe to tell her that *she* was keeping him in Boston—not his father. When the words didn't come, she felt like an idiot. Thank goodness she hadn't voiced her thoughts. It would have embarrassed them both.

"Belle—"

"Yes?" *Say it,* Belle silently urged Ashe. *Get my hopes up. I dare you.*

"We're here."

Blinking, Belle looked around. They were parked outside her office. *That was it? That was all Ashe had to say?* Fine. She could be just as cool and casual as he could. Smiling innocently, Belle grabbed him by the shirt, pulled him close and gave him a scorching hot kiss. Though her legs were a bit wobbly as she left the car, Belle had the satisfaction of seeing Ashe blink, his eyes glazed.

"Thanks for the lift," Belle said, leaning against the door as much for effect as support. "I should be done for the day around five o'clock."

Not waiting for a response, Belle closed her door, walking into the building without a backward glance. Knowing that Ashe watched her every step might have added the extra swish to her hips—just to remind him what he would be missing when he was back in California.

"Good morning, Belle," Pru greeted her as she entered the waiting area outside her office. "You look like you slept well."

Pru's observation couldn't have been further from the truth. Belle hadn't slept well. Ashe wouldn't let her—not that she had any reason to complain. What had begun as a way to soothe Belle's nerves turned into a sexual marathon. Just when she thought Ashe couldn't possibly have anything left in his tank, he would surprise her. Then surprise her again. What Pru saw wasn't a well-rested woman. It was one who was satiated beyond what she had thought humanly possible.

"I had a good night."

"I'll say." Pru followed Belle into her office. "Your skin is glowing."

Considering how the evening had started, Belle's night *had* been good. Ashe used his body to make her forget all about slashed tires and dead cats. She once read that sex was good for the complexion. It that were true, the glow that Pru mentioned should last for the next month—at the very least.

Settling behind her desk, Belle booted her computer, pulling up her emails.

"Your father asked to see you at nine-thirty." Pru handed Belle a small stack of messages. "Other than that, the morning is pretty routine."

"This should be it, Pru." Belle felt a burst of excitement. "Dad must have come to a decision about my proposal. Keep your fingers crossed. If the answer is yes, *Strive* will be fully operational inside of six months."

"I'm crossing my fingers *and* toes. Not that you need any extra luck. There is no way your father can say no."

"I'M NOT SAYING no, Belle."

"You might as well be."

Belle tried to remain calm. She knew that raising her voice would not help—not with her father. He only responded to calmly stated arguments. However, after the news he dropped on her, it was difficult to keep her cool.

"I have agreed to fund your project, just at a smaller initial amount."

"The figures I gave you were already cut to the barest minimum. You've agreed to half. That's not enough."

"I don't agree." Elias Richards tapped his pen on his desk. It was a habit he used when engaged in conversations—over the phone or in person. The dark green blotter that sat in front of him was the only thing that prevented him from damaging the cherry wood desk's glossy surface. "*Strive* is an experimental undertaking. I understand that similar projects have worked, but you are proposing something on a much grander scale. Take the money I'm offering and start small. Show me it can work. In a year, if the numbers show the proper growth, we will revisit the discussion."

"Without the proper initial investment, there won't be enough progress to discuss." Belle stood. If she couldn't shout, at least she could get out her frustration by pacing. "The wheels I have turning are geared toward *that* investment."

"I'm sorry, Belle. My advisors don't think it's doable. They crunched the numbers and feel *Strive* will fail."

168

"I see." Belle took a deep calming breath. "There's something your advisors didn't take into account. I can understand why *they* would overlook it. What I can't figure out is why *you* did."

Elias frowned, the pen in his hand tapping furiously. "I'm not a mind reader, Belle. If you left something out of the report, how am I supposed to see it?"

"It's standing right in front of you." Belle spread her arms, willing her father to look. *Really* look. "You've known me all my life. By now, I shouldn't have to tell you what I'm made of. You taught me well, Dad. *I'm* the reason this project will succeed because I won't accept failure."

Turning on her heel, Belle left the office, not giving her father a chance to respond. What could he say that hadn't already been said? Cutting her proposed budget in half was like a slap in the face, telling Belle that he had no faith in her.

As she walked down the hall, Belle knew she had two choices. She could accept her father's decree. A few years ago, that was what she would have done. However, she was no longer a young woman trying to find her place in her father's company. Belle knew who she was. Strong. Confident. It didn't matter if her father believed in her or not. She believed in herself.

"Well?" Pru asked the second she saw Belle.

"I need a list of donors. Big money, little money. I don't care, just get me names."

"Your father turned you down?"

The disappointment in Pru's voice only strengthened Belle's resolve. Women out there were counting on her. She wasn't going to let a little thing like money stand in the way of helping them.

"He gave me half. The rest is up to us." Belle put out her hand. "Are you with me?"

With a firm nod, Pru's hand grasped Belle's, pumping twice. "I'm with you. All the way."

Belle believed in herself. However, it was good to know somebody had her back. She took her seat, back straight as an arrow.

"It's you and me, Pru. Let's do this."

ASHE ENTERED THE Mathison Building thirty minutes before he was scheduled to meet his father. It wasn't nerves that had him arriving early. He felt surprisingly calm. This was nothing like the drama currently tainting Belle's life. He and his father would find peace— hopefully. If they didn't, Ashe would be sorry. However, it wouldn't be the end of the world. Feelings might be hurt. Physically, they would go on as before. In the end, it was all about perspective.

The building's lobby bustled with the expected mid-afternoon energy. Suited men and women walked with purpose to and from the elevator, phones glued to their ears. It all looked very intense. Ashe knew for a fact that it was mostly for show. In the business world, looking important meant almost as much as the real deal.

Retail merchants occupied the first two floors. Shoppers meandered from place to place, looking more than buying. The crowd was a mixed bag of ages. Babies to senior citizens. This was the first time since Ashe had arrived in Boston that he felt in danger of somebody recognizing him.

It was as much a feeling as a certainty. He knew from experience that the best course of action was to keep his head down, his sunglasses firmly in place and take as short a path as possible from point A—the entrance, to point B—the elevator. After that, it was a quick ride to the tenth floor and his father's office.

Theoretically, it was the perfect plan. Unfortunately, there was no way to anticipate the attention span of teenage girls. One second they were so self-involved it didn't seem possible that they could care about anything that didn't involve their hair, their clothes, or the color of their fingernails. Then bam. In a complete turnaround, the world became clear as a bell—and they noticed everything.

Or—in this case—they noticed the tall, well-built rock star trying his best to remain incognito.

"OMG."

Ashe heard the screech a second before a wide-eyed, ringlet-haired, sky blue-lipped girl jumped in this path. He could have barreled past her—or over her. She couldn't have weighed more than ninety-eight pounds soaking wet. However, that was not an option. Once recognized, that was it. Fans were the lifeblood of any musician. Ashe remembered what it was like to meet an artist he listened to and admired. The ones that took the time to talk and autograph rose in his estimation. The ones that couldn't be bothered? They were a disappointment. It was hard to listen to their music without some of it carrying over.

Before the girl could do more than stare, bouncing on the balls of her feet, Ashe removed his sunglasses and smiled.

"Hello."

For a second, Ashe worried that she was going to collapse at his feet. Her legs wobbled, the color seemed to drain from her face. Just as he reached to prop her up, the exuberance of youth took over. Color popped into her cheeks, her body regained its ability to remain upright. And her unnaturally blue lips curved upward.

"It *is* you," she gasped, signaling to somebody behind Ashe. Before he could blink, three other girls joined her. He should have known. It was an unwritten law. Teenagers almost always traveled in a pack. "I told my friends it was, but Trish said, 'No way, Wendy.' And Paula agreed. Lara said, 'What would Ashe Mathison be doing here?'"

"In the *Mathison* Building?" Ashe teased.

Four sets of eyes grew big. Four mouths dropped open. They looked at him, then at each other, then back at him.

"We didn't think of that," Wendy said as if it were an earth-shaking revelation.

"No reason you would." Ashe nodded toward the phone Wendy clutched with a death grip. "Would you mind if I got some pictures with all of you? My assistant is always on my case because she doesn't have anything to put on my social media pages. I'll give you her Twitter handle. You'd be doing me a big favor if you would shoot her some copies."

They had already started to draw a crowd. When four girls let out a simultaneous scream, everyone in the room took notice. As a result, Ashe had to text his father that he was running behind. It took almost forty-five minutes to take care of the additional requests for autographs and pictures. It might have taken longer, but two security guards came along, dispersing the crowd.

"Thank you so much, Ashe," Wendy shouted as the guard escorted him across the lobby. "We love you!"

"Anytime. I hope to see you the next time we play Boston."

That earned Ashe another high-pitched scream. Chuckling, he waved as the elevator doors closed.

"That was crazy." The guard shook his head. "How do you live with all that attention?"

"It doesn't happen that often." More accurately, Ashe didn't put himself in the position for it to happen very often.

"I suppose it's a small price to pay for all the money. And chicks." The guard whistled, grinning. "Man, I've seen the pictures of the women you date. Katrina Willows? She is the sexiest woman I have ever seen."

Not wanting to burst the guy's fantasy, Ashe merely nodded. Katrina Willows was one of the world's most in-demand models. She was also a world-class bitch. The sex had been memorable because she spent most the time preening as if she were on camera—not sharing Ashe's bed. Once with the crazed diva had been one time too many.

"Here you go." The security guard sent Ashe a sheepish look as the elevator doors opened. "Mr. Mathison. I don't suppose—"

"Get out your camera." Ashe put his arm around the shorter man's shoulders and smiled. One more picture. Not a problem.

The reception area hadn't changed much in ten years. The color of the paint and the furniture looked new. Otherwise, Ashe didn't see a lot that was different. Not even the woman who guarded the entrance to his father's office with the ferocity of a fire-breathing dragon. Tougher men than Ashe quivered at the thought of facing Ms. Matilde Desoto.

"Ashe?"

"Hello, Mattie."

Laughing, the woman rushed to greet him, pulling him into a warm, motherly hug. Unlike other people who looked at Ashe and saw a successful rock star, Mattie couldn't have cared less. To her, he was the same young man who came to work with his father, ran errands after school, and dated her daughter—briefly—during their junior year of high school.

"Now, let me get a good look at you." Mattie held Ashe at arm's length, giving him a thorough once over. "You were always a good-looking boy, Ashe Mathison. But, my, oh my. Up close, I see what all the fuss is about."

"You haven't changed a bit, Mattie."

Still an attractive woman. Slender. She wore her hair in a bun, wound at the base of her neck with ruthless precision. Ashe did the math. Mattie had to be almost in her mid-fifties. She could easily pass for ten years younger.

"Flatterer. Another thing that hasn't changed."

"It isn't flattery if it's true."

"I can't argue with that," Mattie winked.

"How is Arlene?" Ashe and Mattie's daughter had fun, deciding they were better suited as friends.

"Happily married with two little ones and another on the way."

The news made Ashe smile. He remembered that even as a teenager, Arlene knew what she wanted. A husband and children. It was good to know she got her wish.

"If your father knew I was taking up your time, he would have a fit." Mattie pushed Ashe toward the office door. "He's been buzzing me every five minutes asking if you were here yet." On cue, the intercom buzzed. "See?" She hit the intercom button. "He's here." Mattie looked at Ashe. "Go on. What are you waiting for?"

Ashe wiped his hand on his pants. "It's been a while."

"Too long." Mattie gave Ashe another push. "Go on. I don't think you'll be sorry."

Raising his hand to knock, Ashe was surprised when the door opened. Whatever he expected, it wasn't his father, big and robust as ever, holding out his arms in welcome. The tension fell away, and without hesitation, Ashe embraced his father.

"There's my boy." Randall Mathison whispered gruffly, his strong arms keeping Ashe near. "Welcome home, son."

"It's good to be here, Dad."

Somebody sniffled—Mattie. Though Ashe would have sworn he saw a suspicious trace of moisture in his father's eyes, it was hard to tell since he was blinking back a few tears of his own.

"Coffee all around?" Mattie asked, wiping her cheeks.

"Whiskey," Ashe and Randall answered simultaneously. Drawing a smile from Mattie.

"Come in and sit down." Randall closed the door. He went to the wet bar—the one that had been there for generations—and poured the drinks. "I had a speech planned, but suddenly, I can't think of anything to say."

"I know what you mean." Ashe took the glass. Holding it out, he tapped it against his father's. "You look good, Dad."

"Not bad for a sixty-year-old fool?"

"If I didn't know, I would never guess sixty." It was true. Randall sported a full head of hair, liberally laced with silver. He carried a few extra pounds around the middle, but his eyes were clear and his body tall and sturdy. "I'd say the fool part goes both ways."

Randall took a sip of whiskey. "I'm stubborn. That's an important trait in business. Not so much when dealing with an equally stubborn son."

"I used to tell myself that I was nothing like you. I was wrong." They both chuckled.

Ashe was amazed at how natural it felt to sit in his father's office. Where was the stilted awkwardness he had expected? His father seemed a bit nervous—so was he. Was it simply the passage of time? Or had something specific happened to bring this about?

"I imagine you have a few questions." Randall loosened his silk tie, the dark blue perfectly matched to his custom-made navy suit.

"A few," Ashe smiled wryly. "I hate to break our sudden detente. The last time we sat in a room where the atmosphere felt this relaxed..." Ashe shrugged. "Maybe before I turned thirteen."

"Ah, yes. The terrible teens." Randall sighed. "That's when it started. I couldn't figure out what happened to my son. Before, we seemed to be on the same wavelength."

"My ambitions changed, Dad. I didn't know how to tell you."

Randall's eyes narrowed as he lifted his glass, taking a thoughtful sip. "Music."

"Yes."

Ashe waited for what he was certain would follow. This was where his father always sneered, showing his contempt at the thought of anybody attempting to make a living in what he derisively terms *the arts*. Once again, Randall surprised him.

"I wish I had understood, son. You're good. Check that. You're amazing. I had Mattie download all your albums for me."

Ashe couldn't believe his ears. "All of them?"

Randall nodded. "See that?" He pointed to his chest. "It's puffed out with pride. I was on a plane last week. The woman in the seat next to me was reading an article about your band. I pointed to your picture and said, *That's my boy*. To say she was impressed is putting it mildly."

"I'm sorry. This is a bit much to take in all at once." Ashe finished his whiskey in one gulp, the burn helping to focus his thoughts. "When did this happen? Was it gradual or did you have a sudden revelation?"

"Yes, and yes."

"That clears things up." Ashe stood, walking to the decanter. He poured himself another drink. "Dad?"

"No. One is my limit these days." Randall waited until Ashe took his seat. "I've wanted to reconnect with you for some time. However, I will admit it was always with the hope that I could talk you into coming back to the business."

Ashe felt a weight descend into his gut. There it was, he thought. The very thing he had feared. Ten years and all the success Ashe had achieved and his father still believed the business was all that mattered.

"Relax. I don't feel that way any longer."

"What?" Ashe almost dropped his glass. His chin was another matter. At the moment, it was planted firmly on the floor.

"Surprised?" Randall inquired with a grin.

"The hell with a feather. You could knock me over with a look."

"It took a pretty big jolt to make me see the error of my ways." Meeting Ashe's gaze, Randall's expression turned serious. "I had a health scare. The doctors have a fancy name for it, but essentially it was a pre-heart attack."

"Jesus, Dad." Ashe sat forward, setting his glass down with a thud. "Georgia didn't say anything."

"Because she doesn't know. Nobody outside of a hospital in Denver. I had chest pains when I was there on a business trip just after the first of the year."

"You went through it by yourself?" Ashe had a hard time processing the information. "What if it had been serious? What if...?" He couldn't bring himself to say the words.

"What if I had died?" Randall laughed. "I wouldn't have cared, and your mother would have been spared rushing to my bedside only to find out she was too late."

"Are you making a joke?" Ashe couldn't see the humor in the situation. "That's a little morbid, Dad."

"I understand. But I've had longer to live with it. Better to laugh than cry, right?"

That had always been Ashe's theory. However, this was the first time he was faced with his father's potential mortality. Funny it wasn't.

"You're certain it wasn't an actual heart attack?"

"I saw my doctor as soon as I was back in Boston. After a thorough examination, he assured me my heart was fine. And I was damn lucky. It was time to change my lifestyle. Fewer late hours, better nutrition, no more cigars, and only one whiskey a day." His lips twisting,

176

Randall raised his glass. "More than anything, I miss that after-dinner whiskey and cigar. Remember the first—and last—time I shared the ritual with you?"

"I do." Ashe smiled at the memory. At seventeen, he was certain he was ready. A few puffs and couple of sips was all it took for him to heave his guts over the balcony railing. "It took a long time before I could smell cigar smoke without my stomach clenching."

"In retrospect, I'm glad you didn't pick up the habit. Take it from me, you're better off."

"Are you doing okay, Dad?"

Randall nodded. "I had a checkup last week. I've lost a few pounds." He patted his stomach. "I could lose a few more. My cholesterol is down to a reasonable level—as is my blood pressure."

Ashe felt the lump in his throat ease away. "That's good."

"My health is better than it has been in years. I'm grateful. However, something more came out of that scare in Denver. My eyes were opened to how quickly life passes us by." Randall snapped his fingers. "I've missed ten years, Ashe. I'd like to think that I have at least ten more in me. And I hope you'll let me share part of it with you."

"You won't be able to get rid of me again," Ashe assured his father.

Randall nodded, letting out a deep sigh. "Good. Now, about this music career of yours."

Ashe didn't want to upset his father, but he had to make certain there were no misunderstandings between them. "I sing for my supper. Nothing is going to change that."

"I should hope not. You followed your heart—and your destiny. I'm proud of you, Ashe."

They were words Ashe no longer needed. But that didn't make hearing them any less special.

"Thank you, Dad."

"I went to your concert."

Certain he must have misheard, Ashe cupped his ear with his hand. "Excuse me? Would you say that again?"

"I understand musicians sometimes lose their hearing," Randall said, the edge of his eyes crinkling with humor.

"My hearing is fine. There are just some things you never expect your father to say. I went to your concert tops my list."

"Good to know I still have a few surprises left in me."

"A few." Ashe sat back in his chair, shaking his head. "This afternoon has been nothing *but* surprises. Most of them pleasant ones. Now, about this concert. When, where, and what did you think?"

"When? A few months ago. Where? Here in Boston."

Unbelievable. What was with his family? First Georgia, now his father? A few words and there could have been a family reunion. At the very least, Randall could have hitched a ride with his daughter.

"I had Mattie get me a ticket. One for her, too."

"You and Mattie?" It kept getting better and better. "Go on. Tell me what you thought."

Randall put his elbows on the desk, resting his chin on his hands. "There is a song I discovered recently. *Flowers are Red*. Do you know it?"

"Harry Chapin."

"Yes. It touched me in a way that is hard to put into words."

Ashe understood. Harry Chapin had been a master storyteller. *Flowers are Red* was a little-known gem. It told of a boy who looked at the world in a non-traditional way. But his teacher made him conform—flowers are red. Period. After years of this, he was never able to regain his spark of creativity—even when a new teacher told him it was okay to be different.

"You have a gift, Ashe. Can you forgive me for trying to make you believe that flowers can only be red?"

"None of that matters now." Ashe reached across the desk, grasping his father's hand. "You raised me to be an individual. *That* is why I had the strength to go my own way."

"Thank you, son. I don't know if I deserve that much credit, but I'd like to think you are at least partially right."

"What about the business? I'm never coming back."

Randall gave Ashe's hand another squeeze. "I always thought it was my legacy. I was wrong. A hundred years from now, nobody is going to care about how much money I accrued selling and manufacturing do-dads."

Ashe smiled. It was the first time he had heard his father make a joke about his business.

"You should be proud of what you've accomplished, Dad. The business is thriving."

"How do you know?"

"I keep track."

Ashe still watched the stock market. His father's company had grown in worth every year since he had been in charge. In such a volatile economy, that was no small feat.

"I love what I do," Randall told him. "I think your brother will do a good job when he takes over. The thing is, I won't be around to care."

"That's a fatalistic view."

"I prefer realistic." His expression sober, Randall flattened his hands onto the desk with a slap. "You, my boy, *you* are my legacy. The songs that you craft will be here forever. You've done the Mathison name proud."

Those words his father spoke disconcerted Ashe. He swallowed, searching for something to say, finding nothing. Emotions, however, he had in spades. At a loss for something deep and profound, he chose to keep it simple and from the heart.

"I love you, Dad."

"*That* is a legacy any man would envy." Randall cleared his throat, blinking several times. "I love you, Ashe. If you ever doubted that, I'm sorry. Now." This time when he slapped the desk, the sound echoed through the room. "We have some catching up to do. Tell me everything you've been up to."

"It will take a while."

"We have two hours until we have to leave for the party." Randall relaxed, crossing his arms over his chest. "Go on. And don't leave out a single detail."

Stretching out his legs, Ashe thought for a moment, then began. "The day I left home I went to the Greyhound terminal. From there I caught a bus to Chicago."

CHAPTER FIFTEEN

BELLE SMOOTHED THE skirt of her dress, waiting for Theo to get out of the car. She couldn't imagine what was taking him so long. She exchanged impatient looks with the man holding the door. Nigel had worked as a chauffeur for Theo's family for almost a quarter of a century. After all that time, he had no illusions about the heir apparent. He never spoke an unkind word, going about his job with admirable stoicism. However, Belle had noticed that, on occasions like this, he would roll his eyes.

"Theo. There are cars waiting for ours to move." Belle stuck her head in the limousine. "What is taking so long?

"I'm not feeling well."

"Fine. Nigel can take you home."

"Aren't you coming?"

Theo grabbed at Belle's hand, the nail on his index finger leaving a red trail on her skin.

"No, I'm not coming. I have on a new dress." Bought over her lunch hour with Ashe in mind. "There's a party in there, and I'm going."

Belle didn't wait for Theo's answer. She didn't understand his problem—nor did she particularly care. True, she invited herself to be his date for the evening. However, she offered to drive herself—he was the one who insisted on picking Belle up at her apartment. From the moment she entered the back of the limo, Theo had been nothing but a pain in her ass.

"You'll be bored," Theo told her before the car had pulled away from the curb. "It's a sixtieth birthday party. Old people eating old people food."

"What does that mean?"

"I don't know." Theo tugged at his shirt collar, looking uncomfortable. His tuxedo was perfectly tailored, made of the finest materials. He acted as if someone had replaced the suit with off the rack burlap.

"I thought you would be happy. Your parents are always thrilled when we go out together."

181

"Why do you care?" Theo threw back at Belle, his tone belligerent. "You are forcing me to destroy their dreams. Unless you've changed your mind about going through with the wedding?"

The privacy panel was up between them and the driver. Knowing they couldn't be overheard, Belle spoke her mind. "Your parents will survive, Theo. Give them a chance to readjust their dreams. Maybe you and Blaine can adopt. Or hire a surrogate. A little boy with your genes? That might pacify them."

"No. That would send them to an early grave."

"Then what's your plan, Theo? Stay in the closet? Find a woman willing to marry you and act as your lifelong beard?" When Theo merely shrugged, Belle slapped her forehead—she should have slapped him. "Are you actually considering such a harebrained idea? You know what? I don't care."

They had spent the rest of the ride in silence. Belle *didn't* care what Theo did. It was no longer her concern—thank the Lord. Leaving Nigel holding the door, she started up the stairs. She was almost to the Mathison's front door when her soon-to-be ex-fiancé caught up.

"This is not a good idea." Theo took out his handkerchief, wiping the perspiration from his brow.

"I won't force you to stay by my side all night." Belle smiled at the maid who greeted them. "A quick hello to your parents and we can go our separate ways."

"That might help," Theo mumbled to nobody in particular. "But I doubt it."

Shaking her head at his nonsense, Belle took two flutes of champagne from a passing waiter. Her intention was to give one to Theo. Instead, he grabbed both glasses, downing the first in one gulp. The second followed in quick succession.

"Slow down. You know your lips get loose after a few drinks."

"That's the hard stuff. Champagne makes me happy, not talkative." Signaling the waiter, Theo was soon sipping at his refill. "Happy bubbles. Why can't life be all sparkling wine and rainbows?"

"Because that would be weird?" Theo wasn't listening. With a deep sigh, Belle scanned the room. "There are your parents. Come on."

Looping her arm through Theo's, Belle crossed the room, trying hard to camouflage the fact that it was necessary for her to pull him every step of the way.

Belle said her hellos—making them short and sweet—before excusing herself. Thank goodness for the bathroom. It was the universal way to exit any uncomfortable situation gracefully. She could tell that Theo's father wanted to argue. He didn't appreciate Belle abandoning her fiancé. But what could he say? *I refuse to let you leave to empty your bladder?* Well-bred manners and the fact that, in his entire life, the man had probably never spoken to a woman about such things, were Belle's salvation.

Weaving through the crowd, Belle waved at friends and acquaintances, making certain she didn't get close enough to get waylaid. Deciding not to let herself be labeled a liar, she veered to the right and the powder room. Surprised to find it unoccupied, Belle took it as a sign that whatever deity was in charge of such things approved of her need to get away from Theo—and his parents. Not that it mattered, she thought, washing her hands. She didn't feel the slightest twinge of guilt.

Checking her hair, Belle gave herself a quick once over. The dress had been an impulse buy. She had seen it in the window of a boutique as she walked to the toy store. Giving into temptation, she stopped by during her lunch hour to see if it was as perfect as she remembered.

The satin's coppery glow complimented her skin, making it look like rich cream. The fit was loose, purposefully so, skimming her figure as opposed to hugging it. When Belle moved, the material lightly caressed her skin, making her think of Ashe and the way he touched her. Teasingly at first, then with increased purpose. The way he would touch her tonight when they snuck away to be alone.

It was a lovely thought, one that had Belle smiling as she left the bathroom. Scanning the room, she spied Ashe. Gorgeous, as usual. The man was born to wear a tuxedo. Or jeans and a t-shirt. Or nothing at all. She didn't care as long as she was around to enjoy the view.

Ashe mimed raising a drink to his lips. Nodding, she waited while he went to the bar. It took no time for him to make his way toward her, a glass in each hand.

"Hello, Ashe." Belle's smile widened when she saw he held whiskey, not champagne. The man had read her mind.

"Hello, Belle." There was something about the way Ashe said her name. The deep timbre of his voice made her skin tingle. "I saw you arrive with Theo. I somehow pictured someone less buffoon-like."

Belle was in the middle of taking a sip of her drink. She sputtered, barely stopping herself from spewing the liquid onto the floor. Which would have been a shame. The whiskey was excellent. Swallowing, she sighed as it slid smoothly down her throat."

"Theo has turned out to be more toad than Prince Charming," Belle laughed.

"You think it's funny?" From Ashe's snide tone and narrowed gray eyes, it was obvious Ashe did not.

"I stuck myself in a farcical situation." Belle touched her chin with her left hand, subtly wiggling her ring finger, making the diamond flash under the artificial light. "If I didn't laugh, you would find me in a corner, that one over there, crying my eyes out."

"Want a suggestion?"

Looking around to see who might be listening, Belle lowered her voice. "If it involves dumping the ring, then no. You *know* I've already dumped Theo."

"Not to my satisfaction." Ashe's eyes stayed on Belle's face, never slipping to the gaudy piece of jewelry. She knew he hated it—almost as much as she did. Doing them both a favor, he changed the subject. "Would you like to dance?"

"Really?" Most of the men she knew had to be half drunk before they would even consider getting out on a dance floor.

"It's the only way I can publicly hold you in my arms." Ashe motioned for Belle to proceed him.

The dining area had been cleared of the antique table and chairs. The sideboard which had been in the family for generations was now in the library behind a locked door. Empty, the room made a perfectly acceptable dance floor. Several couples were taking advantage of the trio of musicians set up on the patio. Because of their proximity—and with the aid of speakers—the music drifted pleasantly through the house.

Belle smiled when she saw Georgia and her husband swaying together to a romantic song with a nice slow tempo. The look Ashe's sister sent her wasn't exactly cool, but it wasn't as warm as Belle expected.

"Did I do something to offend Georgia?"

Ashe shook his head, drawing Belle into his arms. "She's worried that my interest in you is too... *interested*."

Thinking through yesterday afternoon's visit, Belle couldn't think of anything she and Ashe had done that would draw unwanted attention. "I thought we were perfectly circumspect."

"According to my sister, I couldn't take my eyes off you." Ashe's hand settled at the base of her spine, guiding Belle with ease, pulling her a little closer. "She was right. Though I did my best to deflect her accusations."

The sound of Ashe's voice, the feel of his body swaying against hers. It was a heady combination. Belle closed her eyes and simply let herself enjoy.

"Accusations?" The urge to rest her cheek on Ashe's shoulder almost got the better of Belle. Remembering where they were, she kept her head held high. "What does Georgia think we're doing?"

"Nothing close to the truth," Ashe teased, his laugh low and intimate. "And it is *me*, not *we* that she has a problem with. I assured her that I *do not* seduce engaged women."

There was so much Belle could have said. Though she hadn't admitted it to Ashe, she needed to be honest with herself. She had been the seducer. For all his experience—and her lack of it—Belle was the one who came on to him that night in Los Angeles. She knew what she was doing. At the time, she was an officially engaged woman—a fact she kept from Ashe. There was no way around it. A perfect storm of nostalgia, opportunity, and desire had converged. Belle grabbed the moment. Given the chance, she would do it again—with no regrets. Not now. Not ever.

The music changed to something more up tempo. As the couples around them moved accordingly, Belle threw caution to the wind. She didn't protest when Ashe drew her closer, their bodies gently moving to their own beat. She was past caring. She didn't owe Theo—or anybody else—special consideration. With a contented sigh, she smiled. If people wanted to talk, let them.

"I meant to ask. How did things go with your father?"

Because Belle's hand rested on Ashe's chest, she felt more than heard his deep sigh. The smile that lifted his lips and warmed his eyes was impossible to miss.

"Beyond anything I let myself hope for."

They danced, Belle losing track of the change in songs or how many dancers came and went. She was too busy listening to Ashe. He told her everything from the moment he entered the Mathison building. His encounter with his young fans made her laugh. The reunion with his father brought tears to her eyes.

"Dad blew me away." There was a touch of wonder in Ashe's voice. "It makes me angry with myself for not trying to reconnect sooner."

"I truly believe that most things happen in their own time." Belle squeezed Ashe's hand. "Your father wasn't ready. Neither were you. If you had pushed too soon. A year ago or two, it might have ended disastrously, making today impossible. *This* was *the* perfect time."

Ashe didn't kiss her temple, but the warmth of his breath brushed Belle's skin, sending a pleasant tingle through her body.

"Thank you, Belle. That was perfectly put. Would you mind repeating it to my father?"

Surprised—and flattered—Belle hesitated. She barely knew the man. For whatever reason, the Richards and Mathison families didn't socialize. It would be strange saying something so personal to a man she hadn't spoken to more than a handful of times.

"I think it would be better coming from you," she told Ashe. "However, if you want to tell him it came from me that would be fine."

"I'll do that."

They settled into a contented silence. How long they would have stayed on the dance floor—in each other's arms—Belle couldn't say. Before they could find out, there was a tap on Ashe's shoulder.

186

"Sorry to interrupt." Georgia's tone—and expression—said the opposite. "Didn't you have a special gift you wanted to give Dad before we bring in the cake?"

"It was your idea. I agreed—reluctantly. But thanks for the reminder."

"No problem," Georgia said with a tight smile. "I wasn't sure you were aware of how much time had passed. Or how much attention you had garnered."

Ashe exchanged telling looks with his sister. The message that passed between them wasn't difficult for Belle to read. Georgia was asking Ashe what he was doing. Ashe answered with a definitive mind your own business.

"I'm used to people looking at me." Ashe's tone was cool, his gaze direct. "I rarely notice anymore."

"But Belle isn't."

"Belle is—"

"Right here." Belle refused to let Ashe and Georgia talk as if she wasn't in the room. "I understand what you're saying, Georgia. I think it's time I caught up with my fiancé."

"You don't have to go, Belle."

"You're right." Belle's eyes met Ashe's, aware that Georgia hung on every word. "I don't *have* to do anything. I make my own decisions."

"And?" Ashe knew the answer. The words she spoke were for Georgia's benefit. Belle humored him since it seemed important.

"I made my choice some time ago. Meeting you again simply cemented what I already knew."

"What does that mean?"

Belle heard Georgia's question as she started toward the exit. Neither she nor Ashe could see the upward curve of her lips when he answered.

"Hell if I know."

Leave it to Ashe to make Belle laugh—whether or not that was his intention. She was still chuckling to herself when she spotted Theo across the room. With him was a dark-haired man several inches shorter with a slight build. Their voices didn't carry, but it was obvious from their faces and the gestures Theo made with his hands that the conversation was heated—enough to draw the attention of several party-goers.

Belle didn't need psychic powers to figure out the identity of Theo's companion. It had to be Blaine. Part of her wanted to keep walking. It would have been easier to pretend she didn't see what the others in the room couldn't ignore. When Theo's raised voice reached her, Belle sighed, changing directions.

"There you are." Belle smiled brightly, making certain she could be heard by more than Theo and Blaine. She took her fiancé's arm in what she hoped came across as an affectionate gesture. "Are you enjoying the party?"

Blaine blinked when he realized the question was directed at him. The animosity in his eyes made Belle wonder if he was going to answer. Theo—smart enough to understand Belle's purpose—spoke through gritted teeth.

"Answer, you idiot. And smile. This isn't a funeral."

"Not yet," Blaine muttered, then seeing the way Theo stiffened, gave in. His smile wasn't the least bit genuine, but it was there, his lips barely moving as he spoke, his voice laced with a distinctive Southern twang. "The champagne is first rate."

"My father always says, the secret to a good party is the quality—and quantity—of the alcohol."

Theo laughed, nodding his head. Blaine's eyes narrowed, fixed on his lover.

"I see your mother and father trying to get our attention." It was a lie. She didn't know where Theo's parents were. However, it was the best exit line she could think of.

"Right." Theo seemed relieved. "It was nice seeing you again, Blaine."

"Don't you dare leave with that woman," Blaine hissed under his breath.

When had she become, *that woman,* Belle wondered. For all intents and purposes, she was out of the picture. An illusion of a fiancé.

If Theo was dragging his feet where Blaine was concerned, it had nothing to do with her.

Without another word, Theo walked away, Belle at his side. He tried to steer them toward the open bar. Belle propelled in the opposite direction. From the fumes wafting off him, the last thing Theo needed was another drink. Taking his hand, she pulled him through the open French doors into the cool night air. She didn't stop until they were in a deserted part of the garden, away from prying eyes.

"Thank you, Belle." Closing his eyes, Theo took a deep breath. When he started to sway, he quickly took a seat on a nearby wrought-iron bench. "Blaine isn't normally—"

"I don't care, Theo."

Frowning, Theo shook his head. "You didn't let me finish. Blaine—"

"Listen to me." Belle took a seat next to Theo. Grabbing his shoulders, she gave him a firm shake. "I don't care because this is the end. The end of our fake engagement, the end of us. Period."

"No, that's not right. There's more than a week left in our agreement."

When he whined, Belle wanted to do more than shake Theo. She moved her hands to her side before she slapped him—hard. "Face the facts. I spent most of the evening in the arms of another man. You spent it with your boyfriend. That says it all. First thing in the morning, I'm telling my parents that there will be no wedding."

"Belle—Wait. You were with another man? Who?"

"It doesn't matter." Theo never seemed to grasp the main point. "The fact that there is a man—for either of us—tells the whole story. Two weeks or two years, you were never going to willingly go to your parents. It might not feel like it, but I'm doing you a favor."

"A favor?" Theo's mouth thinned. "More like a kick in the nuts."

"The day I said yes to your marriage proposal, we were friends. At the moment, I don't know what to call us." Belle tilted her head until Theo looked her in the eye. "Do me a favor, walk away with grace while there is still a bit of affection left."

"You can take your affection and shove it up your ass." Theo lurched to his feet. "My world is nothing but rubble as far as the eye can see. And you're the reason. Hurricane Belle."

Belle scoffed. "If that's the rationale you need to make yourself feel better, go for it."

"Fuck you."

Theo staggered into the garden, trampling on a bed of hydrangeas. Watching him go, Belle felt more sympathy for the flowers than for her absolutely, positively, no doubt about it, ex-fiancé.

Taking a minute before returning to the party, Belle looked at her hand. *Well, crap.* She forgot to give Theo back the ring. Since he hadn't consulted her before making the purchase, it was more his taste than hers. Big might be better, but if the day ever came when the man she loved put a ring on her finger, she wanted something less gaudy. Something with character.

Slipping the ring off her finger, Belle dropped it into her purse. Another engagement? What was wrong with her? It was the last thing that should cross her mind. However, she *was* human. Belle knew one thing for certain. This time, it would be for love. She knew the man she wanted. She knew her heart was his for the asking. The question was, would he ever care that much about her? If he didn't, it was hard for Belle to imagine loving somebody else. It seemed her feelings—once fixed—were true blue.

Damn Ashe Mathison. It started as a crush with all the intensity only a teenage girl could harbor. Next came lust. It was mutual and easy. Though not so easily satisfied. Somehow—when she wasn't paying attention—love crept in. It seemed she was back where she started. Her crush had lingered for years—too many years—unrequited. Would the love she felt for Ashe suffer the same fate?

Shaking off her inner turmoil, Belle entered the house. Stopping, Belle noticed a buzz of energy in the room. Around her, the guests huddled in groups, speaking in excited whispers.

Before Belle could ask what was happening, Georgia stepped to the middle of the room carrying a microphone.

190

"I want to thank all of you for joining my family to help us celebrate a very important day. My father's birthday." There was a polite round of applause. This was what had the crowd buzzing? Belle didn't think so. "As many of you know, my brother Ashe is with us for the first time in quite a while."

There it was, Belle thought, grinning when a woman who had to be twice Ashe's age giggled. Not that she was alone. All around, sophisticated society matrons morphed into zealous fangirls. She couldn't wait to see what they did next. Faint from the thrill of it all? Scream Ashe's name? Belle waited with baited breath. After her encounter with Theo, she deserved some entertainment.

"We planned a surprise, but it seems most of you already know about it."

"Ashe Mathison is going to sing." The excited whisper came from behind Belle. "Can you believe it? My sister will die of envy when I tell her."

The woman sounded like she looked forward to her sibling's demise. Belle shook her head. *Charming*.

"As a special present for our father's sixtieth birthday, my brother has agreed to sing a song he wrote." Georgia beamed with pride as Ashe came into view. In one hand, he carried a well-worn acoustic guitar. In the other, a chair. "Ladies. Gentleman. And especially, Dad. I give you Ashe Mathison."

Kissing Georgia's cheek, he acknowledged the wildly enthusiastic round of applause with a wave. Ashe set down the chair, taking a seat in front of an empty microphone stand.

"Whoops." Laughing, Georgie hurried to replace the microphone she still had in her hand. "Sorry."

"Dad?" Ashe strummed a few chords, checking that the guitar was tuned.

"Right here, son." Randall Mathison called out. Belle could see him standing to the side, only a few feet from Ashe.

"This song was featured on *The Ryder Hart Band's* second album." Ashe looked at his father, smiling. "I wish Ryder were here to do it justice, but you're stuck with me."

"I wouldn't have it any other way."

"He has to say that," Ashe told the crowd. "We're related."

It wasn't a great joke, but it garnered the expected round of laughs. They quickly died down when Ashe began to play. From the first note, he had them in the palm of his hand. If he had chosen to play *Mary Had a Little Lamb*, nobody would have complained.

A love song. Not from a man to a woman, but a son to his father. Simple. Eloquent. Emotional. As it came to a close, there were tears on more than one set of cheeks—including Randall Mathison's. Ashe didn't go to his father. He simply held his gaze and nodded.

Belle took a tissue from her purse, dabbing at her eyes. She watched as Ashe made a quick exit. *Smart*, Belle thought. Another minute and he would have been surrounded. After that, who knew when he would get away?

"Excuse me. Ms. Richards?"

Belle turned. The young man wore a black vest and white shirt, identifying him as one of the serving staff.

"Yes?"

"I was asked to give you this."

He handed Belle a piece of paper, leaving before she could ask who it was from. Puzzled, she opened the note.

Meet me at the gazebo in ten minutes. I'm in the mood for a little necking. You won't be able to miss me. I'll be the one with the guitar.

Laughing, Belle tucked the note into her purse. With all the attention still focused on the front of the room, she easily slipped outside without notice. She started down a well-lit path, her mind on her rendezvous with Ashe. But before she could take more than a few steps, a hand covered her mouth. Another hand grabbed her arm, pulling her from the lit path into the shadows, fingers digging into her flesh.

Belle struggled, briefly knocking away his hand. The second her mouth was free, she screamed as loudly as possible. The hand returned but not before hitting Belle on the side of the head. The blow was hard enough to rattle her teeth.

"If you scream again, I swear I'll kill you where you stand."

192

Belle sucked in her breath. Though she had only heard it once before, she immediately recognized the voice laced with a distinctive Southern twang.

"Move it, bitch." Keeping his hand over her mouth, Blaine dragged Belle across the lawn. "I tried to scare you off, but you were determined to keep your claws in Theo." His next words sent a chill down Belle's spine. "If he can't get rid of you, I will."

CHAPTER SIXTEEN

BELLE'S MIND RACED. Theo's Blaine. Why would he care about getting her out of the way? As of tonight, their engagement was over for good. Even if Blaine hadn't heard, he must know about her agreement with Theo. Unless—

Theo hadn't told Blaine.

It was the only explanation. But she couldn't worry about that. Her pressing concern was how to stop Theo's boyfriend from taking her farther into the garden and away from help. Belle searched her memory for anything and everything that would help her get away. Her hands weren't tied. Fingernails could be a weapon. As could the spiked heels on her shoes.

"I can't get rid of you here. Too close to Theo. How would the bitch like a nice long ride in the trunk of my car?"

Blaine seemed to be talking to himself. But his words galvanized Belle. One thing she knew for certain. If she let him put her in that car, she was not coming back alive. Forming a plan, Belle knew she had one shot. Blaine didn't expect her to fight back. That gave her a small advantage. But her biggest weapon was her will to live. Not matter what, she would bite, scratch, and scream to her last breath.

Luck played into Belle's plan. That and a stray cat who chose that moment to streak across the lawn, right into Blaine's path. Already jumpy, he tripped, loosening his hold on Belle. She knew it was now or never.

Digging her nails into his hand, simultaneously Belle raised her foot. With all her might, she brought the heel of her shoe down on his instep. It was enough to break Blaine's hold. As he staggered, Belle rushed forward, leading with her shoulder. With one hard shove, she sent him sprawling into a bed of roses.

Belle didn't wait to see the results. Refusing to be one of those movie victims running like an idiot in high heels, she took just enough time to pull off her shoes. Barefoot, she ran like hell, screaming for help.

ASHE CHECKED HIS watch. He was three minutes late. Not too bad considering. Getting away hadn't been as simple as he anticipated. Who would have guessed the band would have so many fans in this kind of crowd? It just went to prove music knew no boundaries. Any other time, Ashe would have gladly stayed to chat, sign autographs, and take pictures— or all of the above.

Belle was waiting. That superseded anything else. Getting away looked like it was going to be problematic. To his happy surprise, his father turned out to be the solution.

"Want to get away?" Randall asked. The enthusiastic audience hadn't descended on Ashe, but there were rumblings. Any second and the push would begin.

"How did you guess?" Ashe looked right, then left. They were boxed in. Escape seemed impossible.

"Father's intuition?" Randall laughed when Ashe sent him a skeptical look. "I saw you dancing with Belle Richards. And noticed you slip a note to one of the waiters. I can do the math."

Ashe shook his head in admiration. The old man was as eagle eyed as ever.

"Her engagement is a sham." Now that they were reconciled, Ashe didn't want to start out with his father thinking poorly of him.

"Good. I had quite the thing for her mother. Unfortunately, Penelope was in love with Belle's father." Randall sighed at the memory. "But that's a story best left in the past. Head down the hall to my office and slip out the window. You don't want to keep the lady waiting."

Bemused—and grateful—Ashe grabbed his guitar, following his father's instructions. *Belle's mother*? It had always been obvious that Randall and Bonita's marriage was far from a love match. They rubbed along well enough. But this revelation explained a lot. Not that Ashe blamed his father. If Penelope Richards was even a fraction as alluring as her daughter, how could he *not* fall for her?

It was easy to forget that his father was once Ashe's age, filled with desire and need. And it was sad to think he spent most of his life living next door to the woman he could never have. It explained why the families weren't friendly.

Ashe hurried along the path to the gazebo. He didn't want to keep Belle waiting any longer than necessary. His father had missed out on love. He wasn't going to take any chances on it slipping through his fingers.

Jogging the last few yards, Ashe took the gazebo steps two at a time. Ready with an apology, it died on his lips when he found himself alone. He was certain Belle would be here. Perhaps she was delayed by a friend. Or Theo. That wasn't a pleasant thought.

Ashe took a seat. He would give Belle five minutes before he went searching. Taking his guitar, he absently plucked at the strings. Music and moonlight. It was a cliché for a reason. Because it worked. Ashe didn't care if he rushed their relationship. Tonight, he would let Belle know how he felt. If she needed more time, he could live with that.

There was no way in hell Ashe would go back to Los Angeles without putting all his cards on the table. He had no doubts. Belle was his future.

Too impatient to sit, Ashe set his guitar aside. Getting to his feet, he stretched his arms over his head, breathing in the fresh air. That was when he heard the scream.

"Help! Please! Help me!"

Belle. Ashe didn't bother with the gazebo steps. He jumped over the rail, heading in the direction of her voice. Panic added to the surge of adrenaline.

"Belle!" Ashe stopped, listening. "Belle! Where are you?"

"Ashe?" Belle came into view, her hair a wild mess, her clothing torn. Without slowing down, she launched herself into his arms. "Thank God."

Ashe held her tight, burying his face in her neck.

"We need to get help. He's still out there."

"Who?" Ashe turned, his body shielding Belle. "What happened? Are you okay?"

"I'm fine. At least I think I am." Belle's gaze darted toward the dark. "Do you have your phone? I dropped my purse near the house. Call the police. Now."

Belle's word came out in a rush, but her words were clear. Without hesitation, Ashe dialed 911.

"Can you talk to them? I don't know what to say."

Hand shaking, Belle took the phone. Ashe pulled her into the circle of his arms.

"Yes. My name is Belle Richards. I was attacked. Blaine... I don't know his last name. I was able to get away." *Jesus*, Ashe thought. "I shoved him into a rose bed and ran. The address? I..."

After everything Belle had been through, Ashe wasn't surprised when she drew a blank. Gently, he pried the phone from her fingers, then rattled off the address.

"There's a large party in progress. It might be best if the police came to the back entrance."

"Stay on the phone. There is a patrol car in your area. It should be there in a few minutes."

All Ashe wanted to do was get Belle into the house where he could take care of her. Her entire body shook, her arms felt like ice. He lifted her in his arms, following the lit path, his long strides eating up the distance. Ideally, he would have avoided the patio, but it was the fastest way of getting Belle out of the night air. At least a dozen people milled about, drinks in hand, laughing and talking, blissfully unaware that anything was amiss.

Randall was the first to notice Ashe and Belle.

"What happened?" He rushed forward.

"Belle was attacked." There were several gasps. "We called the police but—"

197

The incomprehensible yell of a crazy man filled the air. Blaine, his face and hands scratched and bleeding, rushed onto the patio. There was murder in his eyes, and Belle was his target. Ashe didn't think twice. He handed Belle to his father. Making a fist and leading with his shoulder, he stopped the man in his tracks with one mighty punch.

Blaine crumpled to the ground into a heap. The sound of police sirens filled the air as the patio filled with curious party-goers.

"Nice job, son," Randall said, transferring Belle back to Ashe.

Ashe was aware of the raised phones. Pictures and videos would soon fill the internet. He didn't give a damn. All he cared about was the woman in his arms.

"Can you take care of this?" he asked his father.

"Go. Find a room and lock the door."

Grateful beyond words, Ashe moved through the crowd. He looked down at Belle. She didn't cower or cry. His woman was tougher than that.

"I can walk," Belle informed him, firmly, though her arms didn't move from around his neck.

"I want to carry you. Do you have a problem with that?"

"Nope." With a sigh, Belle laid her head on Ashe's shoulder.

They were almost inside when Theo blindly rushed by, knocking into Ashe in his haste.

"Blaine?" Theo sobbed, dropping to his knees. He grabbed the unconscious man's hand. "What did she do to you?"

"Me?" Ashe felt Belle stiffen. He tightened his grip, worried she might jump from his arms. Instead, she let out an exasperated sigh. "I was engaged to that idiot. What was I thinking?"

"Beats me, sweetheart," Ashe said with feeling. "Beats me."

BELLE SPENT THE next three days handling the aftermath. For her, that mainly involved answering a lot of questions, filling out an official police report, and dealing with her family. Not surprisingly, her father wasn't the least bit upset about the broken engagement. Having her ex-fiancé's boyfriend try to kill his daughter tended to put things like that into perspective.

Letting others fuss over her was nice—for about half a day. After that, Belle kissed her parents, hugged her siblings, then gently—but firmly—pushed them out the door.

"They mean well."

Belle snuggled closer to Ashe. She couldn't get enough of having his arms around her. That wasn't a problem. He hadn't left her side. She knew it couldn't last, but for now, he seemed unwilling to let her out of his sight. Belle was not complaining.

"I love my family. I'm grateful that they love me. But enough was enough. This apartment isn't big enough for all that hovering."

"I hover. Do you want me to go?"

"Absolutely not. You do it just right."

"Good." Ashe kissed the top of her head.

"Would you have gone if I asked?"

Heart pounding, Belle waited for his answer.

"Absolutely not."

Able to breathe again, Belle took Ashe's hand, drawing it to her chest until it rested just above her heart. This was where she needed to be. In her home. With Ashe. Thanks to Tracy, her kitchen was freshly stocked—as was her liquor cabinet. There was no reason for them to budge from the apartment. Except for one thing.

"When do you have to go back?"

"Day after tomorrow. The band has already rescheduled two recording sessions. I can't ask them to do it again."

Belle appreciated Ashe's honesty. She knew he couldn't stay—not permanently. It wouldn't be fair to ask. But she wanted to. More than anything.

"Come with me."

"What?" Belle hadn't expected that. "You want me to go with you to Los Angeles?"

"Yes, I—"

A loud buzz interrupted Ashe. The first day, the entrance to her building had been jammed with reporters trying to get a story. *Ashe Mathison Thwarts Killer*. It was big news. Huge. The headline had blown up the internet. Ashe made it a point of telling his friends that Belle saved herself. His actions came much later.

Ashe stressed that fact to the band's manager. The official press release stressed her heroism—not his. The world didn't seem to care. Ashe was the famous rock star. He was the world's point of interest. Though he raged at the injustice, Belle was more than happy that the spotlight was on him.

As far as Belle was concerned, the fewer people who knew her name and face, the better.

After complaints from the other tenants, Ashe hired around-the-clock security to keep the entrance clear of reporters and rubberneckers. If someone wasn't on the guard's list, he didn't get through.

"I better get that." Belle reluctantly left the sofa. "If it's Mom or Dad, they will never forgive me for not letting them up."

"Let me."

"Ashe—"

"Belle," Ashe teasingly mocked, moving her away from the intercom.

"The time will come when I have to answer that for myself." Belle didn't add, *when you're gone*. There was no need.

Ashe raised an eyebrow, waiting until she returned to the sofa. With an exaggerated huff, Belle plopped down on the cushion. With a satisfied nod, he pushed the button.

"Yes?"

"Mr. Mathison? This is Jamison."

The security guards always identified themselves by name.

200

"Is there a problem?"

"No, sir. There's a man asking to see Ms. Richards. He isn't on the list but—"

"Belle?" The man in question yelled out, effectively circumventing the guard. Let me up. It's Theo."

"You have got to be kidding me." Incredulous, Ashe turned to Belle. "Should I tell Jamison to kick the idiot's ass down the stairs?"

It was tempting. From what Belle had been able to figure out, Theo was a big part of his boyfriend's meltdown. Not that anything excused attempted murder. However, there were some holes that Belle needed him to fill in. With Ashe by her side—and a burly security guard just a call away—she felt talking to Theo one last time might help her peace of mind.

"Let him come up."

"Are you sure?"

"No. But do it anyway."

Belle crossed her legs and waited. She knew how she looked. Exactly like a woman who was hunkered down in her apartment with no intention of leaving anytime soon. That morning, she had taken a shower. Brushed her hair and her teeth. Added a bit of moisturizer to her face. That was it in terms of grooming. She wore her most comfortable jeans and a long-sleeved t-shirt. Ashe was dressed in a similar fashion. Since Belle had no intention of entertaining, she dressed for comfort—not style.

Theo was not a guest. On their best days, she rarely worried about how she looked. Today, she couldn't have cared less.

The knock on the door was tentative. When Ashe answered, Theo had the good sense to hesitate before crossing the threshold.

"Belle?" Tentatively, Theo peeked into the apartment.

"Come in, Theo." The man had been there less than thirty seconds and already he tried her nerves.

If Belle and Ashe were the epitome of stay-at-home casual, Theo looked as if he was going to high tea at Buckingham Palace. Custom-made suit, matching tie, Italian leather shoes buffed to a high-gloss shine. It was an impressive ensemble. If Belle was his target, he had missed the mark by a mile.

"You look—" Theo searched for the right word. "Well."

"What do you want?" Belle's patience was on a short leash. Ashe sat, taking her hand. She didn't ask Theo to sit. Her lack of invitation didn't stop him.

"My father decided not to disown me."

"Okay."

By the look on his face, Theo had expected a more enthusiastic response. He blinked in surprise before continuing.

"In exchange, I am expected to attend a reorientation boot camp."

"What is that?" Belle couldn't help herself—she had to ask.

"According to the brochure, after ten intensive weeks, I will no longer be gay."

That's what Belle got for giving into curiosity. One more example of how crazy people could be.

"I hope you told your father where to stick his boot camp."

"No. I plan to. If you'll help me."

Belle should have known. Theo wasn't here to apologize. Or inquire about how she was doing. He wanted something. Some things never changed.

"Your father won't listen to me."

"My father won't listen to anybody."

"What do you want?" Ashe hadn't spoken until now. The sound of his voice made Theo jump.

"Is it necessary for him to be here?"

"Yes." Belle and Ashe spoke as one.

"Fine." Rubbing his hands on his pants, Theo sighed. "I have the money my grandmother left me. It's only five million."

"Dollars?" Belle exclaimed, exchanging stunned looks with Ashe.

"It may sound like a lot, but it has to last us a long time. I want to leave Boston. Start over. Maybe in Europe. With my inheritance and the money from selling your engagement ring, we should do okay. With time, I hope my father will come around."

"Starting over is a good idea," Belle agreed. "I only have one question. Who are you taking with you?"

"Blaine." Theo stuck out his chin defiantly.

"Is he delusional?" Ashe asked. Belle shrugged.

"You understand that Blaine is in prison. For attempted murder."

"You don't know that he would have gone through with it."

"Yes. I do."

"Besides." Theo rushed ahead as if Belle hadn't spoken. "It's your word against his. Nobody saw what happened."

"A security camera caught him grabbing me and dragging me away. The police have seen the footage, Theo."

"That's unfortunate."

"Unfortunate?" Belle stopped Ashe from jumping to his feet. "You need to leave. Now."

"Belle." Theo sent her a pleading look. "If you drop the charges, they can't hold him."

"Then you and Blaine will disappear, to never again darken my doorstep?"

Theo's eyes lit with hope. "That's right. I promise."

"Are you crazy?" One of them was. Belle's bet was on Theo. "It's not going to happen. Blaine is staying in jail. Hopefully for a long time. I wish I could press charges against you."

"Me? What did I do?"

"You made Blaine believe that I was keeping the two of you apart. That I wouldn't break the engagement. Do you deny that?"

"No. But—"

"Your boyfriend has serious mental problems."

"I couldn't anticipate what he was going to do," Theo whined. "The car and the cat were one thing. He—"

"I knew it!" This time it was Ashe who anchored Belle to the sofa. "Why didn't you tell me what he had done?"

"I didn't want to get him in trouble." Sweat had popped out on Theo's upper lip. From the look of him, he was close to tears. "He kept pressuring me to tell my father that I was gay. It was easier to make you the bad guy."

"You knew he was unstable. Yet you continued to push all his buttons until he went from mildly psychotic to full-fledged whack job." One more minute and Belle wouldn't be responsible for her actions. "Get out!"

"But, Belle—"

"Now, Theo. Never come back. Never."

"You heard her." Ashe grabbed Theo by his perfectly pressed collar, hauling him to the door.

Before Ashe could throw him out, Theo grabbed the door frame. "What about the engagement ring?

"I sold it. I needed the money to help fund *Strive*."

"That ridiculous pet project of yours?" Theo's eyes almost bugged out of his head. "The ring cost seven hundred and fifty thousand dollars."

"I know." Belle smiled smugly. "Thank your father for me."

Applying his foot firmly to Theo's backside, Ashe finished putting out the trash.

"I'm glad I was here to see Theo's face when you dropped the ring bombshell."

"It feels good to know that gaudy piece of crap will help so many women. It almost makes the engagement worth it."

"The hell you say." Ashe stretched out on the sofa, maneuvering until he was on his back, Belle tucked under his arm.

"*Almost*." This was nice. Better than nice. Here, with Ashe, the world was a hazy blip. Theo a distant memory. Belle didn't know if perfection existed. But this was close enough for her.

"I love you."

Belle gasped. There was her answer. Ashe loved her. Perfection *did* exist.

"It took you long enough."

"Thirty-nine days is too long?"

"I've loved you since I was a teenager. A very young teenager."

"I didn't realize this was a contest." Ashe grinned. "Okay. You win. Wait." He moved to his side, sliding down the sofa until he and Belle were face to face. "You love me?"

"Yes."

"Say the words, Belle."

Belle cupped his face with her hand, her gaze unwavering. "I love you, Ashe Mathison. In one way or another, I always have. I guess that makes me a one-man woman."

"One man. One woman." Ashe brushed his lips across hers. "For the rest of our lives."

"That sounded like a statement, not a question."

"Not a statement. Or a question. It's bona fide, set in stone fact. I love you, Belle. Get used to it."

Belle rolled onto Ashe, her body blanketing his. So handsome. So strong. He was hers.

"Say it again."

"I love you."

Belle touched her lips to his. A sweet kiss quickly turning hot, she moaned when Ashe's hands began an intimate exploration. Up her thighs. Cupping her butt. At the small of her back, teasing the sensitive skin as his fingers traveled up her spine, slipping around to her breasts.

Slipping into a fog of pleasure, Belle protested when Ashe's touch suddenly vanished.

"Hey," Belle complained, reaching for Ashe as he moved from the sofa to his feet. "Things were just getting interesting."

"Which is why we're moving to the bedroom." Ashe lifted her. "Any objections?"

"Can I expect more of this?" Belle rained kisses over Ashe's face. "For the rest of my life?"

"Most of it. There may come a time—many, many years down the road—when you may have to settle for walking to bed. Hand in hand. How does that sound?"

Belle was in love. And loved in return. How did it sound? She put her lips close to Ashe's ear, whispering her one-word answer.

"Perfect."

EPILOGUE

"IF THINGS PROGRESS at the same rate, we will see a profit within the year."

Belle waited for the punchline. When none came, she grabbed Mahalia Blanc in her arms, dancing a jig around the office. Out of breath, the head accountant for *Strive* fell into the chair behind her desk.

"A small profit." Mahalia laughed as Belle continued to celebrate by pumping her fists into the air *Rocky* style. Sylvester Stallone in his prime had nothing on her boss.

"I don't care if it's only a penny." Belle didn't sit in a chair. As was her usual practice, she sat on the edge of Mahalia's desk. "Scratch that. I hope it's more, but a profit of any kind will be a huge victory."

Strive had been up and running for six months. With the money Belle's father had provided, some substantial donations, and the sale of Theo's engagement ring, the company had a strong start-up base. But the reason they were doing so well was for one reason. The hard work of her staff and the women who produced the products they sold online. Belle was so proud she felt like bursting.

"If I may make a suggestion, Madam President?"

It had taken some time, but Belle was finally getting used to her new title.

"You know I value your opinion."

"Go home early—for once. Go out to dinner. Have a nice bottle of wine. And stay out of the kitchen." Mahalia patted her well-padded hips. "If you bring any more goodies into the office, I may sue for abuse by baked goods."

Mahalia had become a good friend. Then there was Pru—her right-hand woman. Between finding office space, hiring a staff, and the general headaches involved with starting a business, Belle didn't know what she would have done without them.

"You know that cooking relaxes me," Belle said. "But not tonight. I think I will take your advice. If I can talk a certain man into joining me."

"When has he ever turned you down?"

Smiling, Belle walked to her office. She had her phone out and dialing before she shut the door.

"Belle." Ashe answered on the second ring. "Perfect timing. We just finished rehearsals."

The decision to move to Los Angeles had been an easy one for Belle. Her father had been disappointed when she handed in her resignation, but she left with his blessing. Boston had always been her home. She would miss it—and her family. But making a fresh start felt right. The fact that Tracy followed close behind made the transition that much easier for Belle. Her best friend was tired of the New England winters. Besides, she had run through all the decent men in Boston.

Then there was Ashe. He was based in Los Angeles. She could start her business anywhere. Why not in the same city as the man she loved?

"What are the chances I can talk you into dining out? My treat."

"That depends. What's on the menu for dessert?"

"Let me see." Belle pretended to mull over his question. "Me?"

"My favorite." Ashe's voice had lowered, sending tingles of anticipation across Belle's skin. "When are you leaving the office?"

"I'm out the door."

"Then I'll see you at home." Ashe's downtown condo was now *their* home. "And Belle?"

Belle knew what was coming, but that didn't temper the thrill of anticipation. She was certain it never would.

"Yes?" she whispered.

"I love you."

"I love you too. Drive safe."

"With you waiting to greet me? I would be a fool not to."

Ashe was no fool. Neither was Belle. She finally had the man of her dreams. And she was never letting go.

COMING SOON

*<u>Flowers for Zoe (Hart of Rock and
Roll Book Four)</u>*

AFTER THE RAIN

(One Pass Away Book One)

PROLOGUE

LOGAN. LOGAN. LOGAN.

Logan Price closed his eyes, taking it all in.

"Hear that, kid?" Starting quarterback Gaige Benson slapped him on the back. "Two games under your belt and you're a star. Now let's go out there and add super to the front of it."

The announcer for the team set them in motion down the tunnel with his familiar introduction.

"And now, let's hear it for your division champion SEATTLE KNIGHTS."

The roar of the crowd. There was nothing like it. A packed stadium. Fans chanting his name. Few people would ever experience what it was like to take the field in a professional football game.

Logan Price had been working for this his entire life. He could still remember in exact detail the first game he ever saw. Too small to climb onto the stool in his father's bar by himself, his old man had lifted him onto the seat.

Stay and be quiet.

Not an easy order to follow for an active, inquisitive little boy. One look at the game and for once, Logan had no problem following his father's command. The old TV transported him to a foreign world filled with bright lights and shiny helmeted warriors. Logan didn't know what he was watching. He did know he wanted to be one of those men.

A Sunday afternoon in rural Oklahoma. Lefty's Pub was filled with after-church drinkers who figured they had done their duty to God and family. The rest of the day was their time. A beer. Or two. Or six. Cronies who understood a man's need to unwind before the start of another workweek.

And football.

If the Friday night high school game was their true religion, the Sunday afternoon games were a close second. As Oklahoma boys, they hated anything Texas. The men of Denville gathered every week to root for whichever team was playing the Dallas Cowboys.

No matter how the games ended. Whether the crowd was happy or disgruntled. It meant more drinking. Hours later, husbands, boyfriends, and sons would stumble out, pile into beat-up trucks, and weave their way home to frustrated wives, girlfriends, and mothers.

As he grew older, Logan's view changed. He moved from the stool to behind the bar. And he promised himself one thing. He would never become one of those men. He wouldn't spend the week at a job he hated. His home wouldn't be a semi-wide trailer filled with hand-me-down furniture and a wife to whom he couldn't face going home.

His Sundays were going to be spent playing football, not watching it.

"Ready to take down this vaunted Arizona defense?" Gaige yelled at him, butting helmets.

Vaunted. Good word, Logan thought. His QB liked to use what his granny called highfalutin talk. Must have been that Ivy League education. He knew that Gaige Benson didn't grow up with a silver spoon in his mouth. He came from the mean streets of Brooklyn. He had the scars to prove it.

Like Logan, Gaige had vowed to get out of the life into which he was born. In the process, he polished himself up like a new penny. He took advantage of his full-ride scholarship to Yale. He didn't spend all his time on the football field. Fancy vocabulary. Fancy clothes. Fancy women. They were all part of the package Gaige purposefully fashioned for himself.

Seventeen years after clawing his way out of the tenement that he grew up in, very little of that borough-rat remained. Until game time. No one was tougher than Gaige Benson. Three-time league MVP. Considered one of the best ever to play the game. No one stood in his way when he was playing the game. He had the scars to prove it.

"Gather round."

Knights head coach Harry Coleman gathered the team close. He had to yell over the crowd, but he had the voice to do it. Booming was putting it mildly. The first time Logan heard it, he stood right beside the man. The ringing in his ears didn't go away for three days.

"Divisional game. If I have to say any more than that, you shouldn't be out here. Go kick some ass."

The defense took the field to start the game. Arizona had a rookie quarterback drafted in the second round from a small college in the Midwest. The only reason he was out there was because the regular starter suffered a concussion in last week's game and the regular backup had food poisoning. Thrown into action at the last minute, Logan swore he could see the guy's hands shaking before he took the first snap. When the ball went sailing between his legs, Logan shook his head.

The moment was too big for some people. For Logan, it wasn't big enough. He aimed for the biggest stage of all. The Super Bowl. It wasn't a matter of if he would get there, but when.

"Three and out." Gaige grinned, pulling on his helmet. "Come on, kid. Let's go show them how it's done."

Logan ran onto the field. Kid. He shook his head, grinning. From the first day of training camp, Gaige had hung that moniker on him. Ironic since he was almost twenty-five, a good two years older than most of the other rookies. However, he supposed when someone had been in the league as long as Gaige, all the new guys seemed like kids.

"We're starting on the ground," Gaige instructed them in the huddle. "Sweep out left. Basic. Got it?"

Lining up as he had a thousand other times, Logan checked the defense. He knew he was fast. One of the fastest in the game. What set him apart was his anticipation. He had the uncanny ability to read the guy covering him. He knew when to fake left or when to fake right. Stutter step or flat out, in your face, catch me if you can.

His speed got him out of Denville, Oklahoma. His brains and determination got him to the NFL.

The sounds of the game were as familiar to Logan as the back of his own hand. The call from scrimmage. Each quarterback had his own unique cadence. Gaige was a master of mixing his up. Study him all you want. Good luck figuring it out. His teammates knew. A signal just before they broke the huddle.

Pay attention, you were golden. Slack off even once? Gaige could ream a guy out with the best of them. And he had no problem doing it in the middle of the game.

An entire YouTube channel had been devoted to Gaige and his rants. They were as legendary as the man himself. With a ball in his hand, he was cool as ice. The rest of the time, watch out.

No one would ever accuse Logan of lacking focus. Today was no exception. They were driving down the field. First and ten from the Arizona twenty-yard line. He already had three carries of thirty-five yards. It was going to be a good day.

"Ready to take it in?" Gaige asked.

"Always."

"Then show them what you've got."

A quick snap later, Gaige handed the ball to Logan. The offensive line created a seam. Not a big one. Just big enough. Using the push of his powerful legs, Logan surged through. One more step. They wouldn't catch him. No one could.

Like everything connected with the game, Logan heard the snap of the bone with total clarity. The agony that surged through his body was so intense he almost passed out. In the next few minutes, he was going to wish he had.

"Get back." Logan heard Gaige through the haze of pain. "Goddamn it. Move the hell off."

The three-hundred-and-fifty-pound linebacker didn't get off by standing. He rolled. Crushing Logan's broken leg as he went. He would never know if the move had been deliberate. Now, it was the last thing on his mind. He only cared about two things. How bad was the injury and when would he be able to play again.

"Hold on, kid." Gaige took his hand. "They're bringing the stretcher."

The team doctor checked his eyes. Logan knew he was asked some questions. What they were and how he answered, he would never remember. By the time they carted him off the field, Logan knew the break was bad.

"Gaige." Logan reached for him.

"I'm here, kid."

"Is it over?"

"The game?" Gaige walked with him, his head bent toward Logan. "No. But I promise we're going to win the bastard."

They loaded him onto the open cart. They had him secured and the vehicle rolled away before Logan had his answer. He wasn't wondering about the game. It was his career.

To no one in particular, he whispered the question again.

"Is it over?"

CHAPTER ONE

LOGAN SAT UP in bed, his body covered with a fine coating of sweat.

He glanced at the clock. Three in the fucking morning. On the one night he managed to get to bed at a reasonable hour, he was plagued by the nightmare that had haunted his dreams for the past two years.

Running his hand through his long, damp hair, Logan fell back onto the mattress. His sheets were as wet as he was. With a grimace, he rolled onto the floor. Flexing his stiff knee, he stripped the bed, tossing everything onto a pile of dirty clothes he planned on taking to the laundromat on his day off.

There was an alternative. He could always take Linda Sue Hemmings up on her offer. She would do his laundry anytime. Payment. On-call stud service whenever her husband Darryl was out of town on business. As much as Logan hated folding socks, he decided the price was too high. He had lost a lot in the last few years. He still held onto his dignity. Just barely.

Still groggy, Logan shuffled to the bathroom. Flipping on the light, he grimaced at what the mirror reflected.

Too many late nights followed by not enough sleep. As patterns went, it wasn't a healthy one. Perpetually bloodshot eyes. Dark circles on his dark circles. He needed a haircut. Logan ran his hand over his face. Even more, he needed a shave.

He had to hand it to himself. When he let himself go, he went all the way. All he had to do was stop showering. If he wasn't worried about driving the customers away with his smell, he might have considered it.

The old plumbing rattled with protest when he turned on the faucet. It wasn't a bad place. There were worse. Logan splashed some cold water on his face. He didn't bother with a towel. It would dry soon enough on its own.

He had two choices.

Toss and turn for a couple of hours on the unmade bed – he really needed to get more than one set of sheets.

Or lose himself with an old friend.

Sleep wasn't coming which made the choice an easy one.

Logan pulled on a pair of old shorts, a faded t-shirt and sweatshirt that was too ratty to be called anything as fashionable as a hoodie. After lacing up his sneakers, he hit the road. When he was a kid, he ran for the fun of it. In high school and college, it strengthened his legs and improved his stamina. Now, the only thing it accomplished was getting him a reputation as that half-crazy Price boy. Running the deserted streets at all hours? Maybe his head had been permanently injured along with his leg.

Logan jogged past *Lefty's Pub*. The place where he spent most evenings tending bar. The day he left for college he swore to anyone who would listen that he had served his last beer. Eight years later, here he was, washing glasses and putting up with not so subtle jabs about how the mighty had fallen.

Coming back to Denville was more of an adjustment than Logan anticipated. He expected the cracks about his failed NFL career. Any kind of success tended to breed a certain amount of jealousy and resentment. There were those who reveled in his injury.

Logan Price always thought too much of himself. Denville wasn't good enough for the high school's star running back. He forgot all about us when he made it big.

The sound of his feet pounding on the unpaved side street couldn't keep the usual thoughts from creeping back. Some of what those people said was true. He had been full of himself. At seventeen, one wasn't written up in national magazines without it going to his head.

Logan never tried to hide his plans. A full-ride scholarship to the college of his choice. Then the pros. MVP awards. Super Bowl rings. The cocky attitude of a teenager wasn't any easier to take than if he had been an adult. Most of Denville embraced their golden boy.

216

AFTER ALL THESE YEARS

(One Pass Away Book Two)

PROLOGUE

SEAN McBRIDE WOKE up with a smile on his face. It happened a lot lately. And he thoroughly approved.

He stretched his long, athletic body. Some mornings every inch of him ached. Such was the life of a professional football player. Everything was about preparing for the game. Focus. Concentration. The goal was to be ready for game day.

He had to hold it together for sixty minutes. Pull out a win any way possible. Sacrifice his body to the football Gods and pray he walked away healthy enough to do it all again next week.

Sean dreaded the day after the game. The adrenaline had long ago worn off and he felt all of his thirty years. There were degrees of bad. Sometimes he shuffled to the shower, the aches and pains palpable, but mercifully bearable.

Then there were the bad days. After a day of three-hundred-pound defensive backs using him as their own personal punching bag, he didn't get out of bed—he crawled.

Bruised from top to bottom, his joints creaked and his muscles protested like screeching banshees. Those were the times he wondered why he did it. He could have been a doctor. Or a lawyer. He could have taken his father's advice and gone into the family business. No seventeen-year-old with dreams of glory in the NFL wanted to think about becoming a butcher. But damn. Cutting meat sounded good on those mornings.

This was a good Monday. His body felt lithe—limber. The bruises were there. That was part of his life. However, yesterday had been one of those rare games when every moment fell into place. From the kickoff to the final whistle, the outcome of the game was never in question.

Sean caught every ball thrown his way. He evaded the defense. Fast as the wind. Three touchdowns. One hundred and eighty-two total yards. A damn good day for any wide receiver. He would have had more if Coach Coleman hadn't taken him out of the game in the fourth quarter. With a big lead, there was no reason to risk injury when he wasn't needed.

The after-game celebration moved from the locker room to one of the team's favorite hangouts. Naturally the atmosphere was raucous. Cautiously so.

The Knights were having a stellar season. Ten wins, two losses. Sean and his friends had enough games under their belts to understand how quickly that could turn. Injuries tended to come in bunches. So far, they were healthy. However, that was bound to change. The hope was to get to the playoffs with all their major players on the roster.

After the game, they had a few drinks. Three was Sean's limit these days. A few years ago it was a different story. He would have closed the place down after a win. He and his bed partner of the moment would have moved on to someone's apartment, partying until dawn before going back to her place and fucking like demented rabbits. Then he would go home alone and catch a few hours sleep until it was time to grab a quick shower before heading to the Knights' headquarters to review film from the game.

Those days were over. Sean wasn't a kid anymore, high on his own press clippings and more testosterone than brains. Not that he had settled down completely. He could still party with the best of them. However, he chose his moments—ones that never took place during the season.

Women were another matter. Sean liked sex. Always had. If there were a God, he always would. While his bed partners weren't as varied, they were almost as frequent.

Sean knew players who abstained a few days before the game, saving their *juice*. He wasn't one of them. Sean had plenty of juice, thank you very much. Sex was necessary for a happy and healthy mind. For *his* happy and healthy mind.

A big plus to having sex at night was sex the next morning. It was one of his favorite things. A partner, warm and willing.

The perfect way to start the day.

Speaking of which. Smiling, Sean turned over. His hand reached out, expecting to find a soft, sweet woman. Instead, he found cold sheets. Sitting up, he looked around the room. Like the bed, empty. The bathroom door was open and the light off.

Not bothering to cover up, Sean jumped out of bed. Buck naked, he searched the house. She wasn't in the kitchen. Why would she be? She didn't cook, not even coffee. She was on a first-name basis with half the baristas in Seattle.

Was that it? Would she be back soon with two cups of steaming black caffeine and his favorite muffins? Sean was talking himself into that scenario when he saw the note.

He picked up the paper that had been propped against the lamp by the front door.

Sean.

Thank you for the past few weeks. After years of building it up in my mind, I was worried that it couldn't live up to my expectations. I should have known better. It was everything I had hoped for—and more.

We didn't make any promises. No strings were attached that need to be broken. After all these years, you can finally breathe easy. It's over. We are now friends without the expectation of benefits.

When we see each other, it will be as if it, we, never happened.

Sean read the note. Then read it again.

What the fuck? What was in those drinks?

Sean searched his memory for some kind of clue. The bar. His teammates. Then she was there. They laughed. Everything was smooth and easy. They seemed to be developing a rhythm. In his mind, they were together. Not a man and a woman—a couple.

It sounded good to him. He would have sworn she felt the same. He didn't want another woman. He wanted her. In his arms. In his life.

No expectations? Hell. He woke up with plenty of them, only to find out he was alone. Alone in bed. Alone. Period.

Sean scrubbed a hand over his face. He remembered the way she tasted. The way she melted into his arms. The curves of her luscious body pressed against his. Her sighs. His belief he would never get enough of her.

Crumpling the note into a ball, Sean tossed it across the room. Suddenly he felt every ache. His legs felt like lead. Slowly, he shuffled toward the bathroom. He needed a shower. Long and hot. Determined not to look at the bed, Sean's peripheral vision wouldn't let him off the hook that easily. It captured everything. The rumpled sheet. The pillow still holding the imprint of her head. A slash of red on the floor.

Frowning, Sean picked up the scrap of silk. So small he wondered why she had bothered. The image of her standing in nothing but her heels and the panties popped into his head. Unconsciously, his body tightened with desire.

Right, that was why.

Sean ran the smooth material over his cheek, feeling it catch on his morning stubble. He breathed deeply. He smelled vanilla and spice. Her essence. He would never forget it. As long as he lived, he would be able to close his eyes and conjure up her scent. Her taste.

His eyes popped open. *Friends? Nothing more? Bullshit!*

Keeping the panties in his hand, Sean headed for the shower. This wasn't over. Not by a long shot. It was just the beginning.

AFTER THE FIRE

(One Pass Away Book Three)

PROLOGUE

SHE HAD ONCE asked him if he believed in a higher power.

God? Buddha? Fairies dancing around a blazing fire late at night? Something. Anything bigger than us.

Gaige Benson hadn't known what to say. Not then. But as he stood in the empty open-air stadium—the stars lighting the evening sky—he knew the answer.

Football was his religion. The field he played on and the building surrounding it, his cathedral. If a higher power had a hand in it, then his answer was yes.

He believed.

Walking to the center of the field, Gaige took it all in. He found football at the age of thirteen. A boy who saw his future mapped out. Working in a factory. Drinking away his salary. Divorce. Doling out child support without maintaining a relationship with his children. A weekend father, who half the time didn't bother to show up.

The first time Gaige picked up a football, he felt a connection. The first time he threw it, it wobbled with the grace of a drunk leaving his favorite watering hole on a Saturday night. But it didn't matter. He threw the ball again. And again. Until he taught himself to make it spin in a perfect spiral.

At the time, Gaige didn't know his talent could be useful. Where he came from, Brooklyn kids didn't dream of bigger or better. Most of them didn't dream at all. Gaige was no different.

One day he was passing a playground when a football landed at his feet. The boys on the field yelled for him to toss it back. Without thinking, Gaige sent it sailing, a perfect strike. Then kept walking. He was wary of the man who ran after him. Strangers were the enemy—according to his father. They either wanted money or accused you of something you hadn't done.

Gaige took everything his father said with a big grain of salt. Don Benson didn't have a dime to his name. Why would anyone expect to get money from him? And if a man accused his father of something, chances were he was guilty.

But Gaige was a cautious boy. He fought when necessary and ran when he had no choice. The man trying to get his attention was big. His dark complexion didn't worry Gaige. In his experience, a man was either good or bad. The color of his skin had nothing to do with it.

It turned out that this man wasn't simply good. He was the best thing that ever happened to Gaige.

Terrance Aldridge coached the local Pop Warner football team. A boy with an arm like Gaige's shouldn't let his talent go to waste. Gaige listened. Play football? On a field? With other boys? Was such a thing possible? He didn't know if it were a scam—nor did he care. If there were the slightest chance, he would take it.

The only obstacle was getting a parent's permission. Terrance gave him the papers to be signed, telling Gaige to have his folks call him if they had any questions. Gaige didn't laugh aloud, but he wanted to. His mother never asked questions. Unless they were directed at his father. Wynona Benson hadn't made a move in fifteen years unless she received permission first.

His father was another matter. His word was law. Don Benson could do no wrong. If he drank too much and staggered home two days late, it was his right. If he backhanded his wife—just because—whose business was it? He earned the money. He made the rules. End of discussion.

Gaige hadn't asked his father because he knew what the answer would be. No! Not because he thought there was anything wrong with football. He watched it every Sunday—after laying down a bet that he never won. No, he wouldn't let Gaige play because he was a mean bastard who wanted everyone to be as miserable as he was.

Gaige got around it easily enough. He forged his father's signature. It wasn't the first time and it wouldn't be the last. There was no reason to think anyone would find out. His parents didn't care how he spent his days as long as the police didn't come knocking on the door.

He could steal. Lie. Cheat. Hell, his father wouldn't bat an eye at murder. *Do what you want as long as you don't get caught.* The mantra at the Benson house.

Gaige had no intention of his father finding out. He tried out for the team and made it. The money for equipment was another matter. Gaige didn't steal. Or cheat. Lying was a necessary evil. He would have done almost anything to play but it looked like his first and only dream would die before it had a chance.

Luckily, Terrance was able to dip into a discretionary fund to help boys like Gaige. It rankled to take charity. Especially when the other boys on the team had families to pay their way.

"Don't let it stop you, Gaige," Terrance told him. "Remember. And one day, when you have the means, pay it forward, son."

Twenty-five years later, Gaige hadn't forgotten that kindness and generosity. When he saw someone in need, he did something about it. Over the years, the *Gaige Benson Foundation* paid out millions of dollars to charities and individuals. He had filled the board with people he trusted and could count on to distribute the funds judiciously and without prejudice. The first man he had recruited was the man to whom Gaige owed everything—Terrance Aldridge. Friend. Father figure. Teacher.

"Hey, Gaige." Logan Price called out from high in the stands. "You coming? The guys are waiting to go to dinner."

"Five minutes."

Closing his eyes, Gaige breathed in the air. February in Texas. Tomorrow he would play in his first—and last Super Bowl. Win or lose, he was hanging up his cleats. He was thirty-eight years old. He had more money than he would ever need. He had won every award from Rookie of the Year to league MVP—four times.

This season he put everything on the line to get here—including the possibility that he had lost the only woman he had ever loved.

Gaige Benson was known for his razor-sharp focus. Any distractions off the field were left there as soon as the first whistle blew. It wouldn't be any different tomorrow. Nothing would get in the way.

His gaze drifted to the section where she would be sitting. If she showed up. Gaige planned on going out a winner. But what about the day after? Or the day after that? His future stretched out in front of him. He had plans in place. There were hundreds of options for him to consider.

Do you believe in a higher power?

Her voice and that question had haunted Gaige for almost sixteen years. If there were a God, he prayed the woman he loved would find it in her heart to forgive him. He had a lot of years left. He didn't want to spend them alone.

In his lifetime, Gaige Benson had dreamt of only two things. Playing football. And loving Violet Reed.

DREAMING WITH A BROKEN HEART

(Hollywood Legends Book One

PROLOGUE

THE ROOM WAS dark. Too dark for Garrett's liking. A little stuffy, a slight antiseptic smell with an overlay of sex. That's what you got from a cheap motel and furtive lovemaking. Odors and memories you'd just as soon forget.

The sounds from behind the closed bathroom door indicated his partner was trying to remove all traces of their recent activities. It shouldn't hurt. This wasn't the first time, and damn his weak resolve, it wouldn't be the last.

If he smoked, he would have something to do with his hands. Watching his father struggle with lung cancer put the fear of God in him and his brothers at an early age. All four of them had their vices; smoking wasn't one of them.

Get up. Get dressed. For once, be the first to leave. Even if he could find the balls to walk out on her, he couldn't leave her alone at this time of night. In this part of town.

God, it was like a furnace in here. Despite having the AC wall unit on high, Garrett knew it must be hotter in here than outside. The sheet riding low on his hips was too much. Damn modesty. The room was too dark to see anything; if she didn't like seeing his naked body, she could turn away. Garrett whipped off the coarse cotton material at the same moment the bathroom door opened.

"You don't have to go," Garrett said to the shadowed figure.

"Yes, I do."

She always made sure the light was off. Her silhouette showed a tall woman, thin. Too thin. Even by L.A. standards. She was gaining weight — slowly. Garrett could attest to that. He knew it was a struggle. One she fought every day.

Garrett felt the anger drain from his body — his heart melt. Her demands were not capricious whims. They weren't her attempt to gain the upper hand. Her goal was not to manipulate. She had her reasons. They were real. Legitimate.

"It's still early."

Garrett kept his voice low and even. Shouting didn't help. She never fought back. Retreat. That was her coping mechanism. The last time he blew up it was two weeks before she would take his calls.

"I..." she cleared her voice. "His flight gets in at midnight."

"Don't be there."

"You know how he gets."

Garrett knew all right. She was devoted to a man who treated her like crap, forgot her existence ninety percent of the time, yet expected her to be there when he decided to come home. His fists clenched the mattress. It was the only thing preventing him from grabbing her, begging her to stay. *For once, pick me.*

"I don't know when I can see you again."

I don't know if I ever want to see you again. Garrett thought the words. He would never verbalize them. She was his drug of choice. Weeks passed. The need for her grew. Outwardly, his life looked smooth as glass. Inside, the itch grew.

Garrett became an expert at compartmentalizing. His work never suffered. His family never suspected. No one had the slightest clue about what was raging inside of him. *She* knew. Because she shared his unbreakable habit. Enablers. That's what they were. It was sick. Sometimes, like tonight, he hated himself. He wished he could hate her. Then, maybe, he could walk away.

"I'll be out of town for the next month."

Garrett wished he could see her face. Was she sorry he'd be gone? Relieved? Would she miss him half as much as he was going to miss her?

"Take care."

Garrett waited a second, letting the motel room door close behind her. Jumping up, rushing to the window, he pulled back the thin, dingy curtain. He never walked her to the taxi. Even the minutest chance of them being seen was too much.

The ritual of watching until she was safely inside the vehicle, seat belt on, doors locked, was something he never ignored. Nothing bad would happen to her when he was around. It was when he wasn't there that trouble found her. One more frustration. It wasn't his place to protect her. Knowing that drove him crazy.

Garrett grabbed his jeans from a nearby chair, pulling them on. Unlike her, he wouldn't clean up before he left. He would carry the smell of her with him — let it fill the interior of his car. Tomorrow he would pretend it was still there.

Damn it. Enough. He deserved more than this. They both did. One month. When he got back, one way or another, things were going to change.

CHAPTER ONE

HOLLYWOOD. DREAMS FULFILLED. Dreams crushed. It happened every day. Wide-eyed kids still came hoping to be a star. More often than not, they went back home — a nobody. Iowa, Nebraska, Texas, Georgia. Insert state here. Small town, big city. It didn't matter. The movie industry seemed vast from the outside. In truth, it was the most insular of worlds. Making it took determination, perseverance, and a whole lot of luck. Talent was so far down the list it wasn't funny.

Connections. That was what got you through the door. If you had a recognizable name, the door swung wide, the smiles welcoming. If you couldn't pull your weight once you were inside, no one hesitated to kick you out. That famous name only got you so far. The rest was on your shoulders.

Sink or swim. No life preservers were thrown your way. If anything, you were fitted with cement shoes. The only thing this town loved more than a winner was the child of a Hollywood legend falling flat on his face.

Garrett Landis felt the weight of those expectations every time he stepped on a movie set. His father set the bar so high none of his sons was expected to reach his lofty heights. The fact that all four seemed well on their way to not only matching Caleb Landis' achievements, but surpassing them, caused quite a stir.

Resentment simmered under the surface of hearty backslapping and insincere ass kissing. Their father taught his boys many things. In this business, never turn your back on friend or foe. Treat everyone with respect, from the lowliest crew member to the head of the studio. The most important thing? In this business, trust no one — except brothers. Eight years after making his first low-budget independent film, Garrett followed those rules without question. The Gospel according to Caleb Landis. His father's words were his bible. His brothers were his rock.

Wyatt, the oldest, followed directly in their father's footsteps. He was a hard-ass, bottom-line producer. Nathaniel, Garrett's fraternal twin, was the daredevil of the bunch. He was the most in-demand stuntman in Hollywood. Baby brother Colton was blessed with movie star looks. His charisma leaped off the screen, pulling in even the most cynical audience member. Or so one critic wrote after seeing Colt's first movie. Individually, each Landis brother was formidable. Together, they dominated almost every branch of the industry.

"How can we be behind schedule when we haven't shot a single frame?"

"Welcome to the glamorous world of moviemaking."

Garrett grinned when he answered his assistant director, Hamish Floyd. This was their fourth collaboration. The first two made a nice profit. Number three broke box office records. Expectations for *Exile* went through the roof the second Garrett's name became attached. With Wyatt behind the scenes, the movie's success was practically guaranteed.

Garrett didn't believe in sure things. He worked hard on every project, no matter the size. Bigger budget, more potential headaches. That included a prima donna leading lady who couldn't get her ass on set at the designated hour. Garrett refused to start leaking money on day one.

"You want me to coax America's sweetheart of the week out of her trailer?"

"You'd never get past her PA," Garrett told Hamish. "Lynne Cornish thinks one hit movie and a few magazine covers give her the right to make her own rules. She's going to find out on this movie set, there is only one set of rules — mine."

"She has a contract."

"Wyatt's standard contract. She signed it. Her mistake if her lawyers didn't read the fine print."

Contracts were fluid. *Before* they were finalized. Each actor, depending on their box office leverage, could get their people to make demands, tweak the perks. The basics were non-negotiable. Under no circumstance, barring personal injury, a death in the family, or a genuine nervous breakdown, was an actor allowed to delay production. Once, you were warned. Twice, bye-bye. As far as Garrett's big brother was concerned, potential loss of a lead actor was the reason they paid huge insurance premiums. It hadn't happened to Garrett. Not yet. There was always a first time.

Tim Bodine, Lynne Cornish's PA, waylaid Garrett before he was halfway to her trailer.

229

"Lynne isn't feeling well."

"She was fine an hour ago."

When she was flirting with every man on the set. Apparently, Ms. Cornish could drag herself to any early breakfast if adoring men were present. She found out quickly that Garrett wasn't among them. Whether her sudden *illness* was a result of a hurt ego or plain laziness, he didn't give a damn. Starting right now, Lynne Cornish needed to know who was boss.

"Does she need a doctor?"

"Nooo." Tim drew out the word.

The PA's lack of concern only ratcheted up Garrett's annoyance.

"Five minutes."

"What?" Tim yelled at Garrett's retreating figure. When there was no response, the man hurried to catch up. "She can't make it in five minutes. Lynne doesn't think today will work for her. At all."

Garrett rounded on the smaller man. He topped him by at least eight inches. Tim was slight, Garrett muscular. Yet that wasn't what had the PA stepping back several feet. It was the look in Garrett's steely eyes.

This man exuded confidence. Strength, both physical and psychological, radiated from his core. You didn't mess with Garrett Landis. Not if you had half a brain.

"She was looking a little better when I left her trailer," Tim said, clearing his throat. "She wanted to speak with you. *Privately.*"

Well, shit. Garrett didn't see that coming. Lynne made it clear, early on —she was interested. He made it equally clear he wasn't. End of story. They would have a friendly, professional relationship. Finding out his beautiful leading lady was angling for more didn't hold the thrill it once had. It made Garrett... tired. His personal life was full of enough turmoil — he didn't need the added drama of an on-set romance.

"I don't have the time, or inclination, Tim."

To Garrett's surprise, the PA blushed. In Hollywood, that ability was knocked out of a person fast.

"I can't guarantee anything."

"Then Lynne will be out of a job. How long do you think you'll last after that?"

Tim Bodine looked like a smart man. One capable of cajoling his uncooperative employer. Garrett didn't care what it took to get his star in front of the camera as long as it happened. Immediately.

"Five minutes?" Tim asked, a little panicked.

"I'll give you ten."

Garrett wondered if it was too late to get out of feature films. Animation. That sounded good. No location shoots. Voice-over actors happy to skip wardrobe fittings and hours in the makeup chair. A little direction on his part. Mostly setting the scene. One or two takes. Right now, it sounded like heaven.

"What's the word?" Hamish asked him.

"Bitch?"

"Any chance she'll be joining us in the near future?"

"Your guess is as good as mine."

Garrett looked around. They were ready to go. Cameras primed, leading man looking as impatient as Garrett felt. At least he'd lucked out with Paul McNally. He was a professional through and through. No power plays. No outlandish demands. There was no propositioning the director. Paul's first job was a small part in a Caleb Landis production. He was a great actor. More importantly, he was a friend. Garrett felt lucky to work with him.

"Once again, you've lived up to your reputation," Hamish said with admiration. "You really are a miracle worker."

Garrett looked over his shoulder. Lynne Cornish. In full costume and makeup. A little pouty. He could work with that. It complimented the scene.

"Tell them five."

"We're shooting in five minutes, people," Hamish called out Garrett's directions. "Pee now or forever hold it."

Garrett moved over to camera A, checking the shot. Perfect. This was his world. He knew what he was doing. No one questioned his authority or failed to jump at his command. Unlike his personal life, his professional life stayed on a clear path.

DREAMING WITH MY EYES WIDE OPEN

(Hollywood Legends Book Two)

PROLOGUE

NATE LANDIS NEVER thought much about the way he looked.

Women seemed to like his face. That was genetics. He was the son of Hollywood royalty. Alone, they turned heads. Together, they dazzled. It made sense that they would pass some of that on.

Nate took it in stride. He was strong. Healthy. His body was trained to do what he wanted it to do, under what could only be called extreme situations. He ate right, worked hard, and played harder.

At some point, his lifestyle would catch up with him. Age would take care of that. Right now, he was in his prime. If he wanted to scale a mountain, that's what he did. Jump from a plane? A piece of cake. Race car driving. Deep sea diving. You name it; Nate was the first one in line.

When he was three years old, his mother called him her little daredevil. Fearless, she swore he gave her wrinkles for worrying what he would get into next. Nate would always laugh, peering closely at Callie Flynn's flawless complexion. What wrinkles? In her fifties, she was, and would always be, one of the movie industry's great beauties. Nothing he or his brothers did could alter that.

As Nate stepped to the edge of the cliff, he didn't think about the two-hundred-foot drop. He'd jumped from higher than this. It was what he did. And he did it better than anyone else. For some reason, today he thought about his mother.

Callie never discouraged him from pursuing danger, even though Nate knew she wished he had chosen a safer way to make a living. She didn't say so, but he knew she worried about his safety. It didn't stop him — he seldom thought about it. Until today. As he waited for the director to signal the camera was rolling, for the first time Nate let himself worry about his mother's reaction if something happened to him.

He shook off the morbid thought. Now wasn't the time. He needed to focus. Ninety-nine percent of the time, if something went wrong, it was due to a loss of focus. Nate took a deep breath. He cleared his mind. Three flashes of light. That was his signal. He squared his shoulders, coiled his body. And jumped.

Nate Landis was a stuntman. Some might say it was his calling. If a director needed it done big and done right, that person called him. Nate loved his job.

He let his body relax as he sailed through the air. The count in his head was precise. If he pulled the ripcord too soon, the shot would be ruined. Too late, he risked ending up a pile of broken bones.

Nate planned every stunt. He worked out the timing, the logistics, and the angles. He never let anyone perform a stunt unless he tested it. Over and over again. He refused to rush. Anxious directors. Bottom-line producers. Some tried to push him into cutting corners.

Few things made Nate lose his temper. His brother Garrett claimed Nate had the longest, slowest burning fuse in history. But he had his hot buttons. Endangering himself and his crew was one of them. Last year, a director, trying to save time, ran a stunt when Nate was away from the set. Poorly conceived and executed, two stuntmen went to the hospital with second-degree burns.

Todd Winesap went to the hospital with a broken jaw and a tarnished reputation.

It took a lot to make Nate mad. But watch out when it happened.

Nate ran the count through his head. Eight, nine, ten. He gave the cord a firm, steady pull. Smooth as glass, the chute opened. Even so, he traveled at a high speed. The parachute was safety measure number one. Number two was the large, air-filled target waiting below.

Having done this stunt hundreds of times, Nate knew what to expect and how it should feel. And he knew when something was wrong.

The air bag, that Nate had personally supervised the placement of, wasn't where it was supposed to be. He didn't have the time to wonder how that had happened. If he didn't act fast, he wouldn't be around to beat the shit out of the asshole responsible.

Grabbing the guide strings, Nate pulled a hard right with all his considerable strength — and prayed.

CHAPTER ONE

HOLLYWOOD WAS AN unforgiving town with a long memory.

Drugs could be forgiven. Drunk driving. Spousal abuse. Those things could be forgiven. In the movie industry, your worth was measured by one thing — box office returns. Three strikes, you're out.

Early in his career, Caleb Landis knew the meaning of holding on by his fingertips. He was young, inexperienced, and hungry. That meant working all the angles. No one opened any doors for a dirt-poor would-be producer. That was fine with him. He had no problem barreling his way in. His take no prisoners attitude earned him respect. And enemies.

Hard work. Long hours. Sacrifice. Eventually, it paid off. Caleb's career spanned over four decades. He had money and power. The shelves of his office were lined with every award the industry could give him.

When a movie had the name Landis attached to it, the world knew they were getting quality.

Sitting back, Caleb looked around the table with pride. His family. That was his greatest accomplishment. The fame and money meant nothing compared to the joy of knowing the most important people in the world surrounded him. The people he loved. The people who loved him.

It all started and ended with his Callie.

Screen goddess to the world. To him, protector of his heart.

He had no doubt the first time he saw her. He knew she was the woman he wanted to spend his life with. She was the only woman he would ever love. Their life hadn't been the fairy tale some people made it out to be. They had their ups and downs. But through it all, one thing never changed. Their unshakable love.

His beautiful wife had given him four strong, healthy sons. Men a father could be proud of.

Wyatt was the oldest. Like Caleb, a producer. The difference was *he* trusted his gut. If a project felt right, he fought until he got it made. Wyatt was a thinker. His first concern was the bottom line. They had squared off more than once about artistry versus the almighty dollar.

The end was always the same. He and Wyatt were different enough that butting heads was inevitable. They had enough similarities to put those differences aside. The most important thing was the movie. Together they made art — and money.

Caleb's gaze moved to the other side of the table. The laugh he heard was a deeper version of his sweet Callie's. It made him smile. Colton. The youngest of his four boys. He was the only one to follow his mother's lead, stepping in front of the camera to make his mark. And what a mark it was going to be.

Colt had a face the camera loved. The first offer to put him in the movies came when he was only a year old. The offers kept coming. Callie didn't want any of her sons to be *child stars*. Caleb agreed.

Growing up was hard enough. In Beverly Hills, the temptations were magnified. Caleb and Callie did their best to give their children as normal a childhood as possible. Family dinners. Game night. Backyard barbecues. If that childhood included trips to Cannes and vacations on private yachts, so what? This was their version of normal. It wasn't perfect. But then, what was?

Colton was one of the biggest movie stars in the world. In public, that meant screaming fans and preferential treatment. At dinner with his family, he was expected to set the table and dry the dishes. It was true when he was ten. It was true now, even if his last movie *did* break box office records.

Then there was Garrett. Caleb sat back smiling when he heard his middle son complaining to his mother.

"What is the world coming to when a man's family takes sides against him?"

"First, Jade is your family. And ours." Callie patted Jade's hand. "Second. She's right. You're wrong. End of discussion."

"Hey." Garrett looked at the two women. His mother on his right. The love of his life on his left. There was no rock. No hard place. With a snap of his fingers, there would be a thousand men lined up to take his place. He was no fool. He knew he had it good. "I give up," he said, wisely conceding the point.

Dazzled by Jade's smile, Garrett melted. He tucked a lock of her long, silky red hair behind her ear. The unconsciously intimate gesture had his parents smiling with approval.

"A wise decision, son." Caleb nodded at Garrett with a wink. "When you realize your lady is the brains in the relationship, the sailing will be much smoother."

"Where are you on *Exile*?"

Garrett and Jade were just back from Vancouver where he had finished principal shooting on his current film. His last project had garnered him an Oscar nomination for best director. Caleb believed this one would win his son the statue.

"I'm in the studio next week. The soundtrack needs some tweaking, but the composer assures me it will be ready."

"It better be," Wyatt added. "The Los Angeles Philharmonic doesn't come cheap. You have them for a week. That's all the budget will allow. After that, I'll take it out of your salary."

"It's my own fault for working with family," Garrett sighed. "I could knock any other producer on his ass if he talked to me like that. Mommy would have a fit if I bruised her baby's face."

"Jade, you're marrying an idiot."

"Pardon my French in advance, Mom." Garrett gave Wyatt the finger, and then added, "Fuck you, Wyatt."

"Nice mouth, brother. You might think about washing it out with soap before kissing your woman." Out of Callie's sight, Wyatt flipped Garrett the bird.

"I just brushed. How about kissing me instead?"

"Nate!"

Callie was across the room in a flash. Instead of jumping into his arms, as was her custom, she held back. She knew the doctor said Nate's ribs were healed, but she was his mother. The thought of causing him the slightest pain was unthinkable.

"Where's your sling?"

"Gone for good. Thank God."

Nate's left arm was still in a cast. With little effort, he used his right to swing Callie in a circle. The comforting scent of roses and vanilla drifted around him. As always, it took him back to his childhood when she would tuck him in at night. Burying his face in her hair, he breathed deeply.

Mother. Love. Safety. From the time he was born, she had steered him with a gentle yet firm hand. There was a fine line between controlling and supportive. Callie Flynn showed her sons by example that a woman could thrill the world with her acting and still be the best mother anyone could ask for. Nate affectionately kissed the top of her head. What would he have done without this woman?

"We didn't think you were going to make it." Callie took his good hand, leading him to the table. "Sit. I'll get you a plate. I swear, since the accident you've wasted away to nothing."

Colt snorted in disbelief. "How can you tell? The man is a freaking brick wall."

"Callie's right." Jade smiled at Nate. "You look thinner."

"I knew the woman couldn't keep her eyes off me. Tell me you've finally realized you picked the wrong brother."

"One more word and I'll forget you're my twin." Garrett turned to Jade. "I always felt sorry for him. I got the looks, the brains, and the charm. And Nate got the…? What did Nate get?"

"The ability to kick your ass?" Nate flexed his impressive biceps. "And more women than even Colton could handle."

"Hey," Colt interjected. "That's my reputation as a man-whore you're besmirching. What would the tabloids say if word got out that my brother was getting more women than I was?"

"Don't listen to him, Colt." Garrett loved jabbing at his twin. Just as Nate loved returning the favor. The sport never grew old. "He overcompensated for his shortcomings by living in the gym. I suppose some women find brawn over brains attractive."

"More than a few."

"Enough." Callie chuckled. She had heard this banter for years. "You," she said to Nate, "stop talking — eat. And you," she looked at Garrett. "Leave your brother in peace for five minutes."

Thanking her with a smile, Nate took the plate from his mother. It overflowed with roast beef, mashed potatoes, fresh green beans, all drowned in rich, brown gravy. Adding three fresh baked rolls from the basket on the table, Nate was a happy man.

The truth was, since the accident on the movie set last month, he hadn't been himself. It would be different if he could work. Keeping busy was the best way to calm his mind and body. Unfortunately, the injuries he had sustained kept him sidelined.

Too much time on his hands. Too much time to think about what had gone wrong. The botched stunt could have ended in tragedy. Thanks to his quick reflexes, physical strength, and determination not to end up in a heap of mangled bones, Nate walked away with a few cracked ribs and a broken arm. The only reason he stayed the night in the hospital was to appease his mother. The doctor assured her Nate didn't have a concussion. Callie didn't want to take any chances. One night of observation was a small price to pay for his mother's peace of mind.

It didn't hurt that his nurse was a curvy brunette with warm, soft hands.

"I know that smile." Wyatt shook his head. "Which conquest are you thinking about now?"

"You wouldn't give me such a hard time if you were getting laid more often." Remembering where he was, Nate gave his mother a repentant grin. "Sorry."

"Your brother's love life is his own business," Callie said firmly.

"Thank you." Wyatt gave Nate a *take that* glare.

"Though…"

"Ah, crap." Wyatt's head fell forward, his chin hitting his chest.

"Come on, Wyatt," Garrett laughed with delight. "Every man lives to have his mother discuss his sex life."

DREAMING OF YOUR LOVE

(Hollywood Legends Book

Three

PROLOGUE

LIGHTS FLASHED FROM every direction. It blinded and dazzled all at once.

Screams drowned out every other sound. This was Los Angeles. Busy streets in every direction. Jet patterns overhead. The excited—in some cases rabid—fans that surrounded the roped-off red carpet made it seem like nothing existed but them and the bright lights.

It shouldn't have been a pleasant experience. Alighting from the over-the-top luxury of a Rolls Royce into chaos and mayhem? No normal human being would willingly seek out such an experience.

However, Colton Landis was not a normal human being. He was an actor.

Colt turned his world-famous megawatt smile on the crowd, eliciting another deafening burst of heartfelt screams.

"We need to get inside, Colt. The movie starts in ten minutes."

"Relax, Deb."

Colt's publicist had been with him for five years. Deb Kline knew how to spin a press release like nobody else. They saw eye to eye on most things. Except how much he should expose himself to his fans. If she had her way, he would zip from point A to point B as quickly as humanly possible.

In this case, point A was the limo, and point B was Grauman's Chinese Theater.

"I'll relax when you are safely inside. Have you forgotten Dallas already?"

"Dallas was an anomaly."

Colt continued to wave and smile. Deb wanted him to curb his accessibility. She had always been cautious, but after a fan somehow breached security during a press conference to announce his next movie, she was particularly leery of events like this one.

"Colt."

"Don't go over there, Colt."

Deb knew the second Colt observed the waving autograph books, her words fell on deaf ears. He believed in giving his fans what they wanted. It was one of the things that made Colton Landis a huge movie star. He genuinely loved his fans. He loved meeting them, speaking with them, having his picture taken with them. Most of her clients searched for any reason to avoid these moments. Not Colt. He didn't have a public persona and a private one. What you saw was what you got—twenty-four hours a day, seven days a week.

Colt made her job as a publicist a dream. Keeping him safe was a nightmare.

He refused to have a bodyguard. Part of it was ego—and he had plenty of that. Many of his parts portrayed him as a big, macho, tough guy. How would it look if he had a bigger, more macho, tough guy constantly shadowing him? Not great for his reputation. He would look weak. And in Hollywood, perception was everything.

It was a valid argument. Not so valid? Colt believed that, for the most part, his fans were harmless. Not that he was a naïve Pollyanna. There was no need for Deb to point out the entertainment world's tragic examples of the heinous acts obsessive fans could commit.

Colt lived the life. He grew up watching his superstar mother traverse that fine line between making herself accessible to fans and maintaining some much-needed privacy.

However, he didn't have a family to consider. No wife. No children. His life was his own. A bodyguard would mean he was giving

242

in. Turning his life over to fear instead of embracing every single moment of his fairytale existence.

"Ten minutes."

Deb didn't know if Colt heard her over the screams. Nor did she care. She was getting him into that theater if it meant grabbing his ear and dragging him along like an errant five-year-old. And wouldn't that make a great picture in *People* magazine? Okay. No ears. *Ugh. This man was going to make her old before her time.*

Colt held a woman's phone at arm's length, including himself in a selfie of her and her three friends.

"I love you, Colton."

Colt couldn't single out the speaker. The cry came from every direction. He waved and called out, "I love you, too."

He signed a few more autographs, moving along the line. Deb was right. He needed to get inside. It wasn't fair to keep everyone waiting. Ten more, he promised himself. It killed him to see the expressions on the faces of the fans who were left out.

"Thanks. See you soon," Colt called out to the crowd.

Handing her signed book to a dreamy-eyed woman, Colt gave the crowd a final wave.

"Ready?" Deb tried to maintain the *stern teacher* expression she had spent twenty years cultivating.

Colt had a way of making her professional mask slip. Thank goodness she was old enough to be his youngish grandmother. While his charm was undeniable, her age and experience allowed her to put the sexual pull that radiated around him into perspective.

Until he turned his smile on her. Full blast.

"Am I that big of a pain in the ass?"

There it was. That naughty twinkle in his deep blue eyes that made the world swoon. On screen, it was irresistible. Paired with dark hair and a tall, muscular frame, was it any wonder the camera loved him?

Reluctantly, Deb returned his smile.

Colt was her client. He was also her friend. She knew he wasn't trying to be difficult. He was being himself. For a man who was adored by millions, catered to on a daily basis, and could buy and sell two or three third-world nations without raising a sweat, Colton Landis was surprisingly down to Earth. And hard-headed. And opinionated.

On top of that? On occasions such as this one, a major pain in the ass.

Still, if she were honest, there wasn't a single thing about him that she would change. As movie stars went—hell, as human beings went—Colton Landis was a joy to be around. Not that she would ever tell him that. The last thing he needed was another person extolling his endless virtues. Colt hated that kind of treatment. One of the reasons they worked so well together was because Deb didn't kowtow.

Deb was about to hit him with one of the nifty sarcastic one-liners he loved, when a scream came from the crowd. Not a *we love you* cry, but one of terror. Before she could react, Deb saw a man jump over the velvet rope. He carried a knife.

Colt pushed her to the side, effectively putting himself between her and the attacker. *He isn't after me*, Deb wanted to protest. But everything happened so fast, she didn't have time.

In the blink of an eye, the man raised the knife and stabbed Colt.

IF I LOVED YOU

(Harper Falls Book One)

PROLOGUE

IT WAS SOMETHING out of a fairy tale.

Thousands of flickering lights dazzled her senses, almost as much as the tall, wickedly handsome man who so expertly danced her onto the shadowed balcony. The music that filtered from the nearby ballroom only added to the already magical atmosphere.

Women dreamed their whole lives of a moment like this — a prelude to a happily-ever-after ending. Ever so briefly, she let herself drift into that fantasy as if she was one of those women. For a moment, she let herself pretend that her childhood had been filled with the kind of whimsicality that allowed those fantasies to carry over into adulthood.

But no, she wasn't a romantic, hopeless or otherwise. She didn't want a prince to sweep her into his arms and carry her away on his faithful steed. She was more than capable of rescuing herself. She preferred it that way.

The stars were in the sky, not in her eyes.

"I'm glad you asked me to dance," her partner whispered, pulling her closer.

Suddenly, she was nervous. The champagne she downed earlier had completely worn off. No more floating on a cloud of false courage. If she was going to do this, she was going to have to do it on her own.

"Jack," she said. Damn, it was hard to sound seductive when your voice squeaked. "Jack." That was better, lower, and slightly husky. She'd read somewhere that guys liked husky voices.

"Rose."

"Yes?"

"Nothing, I just thought we were saying each other's names." He put his lips next to her ear. "I like the way you say mine."

"Jack." Good Lord, she had to stop repeating his name. "I need a favor, Jack. A big one." Or should she say, she hoped he *had* a big one. Rose groaned to herself. At least she hadn't said that aloud.

"I'll help if I can."

"You're the only one who *can* help." She took another deep breath. "I need you to take me home and screw my brains out."

www.ingramcontent.com/pod-product-compliance
Lightning Source LLC
Chambersburg PA
CBHW071142170626
46809CB00002B/735